FIRE ON THE WATER

by Clabe Taylor

FIRE ON THE WATER
Copyright © 2014 by Clabe Taylor
A Spymasters Literary Guild Series Book
Clabe Taylor Enterprises
www.clabetaylor.com
www.spymastersguild.com
ISBN 978-0692226346

Printed and Bound in the United States of America

"Vengeance is mine....saith the Lord.

Romans 12:19

PROLOGUE

The smoke from burning incense wafted disembodied and ghostlike across the deck of the Sea Moon II as the 98-foot tuna boat pulled away slowly from Pier 17 in Honolulu. Flowers adorned the wheelhouse and the bow for good luck. Music blared over a loudspeaker while the Vietnamese crew celebrated its departure in a ritual tinged with antiquity and drenched in American beer. Captain Nyugen's radio squawked once with finality, and he pretended to understand Aloha Tower's garbled farewell transmission to the fishermen and nodded his head solemnly.

The water was calm as the boat threaded its way out of the harbor, and only the dissipating wake from the occasional passing ship-assist tugboat disturbed the flat, glassy water. A tall, solitary figure stood onboard apart from the crew and stared blankly at Honolulu's receding skyline and Diamond Head to the southeast. The man swayed slightly as he leaned against the railing of the fishing boat. He gripped the rusting steel tightly until his knuckles turned a pasty white from the effort. He was unsteady on his feet and barely noticed the vague side-to-side motion of the boat.

A three-day binge had taken him on an endless tour of Honolulu's seedy bars and dropped him unceremoniously last night in China Town. His legs shook spasmodically and his stomach churned and was empty from retching. He did not remember his narrow escape from arrest by the Honolulu police in the wee hours of the morning or his role in the fistfight he precipitated by reaching his hand under the skirt of a prim housewife from Des Moines, Iowa. He certainly could not recall how he made his way back to Pier 17 or why his face was bruised and his shirt torn. His head throbbed and he was unshaven, dirty, and stank of rum and unwashed clothes.

He slept almost non-stop for a full day as the Sea Moon II steamed northwest at 6 knots. He got out of his narrow bunk only long enough to vomit or urinate over the side of the boat. A sympathetic Vietnamese fisherman emptied and washed out his shit bucket and occasionally peered into his private cabin with curiosity, wondering who the tall Caucasian was and what he was doing on board a tuna boat. By dawn on the second day, his hangover and seasickness had abated. He appeared on deck, unsteady on quavering legs, and an obliging crew member hosed him down with cool fresh water as he stood naked with his arms outstretched, reveling in his own rejuvenated humanity. He was ravenous and he devoured the stinking fish-head soup simmering on the gas stove as if it were haute cuisine from a five-star restaurant in Paris or Brussels and washed it down with a bitter beer he did not recognize.

The meal made him sleepy again and he lay down, intending to rest for half an hour. When he awoke four hours later, the weather had picked up. He clambered out of his bunk, wrestling with the sleep in his brain and flew catapulted against the thin wood walls of his room. The wind, howling at nearly thirty knots, produced fifteen-foot swells with waves breaking and the foam blowing into streaks in the direction of the wind. One of the Vietnamese crew burst into his room.

"Captain say you stay inside!" The fisherman laughed at the man's startled discomfiture. Then he disappeared, heading in the direction of the wheelhouse.

The man touched a rising lump on his head where his skull had collided with the wall next to his rack. A thin trickle of blood oozed down his forehead. He wiped it off with the back of his hand and fought to stay in his bunk. A new wave of nausea swept over him, and he reached into his duffel bag and located a small plastic bottle with a screw-off childproof top. He pushed down hard on the top, twisted counterclockwise, and removed the top. He popped a white tablet into his mouth and lay down, waiting for sleep to come. He breathed deeply trying to keep down the fish head soup.

When the captain finally appeared in the doorway to his cabin, the wind had subsided and the seas were much diminished. The two looked at each other for a long time without speaking. Finally, the captain motioned him to follow and walked through the house and into the galley towards the stairs that led to the wheelhouse. The man stumbled out of his rack and made his way unsteadily after the captain, slipping and grasping at the sides of the two-tier bunk bed to counter the energetic roll of the boat in the swell. He climbed the five short stairs to the wheelhouse. The captain pointed to the sat phone in its snap-on base and said in barely intelligible English. "Call for you."

The man looked quizzically at the veteran boat captain and shook his head.

"There must be some mistake."

"No mistake….it for you," the captain repeated, this time louder as if the increased volume of his voice could make his passenger understand.

The man retrieved his wallet from the back pocket of his khaki trousers and took out a wad of wet bills. He stretched out his hand and offered the money to the captain.

"Tell them they have the wrong number," he suggested, forcing a smile.

"Too late," the captain replied. "They know you here."

Reluctantly, he took the sat phone from the captain. Its rubber grip was warm and moist.

"Yeah? Who's this?"

"Hello, Mako," said the familiar voice in perfect English. "Looks like we found you."

Chapter 1

"Incoming!" Corporal Vargas threw his short stocky body over the side of the sandbagged bunker, one hand holding his helmet in place and the other poised to break his fall. He hit the ground hard, almost landing on a second soldier already in the bunker. He curled into a protective fetal position a half second before the 60 mm mortar shell exploded in a mesquite thicket one hundred yards from his position. He lay motionless, waiting to hear the telltale cough of another round fired in his direction, but there was only the echo of the first explosion racing away in the distance, its progress impeded only by prickly pear cactus and an occasional scraggly mesquite tree.

He looked over the bunker wall and saw two fishermen on the Mexican side of the river frantically reel in their lines and beat a hasty retreat into the brush, shouting warnings to their friends who looked to be setting a trotline downstream. There was no telling where the *narcotraficantes* had set up their mortar or whether they had moved on. Vargas did not like being in the crosshairs of their target practice. Eventually the marksmanship of the cartel gunners was bound to improve, or they would get lucky. Where were they getting the mortars anyway?

"This is getting old," said Vargas.

"I won't argue with you," replied the other soldier, a tall lanky Anglo in his early twenties with a faded nametag on his filthy fatigues that read "Binkley".

A Ram 3500 pickup approached slowly along the dirt road that ran parallel to the river. Three hundred fifty horsepower of Turbo Diesel muscle rumbled ominously, the truck rocking clumsily from side to side as it traversed deep ruts and splashed puddles left by a rare but recent thunderstorm. Vargas and Binkley could see two men in the front seat and five or six others standing in the bed of the truck, their assault rifles held like a quiver of arrows pointing at the clear South Texas sky. The truck growled to a stop and the men in the back of the pickup jumped down and fanned out towards the river, forming a defensive perimeter between the vehicle and the Mexican side of the Rio Grande.

The two men in the front seat stepped out of the truck and looked towards the river as if they were expecting something. The younger of the two men was dressed in camouflage fatigues and sported a star on each epaulet. The older man wore faded Wrangler jeans, cowboy boots and a felt western hat suitable for the cool weather of early spring in the Rio Grande Valley. His right cheek bulged with a pinch of chewing tobacco and his teeth were stained brown from the juice of the wintergreen-flavored leaves.

"Soldier!" called out the older of the two men, oblivious to the mud creeping over the toes of his boots. A mosquito buzzed annoyingly around his ear, and he slapped at it halfheartedly with his open palm.

"Yes sir!" Vargas climbed out of his sandbagged bunker and walked towards the older man with an apprehensive sidelong glance in the direction of the river. Binkley stayed behind, watching the visitors with his mouth half-open in surprise. Nobody had visited their bunker since the sporadic mortar fire began several days ago.

"You two here alone, son?"

"No, sir. There're five of us. The rest are out on patrol down by the river, trying to spot the gunner."

"How long you been hunkered down?"

"Quite a while, sir. He's not very good, though. Aim's way off."

"Matlock," the older man said as he turned towards his uniformed colleague.

"Right here, Dad."

"How long's this been going on?" asked the older man.

"About two days. Isn't that right, Corporal?"

Vargas recognized the new commander of the Texas National Guard from his photograph in the *Laredo Sun* and snapped to attention.

"Yes sir, they've been firing a 60 mm mortar. About one round every thirty minutes or so pretty much nonstop."

"Nobody's been hurt?" asked the commander.

"No sir, we're all fine. They can't shoot worth a lick."

The older man shook his head and muttered under his breath.

"Isn't there something we can do about this, Matlock?"

"Not unless you want me to take the fight across the river....which I'd be happy to do."

The younger man spat into a mud puddle next to them. His saliva curdled in the water and floated motionless and pale like the barely visible belly of a dead minnow.

"No, not yet. That's got to be the last resort. We don't want to provoke retaliation by the Mexicans. That's probably what they're hoping for," the older man said. "Washington would like that too, I imagine. Give them the excuse they've been looking for to intervene."

The corporal stared at the older man in civilian clothes. The young soldier had not bathed or changed his uniform in several days and he shuffled his feet self-consciously. He brushed his hand over the dark stubble on his chin.

"You're him, aren't you?" Corporal Vargas addressed the older man in awe.

"Depends on which him you mean," he answered.

"You're the governor, aren't you? You're Creed Tucker!"

The older man nodded his head. "You're not going to hold that against me now, are you?" he asked.

"No, sir!" Vargas exclaimed. "I just want to say we're all behind you, no matter what!"

Creed reached out, grabbed the younger man's hand, and shook it roughly.

"I appreciate it, son....*muchas gracias.* Give my regards to the others. You need anything, you let me know."

"*A sus ordenes!*" The corporal grinned broadly and managed a clumsy salute as the two men turned and walked back slowly to their vehicle.

"Dad, I need to get you out of here right away. Those gunners may be off in their aim, but it wouldn't take but one lucky shot, and I'd be hard pressed to explain what the hell I was thinking when I brought the governor of Texas to a forward recon position on the banks of the Rio Grande. Can't imagine what I'd say to Lupe."

"Relax, Matlock! If Lupe's not used to me by now, she never will be. It'll be twenty years on Saturday since I married her. I just never expected to celebrate our anniversary with the *narcotraficantes* squeezing Texas from the south and the U.S. government harassing us from the north. Sometimes I can sort of empathize with Cuba." He looked at the younger man and suppressed a smile.

Matlock looked at his father and pounded him good-naturedly on the back.

"Now I've heard everything. My father, the quintessential conservative anti-government rancher, wins election as the governor of Texas, announces plans to legalize dope, and now declares his sympathy with the communists in Cuba....thought I'd never live to see the day."

Creed laughed and fastened the pickup's seatbelt across his chest. He rolled down the side window and hung his head out into the humid air. He secured his western hat with one hand and sniffed the earthy smell the rain lured from the ground and the faintly fishy odor drifting up from the Rio Grande.

"I always loved the smell of the river in the morning," he said. "Reminds me of working on that *hacienda* south of Nuevo Laredo when I was sixteen. You remember those old black & white photos?"

"Yeah, I saw 'em. You were so skinny that big old Mexican saddle looked like it was going to swallow you right up. I half expected to see Pancho Villa come riding up. You ought to get that photo blown up and framed. Hell, you should have used it for a campaign poster."

Creed took a deep breath. He thought about those days more and more lately.

"Those cows would bed down in the river bottom in the evening, and I'd ride through clouds of mosquitoes and do a count and make sure the calves were with their mommas....I hated making those rounds back then. I'd come back to the bunkhouse with my face all swollen up from the mosquitoes and my eyes red and itching from the gnats. Now I find myself getting nostalgic for the old days."

"Yeah, the old days; the Kennedy assassinations, Watergate, Vietnam, race riots. Sounds great, Dad."

"No, I'm serious. Sometimes I wish we could just go back in time. Things have gotten too complicated. Evil's getting the upper hand, just like the Bible predicted."

Matlock looked at his father, concerned that the never-ending crises of the past two years had beaten the man down and aged him; taken the fight right out of him.

"Well, I doubt the Bible had anything to say about South Texas, but you can't go back, so don't worry yourself about it. Concentrate on how we're going to survive being caught in a vise from two directions."

Creed Tucker pulled out a utility knife from a miniature scabbard in his belt and began paring down his fingernails and picking out pieces of dirt.

"I hope you treat your horses' hooves better than you do your fingernails," said Matlock.

"My, my...we're just full of compliments this morning, aren't we?"

"It's just that time's running out," said Matlock.

"I know it is."

"I mean, look at the situation. The federal government is threatening to cut off aid, and the Mexican cartels are shelling us from across the river while their government looks the other way. That doesn't bode well for a happy ending."

"That's irony for you, isn't it? The Mexican drug cartels and the U.S. government in cahoots."

"I never thought it'd happen either."

"I ain't denying we're in a jam, Matlock. Your troops are the only thing keeping the traffickers from patrolling the streets of South Texas like they did before the autonomy crisis.[1]"

"Well, my troops are running low on supplies, and it's getting hard to find legitimate ways to buy weapons and ammunition."

Creed Tucker sighed and spit a stream of foul-smelling brown liquid out the side window.

"I know, Matlock. We're working on that."

"And where's that Mako Sloane character? He pulled our nuts out of the fire once. Maybe he can do it again."

---

[1] TEXMEX by Clabe Taylor, Legacy Publishers, 2012.

"Well, that's the only bit of good news there is right now," said Creed.

"How's that?"

"They found him, you know. He's on a Vietnamese tuna boat about 300 miles northwest of Oahu."

"Hawaii? What the hell's he doing there?" asked Matlock.

"Too many people want him dead if you ask me. He's probably just looking for some refuge from the storm. Doesn't sound like such a bad idea to me either."

"Well, I hope he likes fish head soup and rice. That's all those slant-eyed little bastards eat. You think he'll cooperate with us?"

"No telling with Mako. His own people are heading towards Oahu to meet the boat when it docks in a couple of weeks. We won't know till then."

Matlock looked at his father, all traces of humor long gone from his face.

"I hope his people are the only ones who got wind of where he is."

Chapter 2

Antonio Salcido respected ritual and custom and believed he had no right to question the accumulated wisdom of those who had come before him. The lack of reverence for one's own history and culture, he argued, was symptomatic of a world strangely out of kilter with itself.

Salcido was a devout Catholic, at first glance an odd thing, given his profession. He loved the solemnity and symbolism of Mexican baptisms above all other rites of the Church, and he accepted with much gravity invitations to stand as godfather to the sons of his most loyal followers. Along with the honor of becoming another man's *compadre* came great responsibility, and Antonio did not take such commitments lightly.

His favorite Mexican holiday was *El Dia de los Muertos,* which he celebrated each year at the beginning of November with his family in Culiacán, Sinaloa. The holiday traced its roots back to an Aztec festival and was a time to pray for and remember relatives and friends who had passed on. The observance of the Day of the Dead together with All Saints' Day and All Souls' Day appealed to his sense of cultural harmony.

"When you take away the material trappings of life," he always told his friends, "a man only has his dignity and his respect for family and traditions."

But dignity was a virtue seemingly in short supply on the evening of his arrival in Mykolaiv, Ukraine, and he was not familiar with the local rituals and customs he witnessed. Antonio remembered clearly the flight from Vienna to Odessa and the comely flight attendant who waited on him with her Yulia Timoshenko look-alike braids piled on top of her head like a coiled snake ready to strike. He remembered seeing his name displayed prominently on a white cardboard sign as he disembarked from the Ukrainian International Boeing 737, and he recalled the van standing off to one side of the tarmac waiting to carry a select group of passengers to the VIP lounge. He knew he slept during most of the two-hour trip in the black Toyota Land Cruiser over rolling hills along the Black Sea coast to the port city of Mykolaiv. He was less clear about how he came to be sitting at a long banquet table in a private dining room at the Black Sea Shipyard, or who his companions were, and why the gathering included a half dozen vodka-swilling women whose plunging necklines and heavy makeup suggested a somewhat different profession than the interpreters and engineers they claimed to be.

He remembered standing up repeatedly to toss down shots of fiery vodka and cognac following banal toasts to everlasting friendship between Ukraine and Mexico. Vague snatches from scenes of singing and dancing swirled through his mind like disjointed excerpts from a novel in a foreign language he only remotely understood. A robust Ukrainian with a shaved head who Antonio suspected was the deputy director of the shipyard sat to his left. On his right a female interpreter kept her lips glued to his ear, alternately translating the deputy director's technical explanations into broken English and whispering her own suggestive promises of favors yet to be dispensed.

The long table sagged with plate upon plate of exotic hors d'oeuvres and fish with gaping mouths and bulging eyes whose identity he could not guess and which he dared not eat. Bottles of vodka, champagne, wine, and cognac stood in strategic clusters along the table. By midnight he was a wreck and waved off his garrulous hosts, who attempted to ply him with more food and drink.

When he woke up the next morning in the shipyard's VIP guestroom, his interpreter lay naked and foul next to him, and the sun was shining through his bedroom window. It bored into his eyes like a malevolent force. He groaned and winced at a debilitating pressure in his temples, his head gripped by the steel vise of a hangover that threatened never to release him.

Antonio cursed the memory of the Russian diplomat he met during the Chamber of Commerce reception at the Maria Isabel Sheraton Hotel in Mexico City some three years before. He had introduced himself to Antonio as

Vladimir, and he spoke at length and with pride of his hometown of Mykolaiv, an important Ukrainian port on the Black Sea located along the estuary of the Yuzhniy Bug. They drank tequila and talked late into the night, leaving the hotel after the reception and closing down a chic bar in Coyoacán just before sunrise. Antonio mainly listened and asked questions. He was good at that. When Vladimir spoke of his father, who had been the director of a military shipbuilding yard for 30 years, Antonio recognized an opportunity and pumped his new friend for information.

Ultimately, it was Vladimir who bore the blame for his presence in Mykolaiv and his raging hangover, Antonio thought. He staggered to the bathroom and removed his clothes, which reeked of pickled herring, cigarette smoke, and someone else's vomit. He turned on the water in the white tile shower, and a thin icy stream that made him gasp gushed from rusty fixtures with ancient enamel faucet handles. He flinched and shivered but stood without moving and greedily gulped the air in spasms as if he had never breathed before.

His interpreter appeared at the door of the bathroom naked, striking a suggestive pose. Her dark hair hung in tangled curls across her shoulders and covered one breast, the other peeking out proudly and beckoning.

"You need company?" she asked in accented English, still playing the poorly conceived role of seductress. The script had bombed the night before and remained unedited and little improved in the morning.

"No, you go home now." He turned off the frigid stream of water.

"I leave?" she answered with surprise.

"You leave."

She tossed her hair impetuously and turned on her heels. He heard the rustling of clothing, the slam of the door, and she was gone.

"Gracias a Dios," he said aloud and managed the semblance of a smile.

He turned on the hot water and reached for the pale bar of nondescript soap on the windowsill, from which he could see blue sky and a courtyard ringed with industrial shops. The temperature of the water did not change. There was no hot water.

"Carajo!"

The green plastic telephone in his bedroom jangled, and he wrapped his nakedness with a thin towel and strode back into the bedroom with a purpose he did not feel. He picked up the headset.

"Yes?"

"Dobrogo ranku, Antonio," boomed a voice full of energy and optimism that seemed foreign to Antonio after last night's ordeal.

"Sorry, I don't speak Russian."

"It's Ukrainian, but don't worry. My English is a bit rusty but I can manage. Can you meet me downstairs in five minutes?"

"Give me ten and I'll be there," said Antonio. He hung up the phone and dressed.

He walked slowly down the two narrow flights of stairs and saw a group of identically dressed men standing in the lobby, talking and smoking cigarettes. Cold air poured into the vestibule as one of the men opened the door and walked out to the street and a black SUV parked next to the curb. Antonio stopped and appraised the men. He recognized his companion with the shaved head from the night before, but he was the only one who looked familiar. Each of the four men wore a black fur hat and a bulky dark leather jacket. Their eyes were bloodshot and their faces ravaged from the bacchanal of the previous night, and when he shook their hands he smelled garlic and alcohol and unwashed bodies. Antonio felt strangely vindicated and relieved. Misery does love company, he thought.

A fifth man burst into the cramped lobby and shouted in English.

"Antonio, there you are! I was beginning to worry you didn't survive your welcoming party."

"And you are...?" Antonio asked curtly.

"You can call me Valeriy. I'm the director of the Black Sea Shipyard. Would you like some hot coffee and breakfast?

"Just show me my submarine, please."

Chapter 3

"Where the hell did this report come from?" asked Harvard Banks, DEA's assistant administrator for intelligence. Banks had arrived in Mexico City from Dallas the night before for a special CIA briefing at the U.S. embassy. The CIA, normally so compartmentalized and territorial, was looking for answers to a puzzle and was offering a quid pro quo. I'll show you mine if you show me yours, went their reasoning.

Banks spent a sleepless night in the Maria Isabel Sheraton Hotel next to the U.S. embassy. The room was comfortable and there was no jet lag involved, but this was Bank's first trip to Mexico and he was nervous. He fantasized that the Sinaloa Cartel would send an assassin to kill him, and he was equally frightened he might get the shits from the Mexican food in the hotel restaurant. Nerves alone were making his bowels rumble ominously. A career analyst in DEA's intelligence division, Banks was not comfortable in the field, especially in the chaotic and unpredictable environment of Mexico City.

"It came from a new source in the Mexican government," answered Cyrus Tinch, a mid-level CIA officer assigned to the Mexico City station and responsible for reporting on government corruption and the narcotics target. The chief of station (COS) sat next to Tinch and stared across the conference table at Banks, trying to judge his reaction.

"Sounds pretty far-fetched," said Banks.

"Maybe, but the source is reliable and has a good track record," interrupted Tinch. "It's one of our most sensitive cases. That's why we had to get a special clearance to brief you."

"Yes," said Banks as he perused the written report. "I appreciate that."

"Besides, we've corroborated the report using both HUMINT and technical means from other sources," added the COS.

Banks squirmed uncomfortably in his swivel chair as another round of stomach cramps almost doubled him over. He clinched his buttocks together to avoid the embarrassment of having to make a run to the men's room in the middle of his briefing.

"ETA's in about ten days. We've got the freighter under satellite surveillance," said the COS. "They have the target completely covered with tarps, but it's on board, no question about it."

"Russian freighter?" asked Banks.

"Ukrainian owned, flying the Panamanian flag," answered Tinch.

"You guys are thorough."

"Got to justify these generous government salaries," joked the COS....."But there's more."

"I was afraid of that," smiled Banks.

"A group of fifteen Ukrainians arrived on an Iberian flight from Madrid last week. We think it might be the crew sent to train the Mexicans. We had a surveillance team follow them to down to Veracruz. Apparently, that's where the freighter's heading," said Cyrus.

Banks put down the two typewritten pages and threw up his hands.

"But what the hell does the Sinaloa Cartel need with a Russian submarine?"

"Technically, it's not Russian....it's Ukrainian," said the COS.

"What's the difference?" Banks replied irritably.

"If I may, sir?" asked Cyrus Tinch.

"Yeah, go ahead, Cyrus," responded the COS.

"Mr. Banks, according to the source....and our station in Kiev has corroborated this intelligence....the submarine comes from the Black Sea Shipyard in Mykolaiv."

"From where?" asked Banks.

"Mykolaiv. It's a Ukrainian city of about six hundred thousand people on the Black Sea, or more precisely, on an estuary that leads to the Black Sea. It's a large port and the city was famous during Soviet times for its shipbuilding industry; mainly for the military. Up until 1990 it was a 'closed city'....closed to foreigners because of all the classified military construction going on. Since the breakup of the USSR, they've been pretty much limited to building yachts for a few wealthy oligarchs and that's about it....until now...or until a few years ago."

"And now?" asked Banks.

"Well, you can see for yourself. The Sinaloa Cartel apparently ordered a custom-built knockoff of the French-made SSK Andrasta submarine, 135 feet long, 800 plus tons of displacement. This is a far cry from the two or four-man homemade subs parked in swampy rivers you guys have been finding in Columbia and Peru."

"Ukraine decided to sell a damned submarine to the cartel?" Banks asked.

"They need the money," said the COS.

Banks was not convinced.

"How do you know it's not for the Mexican navy? This must have cost a pretty penny."

The COS laughed.

"The Sinaloa Cartel isn't exactly in need of shopping coupons to buy whatever the hell it wants," he said. "But we're pretty sure this isn't for the Mexican navy."

"How can you be sure?" asked Banks. "If we alert the administration and you're wrong, we're going to look pretty silly."

Cyrus Tinch reached into a light-green folder in front of him on the table and shuffled through a stack of multi-page documents, most of them with red stamps on their cover sheets.

"A couple of months ago, Antonio Salcido flew from Mexico City to Madrid and then on to Vienna," said Cyrus.

"So?" Banks interrupted. "The man's got a right to travel. Maybe he went to see the Lipizzaner stallions at the Spanish Riding School."

Tinch ignored the satire.

"From Vienna he flew to Odessa, Ukraine. He was picked up at the airport in a black Toyota Land Cruiser that took him to Mykolaiv. Does the man in this photo look familiar?"

Tinch handed Banks an 8 x 10 printout of a digital photo he pulled out of the folder.

"I'll be damned....that's Salcido alright....looks a bit strange in a fur hat," said Banks. "Remind me not to get on the wrong side of you guys. You've got people everywhere, don't you?"

"The man next to him is Valery Sadykov. He's the director of the Black Sea Shipyard."

Banks stared at the COS for a moment and then picked up the report again.

"So how big did you say this sub was?"

"About 135 feet long," answered Tinch.

Banks whistled. "Jesus, that could carry tons and tons of narcotics undetected straight up the East Coast."

"You're missing the point, Mr. Banks," said the COS. "We're not talking about cargo capacity anymore. Even that would be a concern, but the acquisition of this Ukrainian submarine signifies a quantum change in the cartel's strategy."

"Oh, what are we talking about?" Banks was not accustomed to being on the outside looking in.

"Tell him, Cyrus."

"They've declared war," Cyrus said. "We're talking about a $200 million small attack submarine that can accommodate new-generation heavyweight torpedoes like the Black Shark, anti-ship missiles like the Exocet SM-39, and even a mine-laying system."

"The Sinaloa Cartel will have an offensive weapon. If they learn how to operate the submarine and deploy it, they'll be able to blow any ship the U.S. Coast Guard has out of the water and even take on U.S. Navy warships," said the COS emphatically.

"Jesus!" exclaimed Banks. "What the hell for?"

Cyrus and the COS exchanged glances.

"We were hoping you could tell us that," said the COS.

***

Soledad Castillo glanced up at the clock on the wall of her office in the *Procuraduría General de la República,* the Office of the Attorney General. She was running late and that annoyed her. In her thrill at receiving the long-awaited promotion to intelligence analyst in SIEDO, *Subprocuraduría de Investigación Especializada en Delincuencia Organizada,* the organized crime division, Soledad had taken on far more work than she could handle, and she was always in a rush to meet lapsed deadlines. She wanted to impress her supervisor with her analytical ability, but he seemed more interested in looking down her blouse and finding excuses to be alone with her in his office than anything she had to offer in a professional sense. Sometimes she wondered whether it had been her law degree from the *Universidad Nacional Autónoma de Mexico* or her perky cleavage that landed her the much sought-after position in the Office of the Attorney General.

Actually, Soledad did not find her supervisor's prurient interest in her décolletage overly offensive. On the contrary, she encouraged his attentions and got in the habit of unbuttoning the top two buttons of her blouse before she would enter his office. "All men are one-third dog," her late grandmother used to say, and Soledad was not above using that male character trait to her advantage. She had her reasons.

Her supervisor was a short, middle-aged man whose narrow Pedro Infante mustache and rotund silhouette made him more a caricature of the suave, debonair Latin lover than the real thing. He had a constant need to impress Soledad with his importance as a confidante of the attorney general, and she artfully exploited his weakness. When she expressed interest in the information he shared with her, he swelled up with pride like a bantam rooster and told her more. Not that Soledad was any more close-mouthed with the sensitive intelligence than he was, but she, at least, knew exactly what she was doing and why.

In Cyrus Tinch, Soledad found someone who appreciated her for more than her looks. While Soledad talked, Cyrus took copious notes during their meetings each week at the CIA safe house in Cuernavaca, an hour's drive south of Mexico City. Soledad only wished she could tell Cyrus where her supervisor's information came from. That was the riddle, she knew. She often wondered whether the Office of the Attorney General had its own agents inside the Sinaloa Cartel or whether the drug traffickers had penetrated Mexico's top law enforcement agency. In the end, perhaps it mattered little. The intelligence Soledad produced was staggering, both in volume and quality.

Soledad closed her safe and spun the combination lock. She ran her eyes over the top of her desk, looking for any official document she might have inadvertently left out.

At least on the surface, security was tight in her office and violations of security procedures were punished severely. As she rode the elevator down to the lobby, her mind was on the drive to Cuernavaca and the meeting later in the day with Cyrus Tinch. She wished she could meet with him in Mexico City, but he had insisted that personal meetings in the capital with an official from the U.S. embassy would not be safe. He was right, she knew. There were influential and powerful people in both Culiacán and Mexico City who would not appreciate her indiscretions. In fact, they would kill her if they knew.

The elevator doors opened and Soledad walked briskly towards the revolving glass door of the high-rise office building leading out to Paseo de la Reforma. She did not notice the uniformed DHL deliveryman standing off to one side of the exit, studying the address label on a large manila envelope and holding a cell phone to his ear. He stood next to a dolly loaded with cardboard boxes stacked one on top of the other and vaguely glanced at her as she walked by. She turned left as she exited the building and walked towards the curb, intending to wave down one of the hundreds of VW taxis that prowled the streets of Mexico City, incessantly looking for fares. A taxi parked just twenty yards down Paseo de la Reforma caught her eye and she made a beeline towards the yellow VW bug, which she thought must have just let out a passenger. She hurried to catch the taxi before someone else beat her to it. As she approached the taxi, she realized it was empty and noticed the *"Fuera de Servicio"* sign hung on the front windshield. She stopped suddenly and slung her purse over her right shoulder in frustration.

The DHL deliveryman had stepped out of the office building and appeared to ogle Soledad as she walked briskly along the sidewalk in her tight skirt, unconsciously swinging her hips from side to side. He still held the cell phone to his ear, but when Soledad stopped, he quickly keyed in a five-digit code and hurriedly stepped back into the building. He barely made it back through the revolving doors when he heard the explosion and screams from the street.

Chapter 4

Mako Sloane awoke to the sound of Captain Nyugen knocking loudly on the door to the crew's cabin. The skunk smell of coffee drifted in from the galley. He heard the first farts of consciousness from the Vietnamese fishermen as they hauled their exhausted bodies out of two-tiered bunk beds and stumbled into their clothes. Rain fell steadily outside and the crew wore knit caps, sweat pants, and long sleeves under their rain gear despite the tropical latitude. It was the last haul of the voyage, and their clothes stank of fish and sweat and were stiff with sea salt, tolerable shortcomings as long as the clothing was dry. They sucked in the hot coffee greedily with long slurping noises and soon were wide-awake.

It had been only four hours since the end of the last haul, and Mako's shoulders and arms ached from the still unaccustomed effort of coiling the 2 mm monofilament leaders by hand and fighting the tuna, some of the great fish weighing over one hundred pounds and all of them creatures of great beauty and grace. For twenty-eight days he had toiled alongside the younger fishermen and learned the monotonous routine of long-lining and the arcane art of gaffing. He had watched the life blood gush out of the magnificent fish on deck with regret and cringed at the death shudder of the great tuna as the fishermen administered the coup de grâce with a hand-held pike. Mako understood the place of these fish in the food chain, but he came to realize that fishing on this vast scale was not only a business; it was also a methodical taking of souls, and he mourned their passing.

After the final haul, the Sea Moon II turned and steamed back towards the islands, its hold brimming with the carcasses of the great fish. Two days later the boat approached Oahu with Honolulu's skyline appearing phantom-like out of the ethereal early-morning mist that shrouded the island. Mako knew they would be waiting for him at the pier and that he would have to disappoint them.

He released the bungee cords that lashed his nine-foot Stewart Hydro-Hull longboard to the top of the lifeboat and packed his few belongings in a Dakine waterproof pack he slipped over his shoulders. He waved to the crew and the captain, who followed his movements with curious, disbelieving eyes. Then he threw the surfboard off the stern of the fishing boat and jumped in after it. When he looked back, the Sea Moon II was already thirty meters away and moving off at six knots towards port. Mako put his head in the water and dolphin-kicked to where his surfboard lay bobbing in the wake of the fishing boat. He heaved his body on to the board, turned towards Waikiki, and started the long paddle to shore.

An hour later Mako glided towards a group of surfers in the lineup at Threes and eyed the beach suspiciously, looking for anyone who seemed out of place. He saw nothing that concerned him and sat up on his board to catch his breath. His shoulders and back burned from the long paddle and his neck was stiff. He looked back at the swell lines in the distance. The waves were small but they were clean and pure. A light offshore breeze kept the waves glassy, and they formed and rose in predictable succession like the graceful forms of some kind of alien life.

"Whoa, where did you come from?" asked a young surfer in the lineup as he turned his head at the sound of water splashing and caught sight of Mako sitting on his board and breathing hard.

Mako ignored him.

"Pretty mellow day, isn't it?"

"Sure," said Mako.

"You're not a local, are you?" The surfer's short bleach-blond crew cut lay half-spiked and half-plastered down on his head. Indistinct tattoos on his arms and back blended into his sun-darkened complexion.

"No."

"Me neither. Back in Minnesota, my name's Jeremy, but here everyone calls me Keaweaheulu. I think it means 'cool breeze over the mountains' or something like that. I've been here for three months already. I'm never going back." He paddled over to Mako and stuck out his hand in greeting.

"Interesting," replied Mako and shook his hand without conviction. He looked back at a wave beginning to form and started paddling in anticipation.

"Don't drop in on the locals," the surfer warned. "They can get pretty agro here."

"Fuck the locals." Mako's longboard picked up speed, catching the wave and accelerating rapidly forward. Mako popped up effortlessly despite the backpack and worked a small waist-high wave until it gave out about two hundred yards from shore. He paddled the rest of the way to the beach, enjoying the physical exertion and the clear cool water despite the knowledge that someone who wanted to kill him was probably nearby.

Mako walked his surfboard out of the water and approached a solitary figure sitting in the sand, wistfully watching the lineup of surfers.

"Need a longboard?" Mako dropped his surfboard in the sand.

"Are you serious, dude?"

Mako nodded his head and walked off, opening his backpack and removing a t-shirt that still smelled vaguely of fish and slipping the fragrant garment over his head. He caught a taxi on Kalakaua Street for the short ride to the Hale Koa hotel, an unlikely destination for Mako. He knew they would not think of looking for him at the touristy resort.

The next day Mako flew to San Francisco under an assumed name, using a set of false identification documents he had purchased in Honolulu from an obliging Japanese forger, who labored in his smoky studio in a Kaka'ako warehouse loft. The passport and driver's license were expensive, but the people looking for him might have a record of all alias documentation officially issued to him in the past, and he certainly could not travel in true name.

Once in San Francisco, he rented a car at the airport and drove south on Highway 101 towards Monterey. Two hours later Mako sped past the town of Marina, sand dune hills looming at the edge of the beach, and soon saw the Best Western Hotel on the outskirts of Monterey. He rolled down the windows of his rented Mazda and caught the faint stench of rotting kelp on the persistent onshore breeze and he visibly relaxed. Monterey had always produced that narcotic effect on him, even as an eighteen-year old army private studying Russian at the Defense Language Institute forty-some years before. Mako turned right into the large parking lot which half-encircled Fisherman's Wharf. He parked the rented Mazda and strolled over to the fishing pier at the end of Del Monte beach. He walked across the weather-beaten wooden planks, which groaned under his weight, and moved to the far side of the pier past a dozen fishermen, mainly local teenagers with a sprinkling of beach winos angling for surfperch and their supper. He leaned over the railing deep in thought and felt the light mist from the fog on his face.

An unshaven fisherman with a dark complexion staked out his claim to the spot next to Mako and cast his line and shrimp bait into the water below. He held up a brown paper sack to his mouth and drank deeply of whatever the bag contained. He looked over at Mako, who eyed him with curiosity.

"Wanna drink?" the wino offered, speaking with a slight accent.

"What is it?" asked Mako.

"Night Train Express, *amigo.*" He held out the paper sack. "Only the best."

"Sure, why not," said Mako accepting the offering of fortified wine. *"Muchas gracias."*

"¿Hablas español?" asked the man with apparent surprise.

"Claro que sí, hombre. ¿De dónde eres?"

"De Coahuila. ¿La conoces?"

"Por supuesto. Soy de Tejas."

"Ay, por eso. I used to be a lawyer in Mexico," the wino said proudly in Spanish.

"And now?" Mako asked.

"Now I'm just a drunk. This country sucks the life out of you."

"And Mexico doesn't?"

The wino laughed. "*Mexico lindo y querido!* Sure it does. But Mexico doesn't seduce you with false promises of a car in every garage and a chicken in every pot."

"No, I guess Mexico doesn't pretend to be anything other than what it is."

The breeze was cool and wet and Mako turned up his collar for protection against the occasional whisper of fine mist, which the fog carried surreptitiously along the beach. He was enjoying the conversation with the vagrant drunk and wondered what the man was going to say next.

"It never has. Mexico is all chaos and cruelty. Every day something else happens to deprive us more of our humanity. Mexico has fallen into a deep hell where even the sun is silent about our sins....but at least we know what to expect."

Mako glanced over at the drunk with surprise.

"Dante?" he asked.

"*El mismo.*" The wino paused and seemed to study Mako's face and then continued. "What are you running from?"

"Ah, our Mexican philosopher might be drunk, but he sees himself as a shrewd judge of men."

"Don't laugh. I can see it in your eyes. Eyes are like small windows to the soul, don't you think?" asked the Mexican.

"I think you're drunk," Mako looked across the bay towards Santa Cruz.

"I see things others cannot….it's a gift."

"It's the Night Train Express," said Mako.

"I think you've killed many men," said the Mexican mysteriously. "Tell me you haven't."

"Yeah, I've been a regular *desperado.*" Mako leaned over the pier railing and spit into the water far below. He heard the *crack-crack-crack* of a sea otter breaking a shell on a rock. He looked across the marina to the placid water by the boats but could not see the otter.

"You cannot hide the truth with jokes, my friend. I see it in your eyes."

"You see what you gotta see, and I do what I gotta do." Mako laughed and reached for the bottle of wine. The Mexican extended the paper sack reluctantly, as if sacrificing his first-born son.

"That's where you're wrong. You don't *have* to do anything. Everyone makes their own choices." He ignored Mako's attempt at humor. "Don't you believe in human volition?"

"You're an expert on that too, I suppose?" Mako asked.

"Yes, I am. For example, I *choose* to be a drunk. You have chosen a different path, but I think you've disappointed yourself."

"So, you have delusions of being a mind reader, my drunk friend?" Mako tilted his head back and took a long pull of the fortified wine. "What's your name?"

"Armando Trujillo," the wino said, extending his hand. "*Para servirle.*"

"A pleasure.....Mako." They shook hands and stared at each other.

"Like the shark?" asked Armando.

"Like the shark."

"Don't feel bad," said Armando. "I'm running too."

"Oh?"

"Yeah, I was a lawyer in Mexico City and didn't choose my clients well....they were *narcotraficantes*. I knew it but I served them anyway because the money was good."

Mako perked up and looked over at Armando, who stood calmly sipping at the bottle of wine he held in his right hand and gesturing theatrically with his left hand. Sea lions bellowed in the distance by the Coast Guard pier, and a sea gull swooped down to nab a miserly offering of stale bread from a nearby teenage fisherman.

"And what happened?" asked Mako.

"I found out things I didn't need to know."

"That can be risky."

"You know that from experience?" asked Armando.

"Maybe," said Mako.

Armando stared at Mako as if trying to unravel a riddle. Then he continued.

"They were afraid I would go to the *gringos* and tell them what I knew. First, they planted a bomb in my car, but they killed the wrong person. They killed my wife. We had been married for only three months. That's when I ran."

"It's hard to run from the cartel," said Mako.

"I know. They caught up with me in Nuevo Laredo."

"And you're still alive?"

"I agreed to do a job for them."

"One last job?"

"There's never a last one. There's always one more."

"So why did they let you across the border?" asked Mako.

"The cartel?"

"Yeah."

"They have hostages....my parents."

"Hard to refuse an offer like that. And what's the job?"

Armando looked down at his worn-out running shoes and then met Mako's questioning gaze.

"They want me to kill you, Mako."

Chapter 5

As the first vestiges of the steel-gray dawn began to lighten the eastern horizon above the tepid muck of the Gulf of Mexico, the eighty-seven foot United States Coast Guard Cutter *Orca* was cruising at 18 knots heading northeast about two miles due east of Port Aransas, Texas. The coastal patrol boat had been wreaking havoc on drug smugglers for the last two days, interdicting six motorized rubber rafts apparently launched from a larger mother ship, which up to this point had eluded detection. The crew had arrested ten Mexican and four Nicaraguan smugglers and seized several hundred pounds of marijuana. The street value of the dope they seized would not come close to covering the operating costs of the cutter and crew, but the men were in high spirits and believed they were serving their country and doing God's work.

Since the state of Texas announced plans to legalize marijuana three months before, the Coast Guard had seen a marked increase in attempts by the traffickers to smuggle product directly into the Texas coast before the new governor implemented the law and put them out of business. The traffickers were using tactics borrowed from Somali pirates; a mother ship would cruise offshore and dispatch speedy inflatable boats with powerful outboard motors that zipped in to the beach and quickly offloaded the illicit cargo.

Commander Fred Jenkins thought he finally might have the mother ship in sight: a 150-foot hulking ruin of a freighter flying the Liberian flag and moving slowly off to the northeast at five knots. As the *Orca* closed on the cargo vessel, Jenkins watched the ship through binoculars and saw two rubber speedboats brazenly lowered from its deck to the placid surface of the Gulf. Within seconds, the boats were skipping over the water at high speed heading west towards the beach. The commander could see the outlines of large square bundles and the silhouettes of two men in each boat despite the semi-darkness. On the cutter, crewmembers manned the two .50 caliber M2 Browning machine guns on the bow, and the others prepared the rigid hull inflatable boat for launch from the stern.

Commander Jenkins gave the order to send his chase boat after the smugglers' small delivery craft and for the cutter itself to stop the freighter. He alerted the Coast Guard base in Corpus Christi, and they in turn would be sure to alert local law enforcement. With any luck, if one of the smugglers' boats escaped from his men, it would run into an unwelcome welcoming committee on the beach.

As the chase boat sped away in pursuit of the smugglers, all eyes of the Coast Guard crew shifted to the cargo ship as the cutter rapidly closed the gap. So far, the freighter had not complied with Jenkins' instructions to stop or even acknowledged his attempt to communicate. The commander was cautious. He recognized that his small crew and light armament would be no match for a determined resistance by the freighter's crew, which probably had assault rifles and RPGs at their disposal.

"Raise Corpus base and call for helicopter backup," said Jenkins. "We seem to have an uncooperative target."

"Roger," replied his radioman.

The rigid hull inflatable chase boat meanwhile raced over the flat water in pursuit of the smugglers. The two young Coast Guardsmen were already a mile from the *Orca* and closing on one of the smugglers' speed boats when a blinding flash of white light strangely illuminated the early morning sky behind them. Five seconds later the thunderous clap of earsplitting multiple explosions reached them. They turned, yet understanding nothing, and looked in the direction of the *Orca*, or more precisely, where she had been, because in her place they saw nothing but flames and freakish shadows spreading in all directions.

***

"All our information indicates there was no warning at all," said Admiral Jonathon (Johnny) Fontaine, commandant of the United States Coast Guard. "She exploded and went down fast. By the time the pursuit boat circled and returned to her last observed location, there was nothing left but burning debris and a flaming oil slick." He put his briefing notes down and looked around the conference table grimly.

"Theories?" asked Director of the Central Intelligence Agency (D/CIA) Ian McGinnis who was chairing the meeting. "How many agencies do we have investigating the cause of the explosion anyway?" he asked almost as an afterthought.

Fontaine looked around the room, but nobody seemed inclined to speak. All the heavyweights were present at the briefing: anyone with a portfolio related to national security plus Cory Elkins, head of the Drug Enforcement Administration. All were silent, apparently waiting for him to take the lead.

"It might be easier to list the agencies that aren't conducting an investigation," said Fontaine.

"Well, I've got to brief the president this afternoon, and I need your best guess on what sunk the *Orca,*" said the DCI. "Let me hear your theories."

"They run the gamut," continued Fontaine. "All the way from the *Orca* hitting a naval mine that had just been set by the freighter, to an anti-ship missile or a torpedo. We should have some results from forensics later today but not in time for your briefing."

"And who did it?"

"Again, we don't know. Terrorists or drug traffickers would be my best guess. We don't know who or what was on that Liberian freighter. Circumstantial evidence points to her involvement, of course, but we can't be sure."

The D/CIA looked incredulously at Fontaine.

"Are you telling me that we lose a Coast Guard cutter and eight crewmen to possible hostile fire less than two miles off the coast of Texas, and we don't even know who did it? "What the hell happened to the freighter?"

The commandant squirmed uncomfortably in his chair and looked around the room for support. There was none. Each man at the table studied his briefing document intently without raising his eyes.

"The freighter seems to have disappeared into thin air. We think they might have taken her out into international waters and scuttled her, but we haven't found any sign yet."

"Jesus!" exclaimed the D/CIA. "Why do I feel like I've got the Cub Scouts of America defending our coast line? All right, gentlemen. Thanks for coming. I'll be in touch if the president requires anything else."

The D/CIA stood up, adjourning the meeting and called out to the DEA administrator.

"Cory, if you could stay just for a few minutes?"

"Sure."

D/CIA McGinnis waited until only the two of them remained in the conference room. As soon as the door shut, McGinnis turned to Elkins who had been a fixture at DEA for over ten years.

"Are you thinking what I'm thinking?"

Elkins glanced at the door uneasily as if reluctant to answer the director's question.

"Probably."

"How many people do you have on that bigot list?" asked the D/CIA.

"There's only two of us. Besides me, just my assistant administrator for intelligence. You know him….Harvard Banks. He's the one that your people briefed down in Mexico City."

The mention of the name caused the D/CIA to crack a barely perceptible smile.

"Oh yeah. I heard about him. Shit his pants during the briefing, didn't he?"

"Something like that. Harvard has a sensitive stomach, I'm afraid."

"So we agree it was probably the Ukrainian sub that sailed last week out of Veracruz?" asked the D/CIA.

"That'd be my guess.

"I'd bet money forensics comes back today and says they identified fragments from a Black Shark heavy torpedo," speculated the CIA director.

"That submarine can also fire an Exocet SM-39 anti-ship missile if I remember the report correctly," said Elkins. "So what are you going to tell the president?"

"Whatever he wants to hear. Except the truth, of course."

Chapter 6

"Kill me?" Mako's eyes furtively searched the beach and the fishing pier for anyone who might be providing backup for Armando. "I guess you'll have to stand in line. Appreciate the warning, though."

Armando laughed and finished off the bottle of fortified wine. He walked over to one corner of the pier and threw the bottle and brown paper bag into a green plastic garbage can.

"Wanna get some more wine?"

"Don't you have a job to do?" asked Mako.

Armando looked up at Mako with bloodshot, watery eyes and shook his head.

"It can wait."

"Are you alone?"

"No," Armando answered. "How do you think I found you?"

"I've been trying to figure that out."

Armando looked at Mako with surprise.

"I thought you were some kind of super spook."

"I guess that's a matter of opinion," Mako said.

Armando gestured with a barely perceptible movement of his head back down the pier.

"See that Mexican over there fishing by himself?"

Mako shifted his body around and stood with his back to the railing. He crossed one leg over the other and pretended to look down the beach away from the pier. He glanced out of the corner of his eye and saw a Hispanic man casting his line into the water seemingly oblivious to their presence. A blue and white Igloo ice chest stood beside him. Mako doubted it contained ice.

"Yeah, who is he?"

"My cartel associate."

"Oh," he's going to help you kill me?"

 "Sort of. He was going to wire your car to explode in case I failed. Probably already did."

"I see," said Mako. "Now what?"

"That's up to you."

"I'm listening."

"Ever read Cervantes?" Armando asked.

"Don Quixote?"

"Yeah, remember Sancho Panza?" asked Armando.

"Sure."

"Well, there you have it," said Armando mysteriously.

"Have what?" Mako looked at Armando and could not decide whether the man represented a threat or whether he was crazy, just drunk, or maybe all of the above. He could feel the butt of his Browning 9 mm against his hand in the pocket of his windbreaker. It gave him comfort and he watched Armando's every move.

"La tradición manda que todo caballero andante tenga un escudero."[2]

Mako looked at Armando incredulously.

"You want to be my Sancho Panza?"

"Claro," Armando answered. "Maybe we can help each other."

"You think I'm out there joisting with windmills or something?" asked Mako.

"What else? The idealistic but misunderstood CIA man."

"Know what, Armando?"

"What?"

"You're full of shit," Mako said and laughed aloud.

"Maybe, but first things first.....we have to get rid of my friend. Got any ideas?"

"Let's go get that wine. Maybe something will come to me," said Mako.

The two men walked side by side down the pier past Armando's helper, who did his best to avert his eyes and ignore them. As they came down off the pier and headed towards the parking lot by Fisherman's Wharf, they caught sight of a police officer patrolling on foot and pushing his bicycle.

---

[2] Tradition demands that all knights-errant have a squire. - Spanish

"I've got an idea," Mako said to Armando, and he walked casually over to the officer. Armando stood off to one side watching.

"Excuse me, officer," said Mako, switching to English. "I was just up on the fishing pier. There's a Mexican vagrant up there, and it looks like he's got a gun in his ice chest," said Mako.

"Thanks, I'll take a look," said the police officer. As he walked towards the fishing pier, the cop pulled out a handheld radio and spoke quietly into the mouthpiece. Before he even reached the stairs that led up to the pier, another bicycle patrolman arrived, pedaling furiously. Together they walked up the stairs, across the pier, and approached the Mexican cautiously. He was still fishing but turning his head frequently, apparently looking for his partner. As Mako and Armando watched from a distance, one of the policemen grabbed the Mexican roughly by the shoulders, turned him around and pushed him against the pier railing. They spread his legs and frisked him. The other opened the ice chest and retrieved a handgun, holding it by the trigger guard between his thumb and forefinger. A police cruiser pulled into the parking lot a few minutes later, its red light flashing, and the two bicycle cops led their hapless collar to the car for the half-hour ride to the detention center in Salinas. A bust for illegal possession of a firearm in Monterey was heady stuff in comparison with the shoplifting or drunk and disorderly charges they normally dealt with on Fisherman's Wharf.

"I have a new-found respect for the *chota* in your country," said Armando laughing. "That's one down and two to go."

"What are the other two?" asked Mako.

"Well, first there's the bomb that's probably attached to the gas tank of your car."

"Okay, I assume you can take care of that?" asked Mako.

"*Por supuesto*[3].

"And the second thing?"

"We've got to get another bottle of wine."

***

"What do you mean, they missed him?" asked Creed Tucker.

He leaned back in his richly tooled leather chair and stared across the broad oak desk at James Brazzle, director of the People's Intelligence and Security Service. The office of the special South Texas intelligence unit was situated on the twelfth floor of Laredo's Hamilton Hotel, which had been completely remodeled to house the fledgling organization.

---

[3] of course

The local Chamber of Commerce appreciated the unexpected largess from Austin. Creed looked out the window at the traffic below on Salinas Street. The day, which had begun so promisingly, had taken a turn for the worse, something that was happening more and more often.

"Drake Herrin just called from Honolulu," James said.

"Well, that old CIA sonofabitch is the one who told us they knew where Mako was," Creed interrupted. "What'd they do, lose him?"

"Are you going to let me answer?" asked James.

"Sorry. Go ahead."

"Drake has an old colleague who lives on Oahu. He called in a favor and had the guy make some inquiries in the port. That's how they located Mako in the first place. The guy told Drake that a middle-aged Caucasian matching Mako's description paid $5,000 in cash to a Vietnamese tuna boat captain to take him along. The captain left Honolulu four weeks ago with Mako on the Sea Moon II. The boat returned to port yesterday...without our friend."

Creed bent over and reached for the empty Styrofoam coffee cup that stood on the Saltillo tile floor next to his chair and nonchalantly let fly with a brown glob of tobacco juice. He still enjoyed an occasional chew. It was a habit he was unable and perhaps unwilling to give up despite the constant lampooning of the press corps and the almost daily admonishments of his wife Guadalupe.

"Drake's a good man. That should have been enough information to find Mako. Not a lot of places you can hide on a tuna boat in the middle of the Pacific Ocean. How the hell did he give them the slip?" asked Creed.

"How do you think? The Vietnamese captain said he jumped off the boat with his surfboard about a mile out of Honolulu."

Creed grinned despite himself.

"That sounds like Mako," he said. "But where does that leave us? We could sure use him about now."

James leaned forward with his arm propped up on his knee and cupped his chin in his left hand.

"It's not just Drake looking for him either. From what I hear, the cartel has a contract out on him. They blame him for the death last year of Antonio Salcido's brother, Francisco...the original *El Padrino*.[4] But that's all I know. I pretty much depended on Mako for information out of Mexico."

Creed reached for a copy of the *Laredo Morning Times* on top of his desk. He handed the paper to James.

"Does Mexico have anything to do with this?" he asked, jabbing a finger at the lead article on the front page.

---

[4] See TEXMEX by Clabe Taylor, 2013

James glanced down at the folded newspaper.

"U.S. COAST GUARD CUTTER SINKS OFF TEXAS COAST," shouted the headline.

"Did you read this?" asked Creed.

"Of course."

"And?" Creed's legendary impatience was already beginning to redden his face.

"And I don't know who's behind it. I can't imagine the cartel has the firepower for something like that."

"Just reassure me that we didn't have anything to do with this!" demanded Creed.

"Have you lost your mind, Creed? Has high office suddenly made you ignorant or something? Why the hell would we even think about doing that?"

Creed sipped hot coffee from a hand-painted ceramic mug depicting bucking horses and the brands of a dozen legendary South Texas ranches. The famous "running W" of the King Ranch was displayed next to the brand of Creed's own Broken "T". The mug had been a gift from Creed's wife Guadalupe on their tenth anniversary, and Creed refused to drink coffee out of anything else.

"Just making sure, James," he said. "I know how you ex-CIA types are about running your own operations and keeping the powers-that-be in the dark. In the state of Texas, that means me," Creed added.

"Thanks for reminding me," said James.

"This article speculates that our plans to legalize marijuana might have prompted the cartel to sink the Coast Guard cutter. You know, a provocation to give the U.S. government an excuse to step in and stop us. Any truth to that?"

"Maybe," James answered. "They're looking for any reason to intervene. We all know that. Your plans to legalize marijuana have pissed off lots of powerful people in Washington. It's one thing for Colorado or Washington to legalize pot, but Texas has a long border with Mexico. The implications are mind-boggling. Think of the lost revenue and federal jobs that would be lost. The War on Drugs is a cash cow for Washington. Hell, wars have been fought over less."

Both men were silent for a minute.

"So why Mexico? You never answered my question," Creed finally said.

"Just a hunch. I think there's a connection. That's why we need Mako back. With his sources down in Mexico, he might be able to find out what's going on."

"Sure, if the cartel or the U.S. government doesn't kill him first. I don't blame him for disappearing. So what do we do?"

"We wait...looks like he might be on the way back to South Texas after all," he said.

"Why do you say that?" Creed asked.

"I had an interesting text message on my cell phone this morning," replied James. "It said, 'Not too much lime in my Cuba Libre, *por favor*'. I didn't recognize the phone number, but I think I know who it's from."

Chapter 7

Cyrus stood at the first floor window of the fashionable white stucco house, which stood serenely on the corner of a quiet intersection in Cuernavaca, a short drive south from Mexico City. He peered through the vines of blooming purple and white bougainvillea that cascaded down from ceramic planters on the second floor balcony. The street was empty except for a couple of short, squat middle-aged gardeners edging a sidewalk with hand-held clippers across the street. Not at all what he was hoping to see.

Cyrus keyed the miniature handheld walkie-talkie.

"Nothing?" he asked.

"Not yet," came the static-filled squawk of an answer from the counter surveillance team staked out near an intersection about a mile from the entrance to the posh subdivision. Cyrus had positioned the team so they would see her at least five minutes before she arrived at the safe house. If she were dragging anybody behind, the team leader would radio Cyrus, who would place an agreed-upon signal in the window and abort the meeting.

The extra precautionary measure was a tribute to Soledad's value to the CIA. A reliable source on the drug cartels was a rare commodity, and Cyrus had insisted on the counter-surveillance stakeout for the security of the op. He had other reasons as well, but he tried to compartmentalize that part of his life.

Cyrus had no illusions what Soledad's fate would be if the cartel learned of her dalliance with the CIA. He had read the files of some of the classic Cold War cases of CIA agents run in Moscow during Soviet times. The consequence of the cartel catching wind of her relationship with Cyrus would be no less catastrophic than the KGB catching one of its own at a meeting with the CIA. Probably much worse. By comparison, the drug cartels made the KGB look like a bunch of Boy Scouts playing adolescent games. A bullet in the back of the head in the basement of Lefortovo Prison in Moscow would be preferable to what the cartel would have in store for her. Cyrus hated to contemplate that eventuality and always employed textbook tradecraft whenever he met her. The Mexican government did not have much of a counterintelligence service, but Cyrus knew the Sinaloa Cartel jealously guarded its own secrets, assiduously looked for traitors within its ranks, and exacted terrible and swift retribution.

Soledad was punctual, a rare trait in Mexico. When an hour passed and she still had not arrived, the vague concern that nagged Cyrus turned into poorly disguised alarm. He turned off the lights in the safe house, locked the front door, and walked hurriedly out to his car.

"Stand down," he instructed his surveillance team, speaking into the walkie-talkie. "Let's meet up back in Mexico City."

A few minutes later as he exited on the Cuernavaca-Ciudad de Mexico toll road ramp, Cyrus absentmindedly tuned the car radio to the 88.1 FM *Red* news station, expecting to hear yet another report on the mind-numbing traffic jams that clogged the streets of the Mexican capital almost twenty-four hours a day. Instead, he listened with shocked and almost macabre fascination as the sultry voice of the female announcer suddenly transformed his worst fears into nightmarish reality.

"Today at 1600 hours local time, a powerful car bomb exploded in front of the *Procuraduría General de la República,* on Paseo de la Reforma....."

Cyrus got the gist of the report, but felt eerily detached from the stark details the announcer relayed with morbid relish. A car bomb in front of the Attorney General's Office was the only thing he understood. A rushing sound in his ears drowned out the voice of the news anchor as Cyrus realized in shock the likely implications of the explosion. Only one thing seemed to make sense to him: he had to get back to Mexico City immediately.

Cyrus stomped on the accelerator of his Chevy Aveo, rented in alias earlier in the day from a Hertz center on Avenida Miguel Ángel de Quevedo, and sped towards the

Valley of Mexico, his concern over Soledad's no-show for their meeting now threatening to bubble over into overt panic. He had no way of knowing where she had been at the time of the explosion, but the CIA had taught him not to believe in coincidences. A car bomb in front of Soledad's office followed by her failure to appear for a scheduled meeting? Logic led him to only one conclusion, and it was inescapable and the worst of all possible things.

Cyrus knew he faced more than the loss of a highly placed and valuable agent should the dread that gnawed at his gut prove to be justifiable. Contrary to everything he had ever learned in the CIA, Cyrus had dropped his guard with Soledad and had violated one of the most basic tenants of agent recruitment and handling. He had fallen in love with her, and he was wracked with worry.

***

"Coincidence?" Cyrus asked, his voice rising in volume in the enclosed space of the bubble, the secure conference room in the CIA station at the American embassy. "I know you don't believe that!"

The CIA station chief sat across the narrow table from Cyrus. They were the only ones in the cramped room. He looked at Cyrus' grim expression and knew his star case officer was probably right but fought the urge to agree with him.

"There are other explanations, Cyrus. Don't go off half-cocked because of a damned coincidence." He watched Cyrus with increasing concern and noticed the bulging vein on the side of his neck. He needed to calm Cyrus down before he let him back on the streets. No telling what he might do in his current state of mind.

"Isn't that one of our guiding principles?" asked Cyrus. "There is no such thing as a fucking coincidence, right? It's a cliché, but how many times have I heard you say it?"

"Usually not. But we always have to look beyond the obvious. That's our job. Don't start jumping to conclusions here. First, we don't even know who planted the car bomb or who the target was. In addition, we don't know if she was one of the victims. We've got people pounding the pavement trying to find out, but we need some hard information before I'll allow you to start making those kinds of allegations."

Cyrus squirmed uncomfortably in his chair.

"You're right, sorry. It's just that two weeks after we brief the DEA about a penetration of the Attorney General's Office and give them the report on the cartel's attack submarine, a car bomb explodes outside the *Procuraduría,* and the source of that intelligence fails to show for a meeting."

The COS sighed deeply and reached for a cigarette, then remembered he could not smoke in the hermetically sealed bubble. He knew Cyrus was right about the DEA meeting. The CIA had always looked down on the DEA and snickered at their efforts to run covert operations. The agency considered them little better than bumbling traffic cops and had little confidence in their ability to keep a secret or run a secure op. The COS was every bit as frustrated as Cyrus was.

"You're aware we briefed that Harvard Banks character at the specific request of the Director of the Central Intelligence Agency?" For emphasis, the COS used the full title instead of the acronym D/CIA. "We had best have all our ducks in a row before we start making wild accusations about the DEA compromising your source, or both of us will be doing name traces in the basement at Langley for the rest of our careers."

The COS smiled for the first time since early that morning. He could just see Cyrus back at headquarters in a basement cubicle sitting at a computer monitor. He knew that was not a prospect the younger officer would relish. Cyrus had done his share of name traces on a variety of interim assignments before his case officer training ten years ago. It was boring, unrewarding work.

"What about your agent's tradecraft? CI will ask a lot of questions about that before they'll consider a leak at DEA," the COS added.

"All she does is listen to a particularly lecherous supervisor who wants to impress her. The extent of her 'exposure' is to unbutton the top two buttons of her blouse to keep the fat fuck talking. She knows what tradecraft is. She took our counter surveillance course and excelled."

Cyrus opened his mouth to drive his point home but waved his hand in resignation and started to gather the papers on the desk in front of him.

"Go ahead and get it off your chest, Cyrus. I see you've got something else on your mind."

Cyrus hesitated and put the papers down. He studied the COS' face for a few moments before he began.

"You remember the operation we had going a few years ago with the Mexican army?"

"Sure, we worked with DEA on that one, targeting cartel capos," the COS replied. "I was the point man with both the Mexicans and the DEA. I ran the op. I should remember it."

"Well, I've read the file. We spent millions training and equipping a Mexican commando team, right? We even had choppers to carry them into battle."

"So?" replied the COS. "What's the connection?"

"Well, we didn't have the kind of sources to provide targeting information for the op, so we had to depend on DEA."

"Be careful where you take that thought, Cyrus."

Cyrus just nodded his head and bullheadedly continued.

"So we had to trust two things. First, that the DEA's intelligence on the location of these assholes was accurate and secondly, that the cartel didn't have the DEA penetrated. Two very iffy prospects if you ask me."

"Cyrus, make your point and let's get to work on the explosion," said the COS impatiently.

Cyrus stared back at his boss.

"I thought I just did....or don't you remember all the innocent people, who were surprised as all hell to see uniformed men with their heads covered with black balaclavas kick in their bedroom doors and spray them with 5.56 mm rounds as they woke up from a dead sleep? Or the fact that six months after the op began, the Sinaloa Cartel decapitated the army captain who commanded the team?"

The COS clenched his jaw. He had already shared his litany of complaints about the new generation of case officers with Cyrus. The way he saw it, they operated with an arrogant, self-righteous sense of political correctness that denied the very nature of their job.

"Listen," he whispered. "I remember those days. But when you get a presidential directive, you do the best you can. You sure as hell can't make an omelet without breaking eggs."

"So, what now?" asked Cyrus.

"You know the answer to that as well as I do. Keep those thoughts to yourself unless you're looking for an assignment to Ouagadougou for your next tour. Now get the hell out of this station and find out what happened to your girl."

Chapter 8

"What do you mean, she's still alive?" Antonio Salcido posed the question quizzically, a nascent smile of disbelief on his lips that quickly disappeared as he stared at the desperately apologetic figure in front of him. With a shock, he realized the man was telling the truth.

The head of the Sinaloa drug cartel sat behind the vast expanse of a Spanish-crafted mahogany conference table in his personal study and unconsciously, almost with perverse pleasure, caressed the smooth lacquered surface of the wood with his fingertips. Antonio had bought the desk the previous year from a reclusive carpenter he discovered working out of a tiny, dank shop near the Puerta del Sol in Madrid. When the master artisan told him that he only worked with mahogany he personally selected in Cuba, Antonio knew the desk had to be his.

Antonio prided himself on his ability to maintain a detached composure under the direst of circumstances, but what he had just heard stretched the envelope of credulity, even for Culiacán, Sinaloa. He struggled in a fruitless effort to conceal his irritation and sense of betrayal.

"Is this all money can buy these days? You can't even kill a woman for me?" he asked. "With three years of special forces training?"

"The detonation was perfect," the sergeant stammered. "But blast patterns are unpredictable. She must have found a seam."

"Is that a word the CIA taught you?

The sergeant nodded his head.

"I did everything right," he said softly. "According to the manual."

"Yeah, I'm sure you were a star pupil, Juanito," said Salcido. His mocking tone was biting and ominous.

Antonio picked up his cell phone and quick-dialed a preprogrammed number.

"Get everything ready," he said laconically.

With a flick of his wrist, Antonio tossed his cell phone on the conference table. The phone noiselessly slid across the slick surface and came to rest on the far side of the desk. The sergeant stared at the phone with hypnotic fascination; any excuse not to look at Antonio's face.

"Let's see, Juanito," said Salcido in a soft, conciliatory voice. "*¿Cuántos años has trabajado para nosotros?*"[5]

"Since I was fourteen, *patron*," answered the sergeant.

"Hmmm, about twelve years...."

"*Si, patron.*"

---

[5] How many years have you worked for us?

Salcido continued with his questions, his voice quiet and barely audible above the obnoxious hum of the old-fashioned air conditioning unit in the window of the office.

"We had big plans for you, Juanito. The army, your assignment to the *Grupo Aeromóvil de Fuerzas Especiales*[6], your training with the North Americans at Ft. Benning, and then with the CIA at the Farm. Who do you think worked behind the scenes to move your career along?"

"You did, of course, *patron*. I've always been very grateful." The sergeant raised his head slightly and glanced at Salcido.

"Did I fail you in some way? Did I overlook something, perhaps? Maybe I didn't pay you enough, or maybe the roof leaked in the house I built for your parents?" Salcido's voice increased slightly in volume and oozed with a sarcasm the sergeant could not fail to notice.

"Of course, not....." the sergeant stammered. "I've always...."

"*Callate!*[7]" Salcido almost shouted.

A loud knock on the door startled the sergeant, and he looked around wildly for a clue to the sudden interruption. One of the armed guards standing at the entrance to Salcido's study opened the door slightly and

---

[6] Special Forces Airmobile Group
[7] Shut up!

exchanged whispered words with someone outside. The guard turned his pockmarked face towards Salcido and nodded in the direction of the voice from outside.

"*Todo está listo*[8]," he said icily.

Salcido stood up from his desk and spread his arms apart, palms up in an expression of finality and contrived benevolence, almost as a benediction.

"Go with God, Juanito."

"*Está Usted muy lejos de Dios, patrón*[9]," said the Special Forces sergeant. Salcido looked at him and saw the horror of death reflected in his eyes. For Antonio, though, it was a simple business decision. Salcido's chosen few received one chance. This had been Juanito's and he had failed.

Antonio attempted to smile, but a recollection of his appointment later that evening in Mexico City with the Russian distracted him from the inconvenience Juanito had caused with the botched assassination attempt. In the final analysis, Juanito represented nothing more than an unsuccessful investment, an insignificant loss of time and a little money. There were plenty more just like him in the pipeline. The conversation with the Russian, on the other hand, promised to be far more significant and uplifting.

---

[8] Everything's ready
[9] You're very far from God, patron.

Salcido waved his hand dismissively.

"I agree. You're far closer to God than I am." He turned his back on Juanito, and the two guards led the Special Forces sergeant out of the door. A jarring flash of mid-day tropical sun sliced through Salcido's office, and hot humid air gushed into the dimly lit and clammy cool room.

"*Ya viene[10],*" called out a voice in the distance. *¡Arrancala[11]!*

A chainsaw coughed twice and backfired before it burst into the unmistakable *ring-ding-ding* chant of a two-cycle gasoline engine. Someone revved the saw's motor, and it shrieked with a ghoulish intensity, like a demented harbinger of death. Antonio heard the screaming motor and could only guess at what Juanito was thinking. The victims all knew what would happen to their families if they resisted or shamed themselves and their *patron* with a cowardly death. Antonio did not keep that a secret. He saw Juanito cross himself hastily and walk passively towards his executioner.

***

---

[10] Here he comes
[11] Start it up!

Antonio Salcido's King Air C90GT landed at twilight, taxiing slowly to the Culiacán native's private hangar at the Adolfo López Mateos International Airport in Toluca, Mexico. Toluca was a scant forty-minute drive from the outskirts of the capital, and Antonio preferred the relative anonymity offered by its airport. The Benito Juarez International Airport in Mexico City, in comparison, swarmed with security officials hungrily looking for opportunities to augment their meager government salaries. "Why tempt fate?" Antonio always asked and instead quietly bought off the upper echelon of airport management in Toluca, which slavishly catered to his every whim. As the plane lurched to a stop outside the hangar, Antonio glanced at his watch. There was still plenty of time to arrive fashionably late to the Russian embassy reception in the capital.

The Russian embassy in Mexico City was housed in the former residence of the old hacienda of the Countess of Miravalle. The hacienda had produced mainly livestock and *pulque*[12] in the seventeenth and eighteenth centuries, and Antonio thought it ironically apropos that the hard-drinking Russians should have appropriated the locale for its

---

[12] Pulque - a traditional alcoholic beverage made from the fermented sap of the maguey (agave) plant.

embassy in 1942, exchanging the *pulque* of the Mexican peasantry for the vodka of the Russian proletariat.

Antonio's plush Land Rover arrived at the embassy on Calle Jose Vasconelos one hour after the scheduled beginning of the reception in honor of *Den Rossii,* or Russia Day, commemorating Russia's declaration of sovereignty from the USSR in 1990. An impeccably dressed junior diplomat with pronounced high cheekbones met Antonio at the gate and led him through the throng of guests that included accredited businessmen, diplomats, Mexican politicians, and government officials, several of whom were already on Antonio's payroll.

The Russian diplomat walked briskly down a narrow corridor to a double door fashioned from an exotic hardwood Antonio did not recognize. The diplomat opened the door and stood to one side, revealing a short, stocky balding man in a dark suit standing under a life-size portrait of the Russian president.

"Antonio, it's good to see you again," the man said in heavily accented Spanish. "Come in, please. We have much to talk about."

Antonio's eyebrows arched in surprise, but he nodded his head solemnly and walked into the wood-paneled conference room. He shook the man's hand formally and took a seat in an austere and ornately carved wooden chair across the conference table from his host.

"It's been a long time, Vladimir," said Antonio. "I didn't expect to see you here."

"More than three years, I should think," answered the Russian diplomat. "I'm surprised you even recognized me. We had drunk enough vodka and tequila that night to permanently impair our memories."

Antonio winced at the memory. He drank only as the job required, but his body rebelled each time alcohol consumption became a political necessity and he suffered greatly.

"No, I remember it all, Vladimir. I think you were much more clever than drunk. Your mention of the Black Sea Shipyard and its history of military shipbuilding seemed so natural at the time. But it wasn't quite as innocent as I first thought. I realize that now."

Vladimir shrugged his shoulders and smiled.

"I thought you'd appreciate subtlety," he said apologetically. "I think it all worked out rather well, don't you?"

He leaned over the table holding a teapot in his right hand and poured the steaming liquid into a cup with the Russian double-headed eagle stenciled on each side.

"I thought we'd limit ourselves to hot tea this evening," said Vladimir.

Antonio allowed himself the faintest semblance of a smile.

"A humanitarian gesture," he joked. "But let's dispense with the niceties of diplomatic chit-chat, shall we? I'm no diplomat as you know, and now that I realize the SVR[13] Rezident[14] is actually my old friend Vladimir, I think we can get right to the point."

"By all means."

Antonio knew what people like Vladimir really thought of him. He realized that his old friend did not want to prolong the charade of cordiality with the head of the Sinaloa Cartel any longer than necessary. That kind of attitude no longer offended Antonio. He recognized the unspoken hypocrisy behind the SVR Rezident's squeamishness. The SVR itself engaged in unsavory activities and had been doing so for almost a hundred years, under different names, of course, but the notorious Cheka, NKVD, and KGB had been only slightly more ruthless than the current reincarnation of the old Bolshevik and Soviet security services. In fact, the Russians were responsible for death on a scale that he could not imagine. If Vladimir found the cartel's business distasteful, Antonio thought, he should have chosen a different career. Maybe he should have been a soccer coach like his father and

---

[13] SVR –Russian abbreviation for *Sluzhba Vneshney Razvedki,* Foreign Intelligence Service, the Russian equivalent to the Central Intelligence Agency.

[14] Rezident – In Russian, the equivalent to the CIA's Chief of Station.

grandfather. Or maybe that had been a lie too. Antonio realized that Vladimir felt it necessary to conceal the truth on even the most mundane matters.

"We have a saying in Russian," Vladimir began. 'Ruka ruku moyet.' One hand washes the other."

"Don't worry, my friend, I'm not coming with my hat in hand asking for handouts. I don't expect altruistic foreign aid from your country. My organization is sitting on cash reserves that would make many sovereign nations envious."

Vladimir nodded his head.

"I don't doubt that. We know you paid hard cash for the submarine, Antonio, but that's not the point. That was necessary for cover considerations and believe me, our Ukrainian friends are very grateful for your business."

Antonio frowned at the memory of his trip earlier in the year to Ukraine. A wave of nausea swept over him at the mere thought of the late-night revelry at the Black Sea Shipyard.

"Your friends have an odd way of showing their gratitude," he laughed. "They almost killed me with their hospitality."

"Yes, I can sympathize with your suffering. Russia and Ukraine share the same barbaric customs. I know exactly what you went through…..but I believe you're pleased with their work, aren't you?"

Antonio began to relax despite himself.

"You diplomats have a penchant for understatement, don't you? I'm delighted with the product. You know that."

"Good. I'm glad we've established that. Now what can I do for you today?"

Antonio welcomed the abrupt change of subject. He removed a single sheet of paper from the inside of his suit jacket pocket and handed it to Vladimir, who did not seem surprised.

"This is a list of spare parts and armament that we need before the next operation," Antonio stated matter-of-factly. "It came from your own technicians. Then there's the matter of refueling at sea."

Vladimir glanced at the list and looked up.

"Perfect. I can take care of all this, but let's talk first about your next mission. It's time to up the ante."

"Does he choose our targets?" asked Antonio and pointed to the portrait of the Russian president on the wall.

Vladimir hesitated before responding.

"Does it matter? Let's just say that for the first time in history and probably never again, our interests coincide."

The SVR Rezident reached down below the table with his right arm, lifted up a wafer-thin briefcase, and set it on the table with a sigh of exertion. He opened it with two loud clicks of the locks in rapid succession and took out a detailed map of the Texas coast, which he spread on the table so Antonio could see it.

"Have you ever heard of the Houston Ship Channel?"

Chapter 9

"Did you see this?"

Armando pointed to an article in the *Los Angeles Times*. The paper was several days old, but he and Mako had not listened to the radio or read a newspaper since they left Monterey following their odd encounter on Fisherman's Wharf. They had driven slowly south down the Salinas Valley on Highway 101 past King City to Paso Robles, religiously observing the speed limit and trying to avoid the police or anybody else who might be looking for them. They spent the first night in the ramshackle wood barracks of a migrant worker camp on a vegetable farm east of the freeway and shared a dinner of corn tortillas, cabrito, and pinto beans with a crew of Mexican lettuce pickers and their families. The red paint was peeling off the sun-warped wood planking of the one-story building, and it hung down in long shreds like the skin of a molting snake.

"See what?" asked Mako. He was at the wheel of Armando's 1987 two-toned maroon and tan Ford F-150 pickup that tended to shimmy erratically at speeds over 55 mph. In Paso Robles they had taken State Route 46 in the direction of the San Joaquin Valley and Interstate 5. Mako drove carefully and cast a frequent glance in the rear view mirror, looking for suspicious traffic behind them. It was an old habit he could not kick, and now there was good reason to be watching. People wanted him dead, admittedly for different reasons, but that was where he would probably be already if his first would-be killer had not turned out to be a guilt-ridden idealist in search of redemption. Mako needed to be more careful. He had no way of knowing how many more were out there looking for him, hoping to earn a bounty for bringing in his severed finger as proof of his death. Word had reached him of Antonio Salcido's contract on his life.

"It says here a *gringo* coast guard cutter blew up and sank off Padre Island a few days ago. Everybody on board was killed. The federal authorities claim they don't know what happened but I think I do," Armando said and tossed the newspaper in Mako's lap.

Mako braked sharply and skidded to a stop on the gravel shoulder of the highway. He grabbed the newspaper out of Armando's hands and skimmed the text of the article.

"I guess it could have been an accident. Faulty equipment....a fuel leak or something like that."

"Could have been," agreed Armando. "But it wasn't."

Mako turned on the pickup's radio but got only a shrill screech and ear-piercing static for his efforts. He pounded the radio with his fist.

"Nice truck, Armando. I bet Sancho Panza took better care of Don Quixote than this."

"It's the price of traveling incognito," Armando replied. "Who would ever guess that the infamous Mako Sloane is traveling with a Mexican wetback in this old beat-up truck, both men wanted by the Sinaloa Cartel? I think there're others after you too, maybe even your own people."

Mako gave Armando a look of disdain and tossed the newspaper back to him.

"What do you know about this?"

"I know the Sinaloa Cartel sunk that Coast Guard cutter," Armando declared categorically.

Mako glanced at Armando, looking for a smirk or upraised eyebrow, any indication that this startling claim was a feeble attempt at humor rather than the factual bombshell it was.

"I thought we drank the last of the Night Train Express," said Mako. "Or is this your idea of a joke? I suppose you're going to tell me the cartel has acquired some old F-15s or Mirage fighters?"

"No, but they did buy a submarine. That I know. They got it over in Russia or somewhere like that. I think that's what got the Coast Guard cutter."

Mako stared at Armando, not knowing whether to believe the self-confessed assassin or to laugh at his preposterous insinuations.

"If you had a sense of humor, I'd think you were bullshitting me, but I know you don't. So, let's assume for a minute you're telling the truth. How'd you come by this piece of intelligence?"

"This is what they didn't want me telling the *gringos*, remember? When you're the personal attorney for the head of the Sinaloa Cartel, you overhear things....things you'd rather not."

"And Antonio Salcido mentioned a submarine?"

"Many times," replied Armando. "When he wasn't talking about killing you, he was focused on acquiring offensive weapons for the cartel. I know he went over there personally right before they brought the submarine to Mexico."

"And then what?" asked Mako.

"Then they tried to kill me and I had to leave...in a hurry, without saying goodbye. That was the last I heard of it."

"But why would the cartel want a submarine?" Mako asked.

Armando shrugged his shoulders and reached into a brown paper bag on the floor of the truck. He retrieved a can of grapefruit-flavored Jarritos soda he had bought in a tiny, hole-in-the-wall Mexican grocery store in Gonzales that smelled of burnt corn tortillas and chipotle peppers. He popped the top, took a quick drink, and grimaced from the strong carbonation that practically detonated in his nostrils. He wiped his mouth with the back of his hand before answering.

"Antonio Salcido views himself as more than just the head of a drug cartel. He controls half the government in Mexico City and makes more policy decisions that anyone realizes, but he's not satisfied. He hates you and the United States government with a passion you would probably find flattering. He wants you dead, and he wants Washington to kiss his ass and to respect or fear him. He doesn't care which. He's also a cold-blooded killer, but he's limited to AK-47s, chainsaws, and the occasional grenade or car bomb. That cramps his style. He has aspirations to commit murder on a far more grandiose scale and to become a regional geopolitical power, something like the tail wagging the dog or a state within a state. He views the submarine as a tool, a means to an end. Nothing more. You know the man's insane, don't you?"

"Insane?" asked Mako.

"Sure. How else can you describe a man who views himself as the avenging arm of God and justifies his crimes against humanity in self-delusional moralistic terms?"

Mako turned the key in the ignition and the old Ford pickup hesitated for several seconds before the starter clicked loudly and began to whir, coaxing the engine to belch into an uneven hiccup of tired clanking steel.

"Armando, if you use those criteria, you'll have to call every U.S. president in recent memory insane, don't you think?"

"And how far off would that be?" Armando asked as he continued to sip his Jarritos.

"A lot closer than anyone realizes, I'd say," replied Mako.

"The prosecution rests."

Mako was deep in thought as the pickup approached the SR-41 split.

"You know, this is where James Dean died back in 1955," Armando suddenly announced.

"The rebel without a cause?"

"Yeah, just like you, Mako."

"You're wrong, amigo. I've got a cause; truth, justice, and the American way."

"*Puta mierda!* And I thought I was full of shit!"

The men fell silent as the pickup rattled towards the intersection with Interstate 5. Armando was the first to break the silence.

"There's an actor that some people call the 'Mexican James Dean'."

"Who the hell's that?" asked Mako.

"Benicio del Toro."

"You mean the actor who played the Mexican cop in "*Traffic*"?

"That's the one," Armando said. "He also played Che Guevara a few years ago in another movie."

"Armando, that motherfucker is *boricua*. He's Puerto Rican, not Mexican."

"No shit?"

"You don't even know that, and you expect me to believe the Sinaloa Cartel is operating an attack submarine in the Gulf of Mexico?" asked Mako, shaking his head in disbelief.

"One has nothing to do with the other. Maybe I don't read *People en Español*," Armando replied.

"Maybe you should. I might take you more seriously then."

The traffic on Interstate 5 was heavy with long columns of speeding eighteen-wheelers howling past the old Ford 150 pickup and creating a strong backwash, which was testing Mako's driving skills. The poorly aligned tires and bent front axle made the vehicle drift abruptly from side to side in the right lane like a teenager dancing awkwardly on his first date or Joe Cocker twitching on stage at Woodstock.

"We've got to get off this interstate," said Mako. "Check out the road map and find us an alternate route to take us south and into Arizona. It'll be safer too. Too many *chota* patrols on this highway. You never know who they're working for."

"Are you sure?" It'll take longer to get to Texas that way," Armando said.

"Texas? What makes you think we're going to Texas? That'd be like jumping from the frying pan into the fire, wouldn't it?"

"*Si, salir de Guatemala a Guatapeor*[15]." answered Armando.

Mako did not answer.

It took four days to reach Texas in Armando's rattletrap of a truck. They kept to the lesser-travelled state highways and county roads and finally crossed the Texas border south of Loving, New Mexico into country that Mako had not seen since he was a teenager riding saddle broncs at weekend rodeos. Outside of Pecos, Armando almost got himself arrested for sassing a Highway Patrol officer who had stopped them for having a brake light out.

"Armando, *no seas pendejo*[16]," Mako warned. "That wasn't a Mexico City municipal cop back there. You don't talk to the police that way in this country, and you sure as hell don't give them dietary recommendations. You're lucky he didn't ask to see your green card."

"The man had no sense of humor."

"And you do, I suppose?"

---

[15] Spanish version of the "jumping from the frying pan" saying
[16] Don't be an ass

Later in the day, they reached the outskirts of the Hill Country and began to crisscross the Nueces River as it meandered through the hills south of Camp Wood. Mako pulled out his cell phone, which he had not touched since he arrived at the San Francisco airport. Knowing the cartel had found him while traveling under forged identification papers made him reluctant to use his phone. No telling who was listening, he reasoned, or whether they had the capability of pinpointing his position.

"I suppose it's time," he said and began to punch in a telephone number.

"Time for what?" Armando asked.

"You'll see."

A few seconds later, a familiar voice answered.

"Brazzle here."

"You remember how I like my *Flor de Caña*?" asked Mako.

"Where are you, Mako?"

"*¡A la verga!* Your tradecraft sure has gone to hell since you left the Company. No more names, *por favor.*"

"Don't worry. My phone's encrypted."

"Yeah, but mine's not.....where can we meet?" Mako asked.

"Depends on where you are. If you're coming from where I think you are, take Hwy 83 south from Uvalde. I'll meet you at the river in an hour."

"I'll see you there," replied Mako.

"Wait a minute," said Brazzle.

"What now?"

"It'll be good to have you back. The shit's hit the fan."

"So I hear. That's usually what happens when I leave you boys alone."

Chapter 10

"She's alive, *señor.*"

Cyrus Tinch looked across the front seat of the nondescript VW Jetta at the young Mexican in the passenger seat wearing pale blue hospital scrubs and brand-new Nike running shoes. He stared at the man blankly, barely comprehending what he just heard.

He had parked the car on the edge of Chapultepec Park near the Periférico where dozens of picnickers sat on their threadbare cotton blankets in dry, sparse grass, generously littered with pink plastic bags, fast food wrappers, and the occasional pile of animal or human feces. They gnawed on chicken wings, chewed homemade tamales, drank bottles of Fanta soda, and listened to music on battery-operated radios that screeched tinny versions of Mexican pop songs. They paid no attention to the beige VW where Cyrus sat debriefing his agent.

"Did you see her?" finally asked Cyrus.

"No, she's too heavily guarded to get close, but my cousin's a nurse at the Centro Médico ABC. She said the person you asked about arrived yesterday in an ambulance with a police escort. They've cordoned off a whole floor with armed Judicial Police officers at either end. The attorney general is convinced she was the target of the explosion. He says the Sinaloa Cartel tried to kill her."

"How badly is she hurt?" asked Cyrus.

"She'll live, but they don't know if they can save her leg. The main thing is she's safe now unless the cartel can get to her in the hospital. The police doesn't have a good record resisting the cartels, you know, but she has a better chance at the ABC than at the government hospital where she was."

"Thank God," mumbled Cyrus. "Can you get a message to her?"

The agent looked up at Cyrus with surprise.

"Would that be a wise thing to do, *señor*?" he asked.

Cyrus did not respond. He couldn't. His thoughts were jumbled and he had not slept for thirty-six hours. Instead, he watched transfixed, through bleary, bloodshot eyes as an overweight picnicker sitting on a plaid blanket at the side of the road crammed an entire tamale into his mouth using his thumb like a shoehorn in an effort to avoid spillage.

"*¿Señor?*" The young man asked when Cyrus seemed to ignore his question.

"What?" Cyrus shook his head to break the spell and looked back at his agent, trying to focus his thoughts.

"Keep your personal feelings out of this," Cyrus mouthed to himself silently. "Don't be a fool."

"*Señor?*" the man repeated his question for the third time.

"No, never mind." Cyrus handed him a small yellow sheet of stick-um note paper with a phone number scrawled on it.

"If you hear any more news, call this number and leave a message. It'll get to me."

"Si, *señor*," the man nodded. He shook Cyrus' hand and left the car, crossing Chapultepec Park at a brisk walk. He blended into a crowd of cheering Mexicans watching a dusty pick-up game of soccer between two teams of teenage boys, who marked the goals with piles of t-shirts and towels weighted down by rocks.

An hour later Cyrus walked through the gates of the American embassy, showed his black diplomatic passport to the Marine guard, and took the elevator up to the CIA station. He punched in the cipher code to the heavy steel door and waited for the hollow click before entering the station. He walked down the long windowless corridor that led to his functional but dismally austere office. His phone rang with a shrill jangle that made the metallic inbox on his desk rattle faintly. He sat down in the thickly cushioned swivel chair, picked up the receiver, and heard the lilting southern accent of the COS' secretary.

"Cyrus, where on earth have you been? The Chief wants you in his office...now!"

She emphasized "now" with as much authority as her genteel Virginia accent could muster.

"Is he in a bad mood?"

"Have you ever seen him in a good mood?"

Cyrus made his way to the COS' office at the end of the corridor and gently knocked on the door.

"It's open."

Cyrus walked in without greeting his boss and took a seat next to his desk.

"Where have you been?" the COS asked without looking up from a stack of classified cables.

"Working."

"Find out anything?"

"She's alive."

The COS looked up sharply from his paperwork.

"Is the source reliable?"

"Yeah, the information is good. She's at the ABC Centro Médico. The attorney general has armed guards on the floor."

"Good. That's a relief....now you can forget her," the COS said abruptly.

"Forget her? What are you talking about? She's the most productive agent we have."

"You heard me. Those are the instructions I got today from headquarters. Take a look at this cable."

The COS handed Cyrus a single sheet of paper. Cyrus glanced briefly at the list of cryptonyms in the cable heading indicating the agent's codename and the restricted handling status of the case. After reading the text of the cable several times, Cyrus looked up at his boss, who was watching him intently.

"Don't even ask," the COS said grimly.

"Then you tell me," Cyrus said. "She's the most valuable asset the station has ever had on the Mexican narcotics target. Without her, we do not have a single reliable source on the cartels, and they tell us to drop the case? What the hell's going on?"

"Look, I'm not arguing with you, Cyrus. Headquarters is directing us to stand down. That's all I know. They must have their reasons."

"I don't think you believe that."

The COS shifted uncomfortably in his chair and looked down at the stack of cables. When he looked up, his face was flushed.

"The whole thing stinks to high hell," he admitted.

"Conflicting priorities between competing agencies?"

"Maybe," the COS said softly. "But it might be more complex than that. Headquarters seemed to lose interest in our case right after we linked the submarine to the cartel and Antonio Salcido. I don't think that was a coincidence."

"But why would they lose interest? The intelligence was irrefutable," responded Cyrus. "It was a bombshell!"

"That's the question, isn't it? Why indeed? Something doesn't add up. It's like we stumbled on to something they didn't want us to find out."

"Is it too early for theories?"

"Yes and no," said the COS. "When I read the cable from headquarters, I had an eerie sense of *déjà vu*."

He paused, opened the lower right-hand drawer to his desk, and pulled out a half-empty bottle of Los Danzantes one-year old mescal. He placed the bottle on the government-issue wooden table and glanced at Cyrus with an unspoken invitation. The amber mescal was almost luminescent under the light emanating from a gaudy crystal chandelier that hung from the ceiling, the previous occupant's idea of chic décor. He stood up and walked to an oak sideboard that stood along the rear wall of his office and retrieved two cut-glass shot glasses from the top shelf. He placed them on the desk, poured two shots, and handed one to Cyrus. He had not even asked whether Cyrus would like to join him.

"You've seen something like this before?" asked Cyrus.

"Maybe...ever heard of Mako Sloane?"

"Yeah, who hasn't?"

"I was still working the Russian target when they arrested Sloane not too long after 9/11. The story was that he went rogue. They said he was selling arms a retired Russian general supplied him, and they were stashing the money in offshore accounts. But it wasn't true...we only found that out later."

"What really happened?" asked Cyrus.

"Nobody knows for sure, or at least I don't. But one thing was clear. Sloane had been submitting intel reports from Moscow nobody wanted to see. They were too explosive. Someone decided to quash the reports. The rest is history. Sloane did seven years in the joint, some of it at Guantanamo...they say the cocksuckers even waterboarded him."

Cyrus whistled.

"So where's the similarity? Where's the déjà vu?"

"Where do you think? We provide break-through intelligence, and headquarters tells us to drop the case. No explanation. Something's not kosher, but that's all I can say at this point."

"Well, that's the only the tip of the iceberg if you ask me," ventured Cyrus. "A couple of months after we connect the Ukrainian submarine to the cartel, the *Orca* mysteriously explodes off the Texas coast, but all we've seen so far is open-source reporting on the sinking. Only what CNN, Fox, and the *New York Times* are reporting.

There's been nothing in back-channel traffic and nothing in the daily intelligence summaries out of headquarters....zilch. And they haven't tasked us with investigating the incident. That doesn't strike you as odd?" asked Cyrus.

"Yeah, it's almost like Langley doesn't want to know what happened or want anybody else to know."

"But why?" Cyrus asked.

"I don't know," replied the COS. "But I think we know what sunk that Coast Guard cutter."

Cyrus paused, raised his shot glass in a silent toast, and drank. He held out the glass for a refill.

"Put it down on the desk. It's bad luck to fill a glass when it's in mid-air."

"Moscow superstition?"

"Yeah, you can't teach an old dog new tricks."

Cyrus put the shot glass on the desk, and the COS reached out with the bottle of Los Danzantes and poured the mescal. This time both men drank.

"Well, none of that makes any sense at all," said Cyrus. "That report was an intelligence coup. It should have been enough to make our careers. If the sub came from Ukraine, we all know there'd have to be a Russian connection. Ukraine wouldn't dare get involved in a hair-brained operation like that by itself. A report like that should land on the president's desk. If Russia's behind the sinking of the Coast Guard cutter, that's an act of war."

The COS did not reply.

"So what do we do?" asked Cyrus.

"I tell you what we're going to do; I want you to dig into the Russian connection to the cartel submarine. That's your highest priority starting right now. I'll reassign your other cases. Let's get to the bottom of this."

"We're going to ignore the cable from headquarters?"

"Let me worry about that," said the COS.

Chapter 11

"That's the Bolivar Roads Alternate Inbound Route down there," called out Lieutenant Bill Jacobson, public affairs officer at the Houston Coast Guard Air Station. "The oil tankers can take this route and avoid the 105 degree turn at the Bolivar Roads intersection with the Houston Ship Channel. Helps out quite a bit with congestion. It's a long name, but it's basically like an entrance ramp to the freeway."

The CNN reporter and his cameraman peered out the window of the French-made H-65 helicopter at the blue coastal waters of the Gulf of Mexico below. The lieutenant looked back at his "VIP" passengers. The cameraman looked a little queasy as the helicopter banked steeply and dove to get a closer look at the oil tankers traversing the sea portion of the Houston Ship Channel. Jacobson smiled to himself. Occasionally his PR assignments were intellectually stimulating, like the time he gave a guided tour of New York harbor to former Secretary of State Hillary Clinton. She had done her homework so well she could have given the tour, he recalled. It almost made him feel inadequate. Today, he knew, was going to fall short of those cerebral heights. His guests were looking for sound bites that tended more towards the sensational rather than the detail-rich type of briefing he was used to giving.

"Back in 2005 they completed the dredging of the main channel to a project depth of 45 feet and a width of 530 feet. The entire channel is 50 miles long. Now the Houston Ship Channel can even handle the huge Suezmax tankers. Those ships you see down there are much smaller. As a matter of fact, that looks like the *Ostap Bender* right below us. She's a Bahamian flagged oil tanker owned by a Russian oligarch. Probably carrying about 40,000 metric tons of Venezuelan heavy crude for an oil refinery here in the Houston area."

"I think our viewers are more interested in seeing where the *Orca* went down," said the reporter without any preamble or attempt at diplomacy. "How long before we can get there?"

Jacobson bit his tongue and tried to recall details of his job description that emphasized interpersonal skills and diplomacy under stressful circumstances.

"The location of the *Orca* sinking is at the limit of our range. We'd have to refuel to get back. My instructions were to give you a tour of the ship channel. I thought you were doing a story on potential strategic targets for terrorists."

"I changed my mind," said the middle-aged reporter. "We need something sexier. Our ratings are down."

"I'm sorry but I don't have authorization for that. The Coast Guard isn't big on unauthorized flights using its helicopters."

"Well, don't waste any more of my time then. You're putting me to sleep."

Jacobson found the reporter's tone presumptuous and dismissive although he knew the older man meant nothing personal by his manner. At his age, he should have been hosting a prime-time news show. The lieutenant suspected that his lack of tact was merely a reflection of his frustration over a media career in a tailspin. Every routine assignment likely poured salt in the wound of a deflated ego and served as a reminder of his own mediocrity.

"Holy shit!" exclaimed the CNN reporter without warning as the helicopter completed a tight circle above the Houston Ship Channel and set its return course back to the air station. Lieutenant Jacobson turned and followed the reporter's gaze as he stared to the east at two rapidly approaching objects skimming over the sea surface.

"What the hell is that?" asked the lieutenant.

"Incoming missiles," yelled the reporter. "I've seen it before. Tell the pilot to get the fuck out of here!"

The pilot instinctively turned 90 degrees away from the incoming objects and increased his rate of ascent dramatically. The two elongated objects whizzed under them at more than 1,000 feet per second just above the water's surface, barely visible in the early morning haze that hung over the gulf. As Lieutenant Jacobson and the CNN reporter watched with disbelieving eyes, the fifteen foot long SM-39 Exocet missiles slammed into the *Ostap Bender*'s port side two seconds apart, their 360 pound high-explosive warheads detonating a fraction of a second later. The tanker disappeared from view in a massive fireball of orange flame and black smoke. The helicopter shuddered from the shock wave. Moments later a series of secondary explosions boomed in quick succession.

"Did you get that on film?" the reporter shouted to the cameraman. "Keep shooting! Jesus F. Christ! What the hell is happening?"

"Where do you want me to go?" called the pilot.

"Make a circle.....we'll need some photos of this!" replied Lieutenant Jacobson. "Get the Houston air station on the radio!"

"Give that tanker a wide berth," shouted the CNN reporter. "There might be more incoming missiles. I saw this back in 1982 when the Argies hit the Sheffield with an Exocet missle. She burned and sank eight days later."

"Who the hell is doing this?" asked the lieutenant of nobody in particular. "First the *Orca* and now the *Ostap Bender*....people are dying! Who's killing them?"

***

Bulat Mikoyan was short with the dark complexion of a *mestizo*. He affected the ubiquitous macho moustache of Latin America and in the right clothing looked more *mexicano* than a taco vender on the streets of Tijuana. That had been part of the plan. The fact that Bulat spoke not a word of Spanish did not worry his mentors in Moscow. Everything else was perfect and besides, there were not many former Soviet submarine commanders who spoke Spanish.

Because of the sensitive nature of his sojourn in Mexico, Bulat avoided contact with the local population in Veracruz and rarely ventured out of the heavily guarded compound where he lived with the rest of his crew just beyond the shipyard. His Armenian father had given him his swarthy pigmentation, and an unfortunate cast of the genetic dice had cursed him with the height of his diminutive Russian mother. At 1.65 meters, or five feet five inches tall, Bulat Mikoyan always felt at a distinct disadvantage in any physical endeavor growing up in Yerevan during Soviet times. As a young man, however, Bulat had shown an enviable aptitude for math and physics and became one of the few representatives of a national minority to obtain a naval commission and later enter the Leninskiy Komsomol Higher School of Submarines in Leningrad. It was the first time in his life Bulat felt as if the tables had been turned, as if luck had smiled on him at last.

He laughed at his taller comrades when they forgot to duck moving from one compartment to another on board the training submarine and smashed their heads painfully on the unforgiving steel of a bulkhead. Bulat had no such difficulties and scampered around the cramped quarters of the submarines as if he had been born onboard one of the underwater death traps. He mind was as dexterous as his lithe body, and he excelled in the tedious technical training. His abilities and assiduousness were amply rewarded, and he advanced rapidly in the elite corps of submarine officers, eventually becoming the youngest submarine commander in the Soviet Navy.

Such was Bulat's reputation that he was able to prosper in the years following the breakup of the USSR and the disintegration of the country's armed forces. He managed to keep his job despite the catastrophic cutbacks in defense spending, and his career continued to advance. Finally, after twenty years commanding the full array of Soviet and Russian submarines in the fleet, Bulat retired to a pittance of a government pension on a small dacha not far from where the Volkhov River flows into Lake Ladoga about 140 kilometers east of St. Petersburg. He blamed himself rather than the Russian government for his impoverished circumstances. He simply had not had the foresight or perhaps the necessary moxie to make the fortunes that some of his ex-military colleagues had already done, selling surplus weaponry or peddling their skills as mercenaries to third world despots. When the SVR contacted him a few years ago with an offer that promised both a return to the sea and a generous salary with benefits, Bulat had asked few questions and accepted the SVR recruitment pitch on the spot.

"What progress have you made training the Mexican crew?" asked Vladimir in the same conference room of the Russian embassy where the SVR Rezident had met with Antonio Salcido the previous week.

Bulat looked up from the computer monitor that displayed close-up satellite photography of the Houston Ship Channel taken four days before by a Persona-3A, the best reconnaissance satellite Russian technology had ever produced. The satellite had been launched earlier in the year from the LC-43/4 launch site at the Plesetsk Cosmodrome about 800 kilometers north of Moscow. Bulat was getting his first view of the lethal handiwork of his weapons officer and he nodded his head in appreciation of the man's skills. In the photograph shown on the monitor, black smoke and flames still engulfed the *Ostap Bender* two hours after the attack. She was listing heavily to starboard and appeared to be sinking rapidly.

"The Mexicans are hopeless." Bulat looked into the eyes of the SVR Rezident without flinching, the smile on his face disappearing instantly as the subject of conversation turned to his trainees.

"That's not exactly the answer I was hoping for," said Vladimir.

Bulat examined Vladimir from head to toe out of the corner of his eye. The SVR Rezident's clothes, his demeanor, and Moscow accent reeked of privilege. He pretended to speak to Bulat as an equal, but the half-Armenian retired naval officer knew what most Russians thought of his brethren and how they referred to them in Russian: *"chernozhopaya mraz,"* black-assed scum. It was the "N" word in Russian, but Moscow, unlike Washington, had little or no political correctness to contend with, and unconcealed racism towards the former Soviet republics to the south and Central Asia to the east was rampant and almost universal.

"You did want the truth, didn't you? Surely you didn't expect a Mexican crew of homicidal troglodytes to learn to operate a modern attack submarine in a few months?" Bulat asked sarcastically. "Even the ones with naval training are complete morons. I need another six months to even cut my training staff by half."

"I did have my hopes, based on how highly you came recommended, Captain Mikoyan. Not to mention the expectations of some important people in Moscow. You can have three more months. We need to get our people out of the operation."

"You know, there was a reason it was so hard to gain acceptance to the Frunze Higher Naval School in Leningrad," said Bulat. "You can mold good raw material into whatever you want. I can do little with these mindless peasants. There are only two of them with a university education."

Bulat could see the SVR Rezident was not pleased with the news, but he could not conceal the abject failure of the training program so far. In fact, Bulat did not think the candidates would ever be able to operate the submarine's complex navigation and weapons systems.

"Let me put it this way, Captain Mikoyan." The SVR Rezident stood up and took out a carafe of vodka from the elegant but slightly rustic wood sideboard. He filled the two shot glasses he retrieved from his briefcase on the floor.

"The sinking of the *Ostap Bender* has closed the Houston Ship Channel for at least three weeks. The Americans are scurrying to reassure the world that its shipping lanes are safe, but they have no earthly idea who was behind the attack. The Gulf of Mexico is swarming with U.S. Navy warships and planes that have no idea what they're looking for! A dozen terrorist organizations around the world have claimed responsibility for the sinking as we predicted. Even when the Houston Ship Channel reopens, insurance premiums for incoming oil tankers will go through the roof. The price of crude has already reached $200 per barrel since the attack and will undoubtedly continue to rise. Need I remind you how this enriches the coffers of the Russian national treasury?" the SVR Rezident asked.

He raised his glass of vodka in Bulat's direction.

"I salute you, Captain Mikoyan. In one fell swoop, we have struck a blow to the U.S. economy that will cost those bastards billions of their precious dollars."

And sown the seeds for WWIII if we're not careful, thought Bulat. What the hell have I gotten myself into?

Chapter 12

"That's quite a story."

Mako sat deep in thought across from Creed Tucker and James Brazzle in the living room of the Broken "T" ranch headquarters five miles south of Cotulla, Texas. The same clanking ceiling fan he remembered from his last visit vaguely stirred the warm humid air in the living room. A clump of dog hair blew slowly across the rust-red Saltillo tile on the floor in front of him. He saw Creed's Blue Heeler curled up in the farthest corner, warily observing the two-legged interlopers who had invaded his territory. Mako smelled skunk and figured the heeler had been out hunting the night before and had run into something unexpected.

"You think it's safe to have that Mexican staying out there in the bunkhouse?" Creed asked. "You *did* say he used to be the cartel's head attorney?"

"Don't worry about Armando. He had the chance to kill me back in Monterey. He's sort of my superhero sidekick now. You know, like Sancho Panza and Don Quixote."

"Last I heard, Don Quixote wasn't exactly a superhero," ventured Creed. "We were hoping you still had some of your famous espionage skills."

Mako laughed.

"So, what do you think?" asked James Brazzle.

"Well, I knew some of the story already," answered Mako. "Obviously Creed's harebrained decision to legalize marijuana was not going to go over big in Washington or with the cartels. You've accomplished the unthinkable: got the USG and the drug cartels on the same side."

"Come on, Mako," argued Creed. "They've always been on the same side. The War on Drugs meets both their needs. It props up the price of dope for the cartel and keeps people employed for the U.S. government. Not to mention a source of extra income for some powerful people in Washington and probably my own administration in Austin. A few minor fall-guys every now and then and everyone's happy."

Mako studied Creed's face. The new governor of Texas never ceased to amaze him. You could not find a more traditional, conservative Texan than Creed Tucker. He had raised cattle and trained horses his whole life. He had voted the straight Republican ticket since 1980 and never smoked anything stronger than an unfiltered Camel. Yet the man had proposed revolutionary legislation that had shaken official Washington to its foundations and reverberated in like-minded states around the country. It actually made a lot of sense unless it caused the federal government to send troops into Texas for the second time in two years[17], a possibility that was still on the table.

"You're right, Creed. I'm not arguing with you. I'm just saying that sometimes waving a red flag at a raging bull is not the best thing to do," said Mako.

"What's done is done," said James. "Let's concentrate now on dealing with the consequences. We need to find out what Antonio Salcido is up to."

"And don't forget the damned U.S. government," added Creed. "You can bet your bottom dollar they're in it up to their necks."

"Yeah, they usually are," agreed Mako. "But let's not jump to conclusions yet."

"So, here's our dilemma as I see it," began James. "If Armando is right and Antonio Salcido acquired a submarine from Russia or someplace over there, I can see those crazy bastards sinking the coast guard cutter. It sends a not-so-subtle message not to fuck with the status quo. On the other hand, why would they want to rock the boat and threaten a balance of power that already favors their interests?

"I agree. Why declare war on the U.S. when the feds give them most of what they want anyway?" said Mako. "Unless....."

---

[17] See TEXMEX by Clabe Taylor, Legacy Publishers, 2012.

"Unless they're trying to provoke the U.S. government to take action against us," interrupted Creed.

"Yeah, they don't want us to legalize pot. Maybe they figure they can escalate the violence and force the USG to act," said James.

"So far so good," said Mako. But then how does the sinking of the oil tanker in the Houston ship channel fit into that matrix? Was it the submarine again? How would that serve their purpose?"

"Could it have been terrorists?" asked Creed.

"I doubt terrorists could muster the resources right now," answered Mako. "But someone else has their hand in this besides Salcido. Think of the technical obstacles. The cartel may have the money to buy a submarine, but they sure don't have the expertise to operate one."

"Well, who's behind it then?" asked Creed.

Mako had his theories. He always did. To him it seemed obvious, especially in light of the conversations Armando had overheard. There was only one country and one organization in the world that had the technological wherewithal and the *cojones* to pull off something like this. Mako wondered whether the Russian president had laughed when he saw the photograph of the sinking *Ostap Bender.*

***

Mako arrived at Benito Juarez International Airport in Mexico City late in the afternoon on an Aeromexico flight out of Juarez using an alias passport, which James Brazzle had thoughtfully provided. No use setting off any alarm bells in Mexico City or letting Antonio Salcido know that his archenemy was in country. Mako knew the cartel leader had the capability to monitor international arrivals and check his name against a watch list.

From the airport, he took a rust bucket of a VW taxi to a working-class bar on Insurgentes Sur Avenue with the unassuming name of *El Guajolote,* The Turkey. He planned to have a cold beer while he waited for Armando to arrive on a later flight out of Matamoros. If Armando did not show today, their commo plan called for a meeting in the same bar an hour later the next day. Both had agreed it would be best if they arrived on different flights.

Mako sipped his cold Modelo Especial and dipped a *totopo*[18] in a saucer of the hottest salsa he had tried in months. He looked around the darkened bar at the cheap faux-wood paneling already beginning to peel off the walls. The bar reeked of cigarette smoke and rotisserie chicken. Shallow glass jars filled with carrot slices, onions, and peppers in a fragrant jalapeño-vinegar concoction had been placed in the middle of each table. The almost mandatory

---

[18] fried corn chip

photographs of Pancho Villa on horseback and other sepia-tone scenes from the Mexican Revolution decorated the modest eating and drinking establishment, a bit of a cliché, but appealing nonetheless, albeit in a Carlos Fuentes – *Old Gringo* sort of way.

Mako thought how little Mexico had really changed since those chaotic and violent days so many years ago. Maybe things would never change in this country. He remembered the words of Porfirio Diaz, Mexico's president who was toppled from power during the revolution in 1911: "Poor Mexico, so far from God and so close to the United States." Nowadays the cynically altered mariachi song title, *"Mexico lindo y jodido[19]*," put it more succinctly. All pretentions to eloquence aside, not much progress in one hundred years.

Mako had stayed in South Texas for three long days, delayed by the need to bring Armando's parents across the Rio Grande to the safety of the United States before the two men embarked on their fact-finding mission to Mexico City. Creed authorized the unofficial cross-border rescue mission without consultation with federal authorities, and James Brazzle lent a dozen former Special Forces troops from his elite South Texas intelligence unit, who were itching to get into action against the cartel.

---

[19] Mexico – beautiful and fucked

As they had climbed into the two SUVS that would take them into Nuevo Laredo, Mako had deadpanned, "As always, if any member of your team be caught or killed, the secretary will disavow any knowledge of your actions..." No one had laughed at the old *Mission Impossible* disclaimer. It was all too true.

In the end, the raid turned out to be an exercise in over-kill as Mako and his team found only two sleepy, overweight guards outside the small stucco cement-block house where Armando's parents lived. As Mako cut the barbed wire on top of the security wall that surrounded the house and prepared to scale the wall, Armando stopped him with an upraised hand and a slight inclination of his head in the opposite direction.

"They're mine," Armando had pantomimed.

Mako understood immediately and sympathized with Armando's proprietary interest in the fate of the cartel guards. After all, these were the men who had physically imprisoned his parents and kept them hostage to one condition: his own obsequious obedience to Antonio Salcido. Mako slid quietly down the wall, relinquishing his unspoken leadership and allowing Armando to move forward in his place. A few minutes later, Mako was shocked at the relish with which his scholarly Sancho Panza cut the throats of both guards as they slept. Mako realized then that Armando must have earned his bones as a cartel *sicario* killer before *El Padrino* selected him for higher education and to serve the cartel's loftier, white-collar goals. Armando was a renaissance man in the feral context of a modern Mexican drug cartel.

That was two days ago and today Mako was confident Armando would show up on time at the rendezvous point. He had already been impressed with his sidekick's intellectual depth, and now his Mexican friend had shown a different facet of his skills repertoire. Mako had not realized what danger he actually had been in on Fisherman's Wharf that day.

A full hour passed, however, and Armando was a no-show. Mako would normally have aborted the meeting and tried the next day an hour later according to their commo plan, but something made him order a third and then a fourth Modelo Especial as he calmly watched the desultory pedestrian traffic outside. When Mako finally saw Armando alight from a crowded passenger bus a block down from the restaurant and sprint towards *El Guajolote*, he was relieved. Armando had become more than a mere professional contact to the ex-CIA operative.

"You had me worried," Mako said as he greeted his friend.

"Worried....why?" he asked. "If anything had happened to me, I would still live on in your memory, wouldn't I?"

"I suppose so."

"Then I'm immortal. At least temporarily," Armando joked. "What is life anyway but a memory? When the memory dies, that's when I die, not before."

"I love listening to your philosophical bullshit, Armando, but we have other things to do today," said Mako. "Why were you so late?"

"That's the good news. I've been working while you've been swilling Mexican beer."

"And?"

"Did you hear about the explosion in front of the attorney general's office two weeks ago?"

"Sure, James briefed me on it. Sounds like the cartel's fighting a war on two fronts."

"Well, the target of the attack was my cousin Soledad. She barely survived."

"She worked in the attorney general's office?" asked Mako.

"Yeah, in the special organized crime department. She knew a lot about the cartels."

"Too much?" asked Mako.

"Apparently so. Or maybe shared it with the wrong person. I just visited her at the ABC Centro Médico. Ever heard of a *gringo* named Cyrus Tinch?"

Chapter 13

Cyrus threw his wet towel into a dirty laundry bin on wheels and walked out of the men's locker room at the Club Mundet in Polanco, a fashionable district of Mexico City a short drive from the American embassy. He felt refreshed, almost rejuvenated, and his nagging headache was gone. A tennis lesson on a freshly raked red clay court and a 1,500-meter swim in the club's Olympic-size pool served as a much-needed distraction. He was mentally exhausted after a desperate week of meetings both in Mexico City and in the hinterlands with agents of varying ilk and nationality.

To Cyrus, the Russian connection to the cartel's purchase of the Andastra knock-off submarine and its role in the mysterious sinking of the U.S. Coast Guard cutter and the oil tanker was irrefutable. However, the station's stable of covert assets had not provided a single kernel of intelligence on the subject. Quite the contrary, most parroted the unlikely conspiracy theory that the new governor of Texas and his rogue band of ex-CIA officers who ran the special South Texas intelligence unit were somehow complicit in the sinking of the hapless Coast Guard cutter. The subsequent sinking of the Russian oil tanker left even the conspiracy theorists stunned, but most continued to stubbornly believe that this was somehow part of a complex scenario of political intrigue involving the increasingly hostile confrontation between Texas and the United States government. The fact that the sinking of the *Ostap Bender* inflicted vast economic losses on both Texas and the rest of the United States did little to dampen the enthusiasm of Mexican political pundits and a populace thirsting for political scandal, conspiracy, and ghoulish scenes of death and mayhem.

Cyrus shouldered his old-school blue canvas gym bag and walked across the parking lot to his modest Volkswagen Passat, a metallic silver sedan purchased by the CIA station for operational purposes. Its *Distrito Federal* "civilian" license plates were supposed to render the vehicle less visible than the personal vehicles of the U.S. embassy officers, which sported highly visible and recognizable diplomatic license plates.

Cyrus glanced towards the obscured mountains on the horizon, which at this hour were shrouded in a rank yellowish haze that stank of noxious automobile exhaust. Mexico City allegedly had done wonders in cleaning up its atmosphere since the 1990s by replacing its pollution-belching old cars and removing lead from its gasoline, but the city was having a bad-air day despite the heart-warming environmental statistics, probably bought and paid for by the Mexican government.

As he approached his Passat, Cyrus caught sight of a tall middle-aged man with an athletic build dressed in a tight black t-shirt, faded jeans and cowboy boots leaning against a Toyota Land Cruiser parked next to his car. The man looked American and had longish blond hair pulled back in a short ponytail. His casual dress and demeanor marked him as a tourist, probably making a stopover in the capital before hitting some of the surf breaks on the Pacific coast. He had that look about him. Something appeared vaguely familiar about the man, but Cyrus chalked up the false sense of recognition to his own nagging preference to be on vacation as well, sipping an ice-cold Modelo and lounging on a sandy beach somewhere in Puerto Escondido or Zihuatanejo.

"Cyrus, could I have a word with you?" the man with the ponytail suddenly asked in English.

Cyrus froze as he heard his name roll off the lips of a perfect stranger, and a chill ran down his back. He cursed silently, recalling that he had carelessly placed his government-issue Browning 9 mm at the bottom of his canvas gym bag, an unforgivable oversight for a case officer with his breadth of experience, especially one working the narcotics target. Cyrus turned slowly toward the man who had addressed him, scanning the area for anybody else who might be with him.

"Do we know each other?" asked Cyrus, relaxing a bit as he saw the tall stranger smile and hold out both hands with his palms up. The hands were empty and Cyrus saw nothing suspicious in the small parking lot of the exclusive sports club.

"No, not really, but a patient at the ABC Centro Médico spoke highly of you and suggested we meet. I'm Mako Sloane. Maybe the name means something to you?"

Cyrus stared in disbelief at the man in front of him, who claimed to be the notorious ex-CIA operative who allegedly killed the head of the Sinaloa Cartel a year ago in South Texas.[20] The name was a legend in the hallways of CIA headquarters and the subject of a thousand whispered rumors and unconfirmed innuendo. Sloane was an enigma, lionized by those close to him, but reviled by an equal number of detractors and a disturbing number of enemies who would prefer to see him dead. There seemed to be no middle ground as far as Mako Sloane was concerned. He was in and out of operational vogue as often as the political winds shifted inside the beltway.

"Maybe, but how do I know that's who you are?"

"Who else would risk coming to Mexico knowing the Sinaloa Cartel has a contract out on his life? Or know to look up Cyrus Tinch, who up until two weeks ago was

---

[20] See TEXMEX by Clabe Taylor, 2013.

running an agent in the Attorney General's Office named Soledad Castillo?"

Again, the familiar chill down his back. It was an unpleasant sensation he always felt when confronted with the realization that his activities were not always as clandestine and anonymous as he might think. Every CIA officer knew the feeling. Cyrus looked at Mako Sloane and made his decision.

"Okay, I take it you're buying?" He walked toward Mako with his right hand extended in greeting.

***

"Mako, are you freelancing here in Mexico City or is this official?" Cyrus clinked Mako's proffered shot glass and threw back a shot of tequila, his eyes tearing slightly. They sat around a small round table in the well-lit lounge of the Nikko Hotel. Cyrus glanced around the room at the foreign tourists and well-heeled Mexicans sipping their tequila sunrises and vodka martinis.

The Mexicans were mostly middle-aged men sporting respectable paunches in the company of much younger women, probably their mistresses. Cyrus knew the type. After a few drinks, there would be a hurried tryst in a hotel room upstairs, and then the men would drive back to their luxurious houses in the well-to-do residential communities of Lomas de Chapultepec and Coyoacán or a dozen others like them where their wives and nannies stayed home with the kids. The Nikko Hotel was not exactly a classic venue for a clandestine meeting, but it was a perfect place for two *gringos* to have a drink, unnoticed by the staff or other customers. Sometimes a crowd is the best guarantor of anonymity.

"The last time I did something for the government it landed me in prison for seven years, Cyrus," answered Mako. "This is unofficial, I can assure you."

"Then you know I'm risking my career by even speaking with you."

Cyrus was nonplussed despite getting the answer he expected. He was bursting with curiosity about the man sitting across the table, and he was certain Mako Sloane had submarines on his mind. Cyrus sensed Sloane knew about Russia's alliance with the Sinaloa drug cartel, and he was dying to share the station's latest intelligence with him. Cyrus knew he was courting professional hari-kari if this contact came to anyone's attention at the station or back in Langley, but he was at a dead end and looking for a lead.

"I won't tell if you won't," smiled Mako.

"This is starting to sound like a recruitment pitch. Next thing, you'll be telling me that my security is your paramount concern. I've used that hackneyed line a few times myself."

"No, that would be too much of a crock of shit even for me." said Mako.

Cyrus looked intensely at Mako and liked what he saw. The man's disarming honesty was refreshing in a profession based on lies and false promises of fealty that rarely materialized.

Mako raised his arm and waved at a passing waiter. *"Dos tequilas más, por favor,"* he said.

"It's a good thing you're paying," said Cyrus. "Imagine the reaction at the station if my monthly accounting showed that I bought drinks for Mako Sloane in the Nikko Hotel."

"Yeah, they'd probably send you back to headquarters on the first available flight for a polygraph and a CI interview," said Mako with a straight face. Cyrus knew he was only half-joking and neither man smiled.

"If Soledad gave you my name, I think I know what you want to talk about."

"After the sinking of the oil tanker in the Houston ship channel, it's the only thing anybody's talking about," replied Mako. "I've got a piece of the picture, but I'm hoping you can fill in the blanks. Actually, I'm hoping you'll tell me I'm full of it. I've never wanted so badly to be wrong."

"Let me make it easy for both of us. How does an alliance between the Sinaloa Cartel and Russia sound?"

"Jesus!" mumbled Mako under his breath. "So Armando was right all along."

"Who's Armando?"

"A wise man who was supposed to kill me," answered Mako. "He's Soledad's cousin. He's also Antonio Salcido's former attorney."

Cyrus whistled softly.

"Must be one of her sources."

The waiter in a black vest and bow tie approached and gallantly set two shots of tequila and a saucer of fresh lime slices on the table in front of the men.

"*Salud.*" Mako offered a simple toast, and the two men clinked glasses and drank once more. The waiter hovered nearby in servile expectation and Mako nodded to him, ordering another round with a circular motion of his upraised index finger. A piano player with a shaved head and neatly trimmed goatee labored over a Rachmaninoff piano concerto at a black Yamaha baby grand, but his mistakes and technical imperfections grated on Cyrus, who tried to tune out the music and instead waited for the question from Sloane he was sure would come. He did not have to wait long.

"So what does the station know about the Russia – cartel connection?"

Cyrus pursed his lips in one last moment of hesitation and then his resolve crumbled. He sighed deeply and drank the third shot of tequila the waiter had placed in front of him without even waiting for Mako to join him. Dropping all pretenses to caution, Cyrus told Mako everything he knew about the submarine purchase: Antonio Salcido's trip to Mykolaiv, the technical specifications and attack capabilities of the Andastra knock-off, the Ukrainian training crew, and the satellite tracking of the freighter carrying the submarine to Veracruz.

For Cyrus, the most compelling and frightening circumstances, though, lay elsewhere. He described to Mako the briefing of Harvard Banks, DEA's assistant administrator for intelligence and the coincidence of the car bomb attack on Soledad Castillo a mere two weeks later. Most perplexing of all was the morgue-like silence of headquarters regarding the demise of the *Orca* and *Ostap Bender* and Langley's explicit instructions to mothball Soledad Castillo as a source.

"You think I'm jumping to conclusions?" asked Cyrus.

"No," replied Mako laconically. "But your theory raises more questions than it answers."

"Yeah, what motivation would the government or somebody in the government have for concealing what we reported on the operation? Why has there been no follow-up? And why were we ordered to stand down?"

"It sounds like you're suggesting that the U.S. Navy armada combing the Gulf of Mexico right now is a red herring? Out there just for show?"

Cyrus sat back and unconsciously ran the back of his right hand over his two-day growth of beard and grimaced slightly at the thought of what he now firmly believed.

"Yeah. I'm saying they should be looking for that submarine in Veracruz or camouflaged in some lagoon along the Mexican coast, and I think they know it! Or at least somebody does."

Chapter 14

Harvard Banks hoped he had seen the last of Mexico. Every time the DEA assistant administrator for intelligence recalled his embarrassing debriefing at the CIA station in Mexico City, his fleshy jowls turned bright crimson and he shuddered inwardly. Word had gotten around too. Not about the briefing, though. That subject was limited to a very exclusive bigot list, but rather how Harvard soiled his trousers in the bubble at the end of the briefing despite his heroic efforts to prevent, and then when that failed, to contain the malodorous spill. Maybe it was the CIA's surprise revelation about Antonio Salcido's trip to Ukraine that had loosened Harvard's bowels or maybe it was just the damned Mexican food. Jimmy Carter was right to joke about Montezuma's revenge. You could not drink a glass of water in this god-forsaken country without shitting your brains out the next day.

Then there was his role as a messenger boy. Harvard chafed at DEA administrator Cory Elkins' insistence that he be the one to carry a personal message to the head of the Sinaloa Cartel. For Christ's sake, he was the DEA's assistant administrator for intelligence, not some kind of field agent or messenger boy! He should be sitting behind his computer at DEA headquarters in Washington, not cooling his heels in a hotel room in Mazatlán, Sinaloa running to the toilet every fifteen minutes and waiting for someone to knock on his door. And what the hell was Cory Elkins up to anyway? Why was the head of DEA communicating directly with Antonio Salcido? Something stank, but Harvard for the life of him could not figure it out despite his impressive credentials as DEA's top analyst.

Harvard's room at the El Cid hotel along the strip in Mazatlán was pleasantly cool from the overworked air conditioner, but the years of constant humidity had made the room clammy and dank. The dim lighting exacerbated the dismal ambience, and the furniture upholstery and the bed linen exuded a tomb-like mustiness that offended Harvard's delicate sensibilities.

As time passed, Harvard had become increasingly uncomfortable over the secret he knew and could not reveal. To his knowledge, besides the two CIA officers in Mexico City only two other individuals in the U.S. government shared the secret: DEA Administrator Cory Elkins and Director of the Central Intelligence Agency Ian McGinniss. When Harvard learned of the *Orca's* fate, he knew instinctively who was behind the atrocity, and he awaited the wrathful vengeance of the United States with barely concealed glee. When the members of the president's national security team shrugged their shoulders behind closed doors and professed ignorance about possible perpetrators of the outrage, Harvard knew that there must be a deeper, more strategic reason for the government's inaction. He was certain there had to be more to the story, but he respected the "need-to-know" principle and asked no questions.

When the *Ostap Bender* sunk under similar circumstances, Harvard watched with shock as the price of oil skyrocketed and the stock market fell precipitously. He was even more dismayed at the obvious connection between the two sinkings and the still inexplicable inaction of the government he loved and revered. Harvard began to doubt the existence of any longer-term thinking, and he smelled a rat.

Harvard shared his fears with Cory Elkins who dismissively told him that the matter was above his pay grade and to shut the fuck up. Two days later, he received the unexpected assignment to travel to Mazatlán to deliver the coded message he now carried in his briefcase. He had no idea how to read the encrypted message, but he had a premonition that his life was careening out of control. The head DEA analyst wished he were back home trimming the azaleas that surrounded his suburban home on the banks of Lake Barcroft in Falls Church, Virginia.

A loud knock on his door startled Harvard, and his heart involuntarily raced as he walked across the tile floor and peered through the peephole in the door. He could discern the distorted shapes of two mustachioed Mexicans standing in the corridor.

"Yes?" he called out.

"Señor Banks," abre la puerta, por favor. Somos amigos[21]."

"Speak English," called out Harvard. "Where is Mr. Salcido?"

Harvard heard snickering in the hallway and indistinct words spoken in whispered Spanish.

"We're here to take you to *El Padrino*," one of the voices finally said in accented English.

Harvard mustered what courage he could and opened the door, revealing two of Salcido's low-level employees, both dressed in baggy jeans and wrinkled Chinese versions of Ralph Lauren Polo shirts. Harvard had never been so frightened in his life. Last Sunday's sermon at the Falls Church Baptist Church on West Columbia Street about Daniel being cast into the lions' den came to mind, but he gritted his teeth and followed his hosts to the parking lot and their nondescript white delivery van.

He felt far more like a hostage than a VIP guest from Washington, especially when Salcido's henchmen hustled him into the back of the van and shut and locked the door from the outside. Harvard's panic increased as the van

---

[21] Open the door, please. We're friends.

trundled noisily across town and came to an abrupt halt after only a few minutes. There was no air conditioning in the back of the van, and Harvard was sweating. A claustrophobic panic had begun to spread in his gut when one of Salcido's men finally opened the back of the van. Even the sweltering and sticky tropical air was a relief. He gasped for air, uncomprehending and suddenly fearful for his life. Cory Elkins had said nothing about the possibility of this kind of reception. Harvard looked at his leering hosts and felt certain they did not share his vision of life everlasting or his hopes for a Redskins' Super Bowl appearance in January.

The van stood in a parking lot adjacent to the Mazatlán Marina. Salcido's men walked on either side of Banks and pushed him along roughly, holding him tightly by the elbows. They accompanied the DEA official, stumbling and protesting to the boarding ramp leading to an 80-foot yacht with the name *High Jinks.*

"Harvard, is that you? Come on up!" a voice shouted.

Banks looked up to the fly bridge and saw a jauntily dressed man about forty years old waving to him and standing beside two shapely women in bikinis and high heels. Salcido, he thought with relief. Now things will go as planned. He would pass the message, return to his hotel, and take a taxi to the airport for the afternoon flight back to Dallas. The fact that the twin 425 horsepower diesel engines were warming up did not register in his brain. He was relieved to be alive and was not paying attention to his surroundings. He looked up at Salcido and waved to his savior.

An hour later Harvard Banks sat together with Antonio Salcido on the fly bridge in a pair of borrowed swimming trunks and baby blue Polo shirt, drinking cold beer and discussing American football as the *High Jinks* steamed west into the Sea of Cortez. Salcido was a gracious and garrulous host, and Harvard found himself liking the man who now sat across from him. He was enjoying the unexpected cruise. Harvard had difficulty taking his eyes off Salcido's female companions, who had doffed their bikini tops and pranced about the fly bridge with their taut breasts bouncing like coiled springs. Harvard was embarrassed at the unexpected stirring in his borrowed tropical-weight shorts and crossed his legs to conceal any sign of his arousal.

Banks knew more about Salcido's violent side than any other man in the U.S. government and found it incongruent that his urbane host could be the same man whose very name infused cold-blooded terror into his allies and rivals alike. Several of Salcido's deckhands had joined them on the fly bridge, and they were generously dispensing a mixture of chum made from bloody tuna chunks and fish oil overboard.

"You're a fisherman?" asked Harvard, stating the obvious.

"Oh yes," replied Salcido. "And I expect some exceptional fishing today."

"What are you going after?" Harvard asked, walking over to the railing and peering over the side of the yacht, which had stopped and was now drifting slowly in the offshore current. Pieces of bloody tuna floated off the starboard side, and Harvard thought he saw several large fish swimming in circles in the water just below the surface.

"We're hoping to attract some hammerheads today," replied Salcido. "Looks like a few have arrived already."

Harvard watched with fascination as the number of sharks in the water multiplied rapidly, and within fifteen minutes all the men stood at the rail, pointing to the surface of the Sea of Cortez, which roiled in confused bubbling motion as the hammerheads gradually worked themselves into a feeding frenzy.

"I think these are scalloped hammerheads. The Latin name is *Sphyrna lewini,*" said Salcido. "They're not as dangerous as a bull shark or a great white, but when they get into a frenzy like this, you don't want to be anywhere near. Would you like to take a swim, Harvard?"

Harvard laughed. "Not today, thanks," he joked.

"Come now, where's your sense of adventure?" asked Salcido. "These sharks look pretty small. They can get to about fourteen feet long, but I don't see anything longer than six or eight feet out there."

He nodded to his deckhands who suddenly took hold of Harvard's elbows from behind as he peered over the railing.

"What's going on, Antonio?" shouted Harvard as the deckhands wrestled with him, lifting his body halfway across the guardrail that ran around the perimeter of the fly bridge. "Is this your idea of a joke?" he cried out in alarm. The two women shrieked and then laughed nervously.

"Just following orders, Harvard." Antonio laughed. "Nothing personal, but it seems your boss thinks you have a big mouth."

"Please," begged Harvard. He was scared now and he felt his bowels release in protest. He desperately grabbed at the guardrail as the deckhands tried to pry his hands loose. One of them punched Harvard in the face and blood poured from his nose.

"Wait, I've got a family!" protested Harvard, tears coming to his eyes and he began to sob. He looked over at the half-naked women, hoping for sympathetic intervention, but they stared with a cruel delight that was almost sexual.

"Se cagó este gringo[22]," shouted one of the deckhands, wrinkling his nose at the putrid brown stream pouring out of the borrowed shorts and down Harvard's legs.

Salcido nodded to a third deckhand who rushed to the assistance of his struggling friends. He carried a small wrench and smashed it repeatedly against Harvard's hands that tenaciously clung to the guardrail. Harvard bellowed and cursed and then released his crushed fingers. He felt his body hurtle through the air and then collide painfully against the railing of the lower deck before hitting the water with a hollow slap and submerging. As he struggled to surface, Harvard knew he had broken several ribs in the fall, and each desperate stroke produced excruciating pain. When he at last broke the surface of the Sea of Cortez, he gasped for air and inadvertently swallowed a nauseating mixture of salt water and bloody chum slick. He gagged and choked, and the pain in his ribs was so sharp it distracted him from his immediate problem: dozens of hammerhead sharks were churning the water around him into a pink frothy whirlpool of lethal confusion.

Harvard heard the twin diesel engines cough into a smooth rhythm and watched in abject horror as the 80-foot yacht pulled away slowly. He screamed and his jumbled

---

[22] The gringo shit himself.

thoughts coalesced for one brief moment, and he cursed the perfidy of human nature. Then he saw the excited hammerheads swimming in ever-decreasing concentric circles him. Harvard began to pray.

Chapter 15

Antonio Salcido put down his gin and tonic and reached for the pair of Steiner 7/50 marine binoculars on top of the built-in bar at the front of the fly bridge. He liked the convenience of the black rubber armoring on the binoculars for use at sea, and he appreciated the fact that they were manufactured in Germany. He would buy anything as long as it was not made in the United States.

The *High Jinks* was already several hundred yards from the spot where Harvard Banks went overboard, and Antonio could no longer distinguish a human body in the crimson water, which still churned and roiled like a gigantic jacuzzi. He was inured to violent death, but he shuddered despite himself as he recalled Banks' panicked screams. The method he chose for Bank's death truly had been an inspiration, but Banks had spoiled the artistry of the execution by his cowardice and clumsy fall from the fly bridge. Antonio replaced the binoculars on the bar and skillfully descended the spiral stairs to the main salon where his guest waited patiently, watching CNN International via the Thrane & Thrane Sailor 60 Satellite TV system installed on the yacht.

"Is it over?" asked the guest in English and turned off the television with the remote control.

"Yeah, he didn't last long. Those hammerheads were ravenous today although as a rule they much prefer tuna to human flesh," said Antonio.

"I was hoping for a more traditional method, something quicker and cleaner," the guest commented.

"Mr. Elkins, please. I am an artist. Life must be entertaining, even when it ends, or why bother getting up in the morning?"

"Remind me not to get on your bad side."

"Don't pretend to be shocked. I've heard about some of your DEA-sponsored murders on Mexican soil. Messy, amateurish affairs, every one of them."

"Don't get me wrong," said Cory Elkins. "I appreciate your assistance. Harvard was a security risk. I made a careless mistake using him as a conduit with the CIA. It was time for his departure."

"Do you have anyone else you want me to 'depart'?" joked Antonio.

Elkins shifted uncomfortably in the built-in leather sofa. Salcido looked at him and smiled inwardly. He knew the DEA administrator was uneasy being alone on a yacht in the Sea of Cortez with the head of the Sinaloa Cartel. Antonio did not blame him. He could not imagine himself traveling to Washington to meet with Elkins in a Georgetown bar.

"No, but we need to discuss the operation," Elkins stated without emotion.

"What's there to discuss? We're fulfilling our half of the bargain. I think things are going quite well."

"You're doing more than that! We agreed to keep each other in the loop....no private agendas, remember?"

"You presume to rebuke me on my own yacht?" Antonio looked at Elkins, and his visceral dislike of *norteamericanos* threatened to overpower his need for a more diplomatic and practical approach, at least today. He hated to admit it, but he still needed the *gringo*.

"Look, Antonio, I don't mind passing you information on the whereabouts of a few Coast Guard cutters on interdiction missions. That's part of our strategy to shut down Texas, right? We can't have a border state legalizing marijuana on its own, period. The rest of the states would follow like a bunch of falling dominoes. Can you imagine what that'll do to your bottom line and the size of my budget?"

Salcido had heard Elkin's pitch before and knew it by heart, but he let the DEA official continue, more out of professional courtesy than anything. He suppressed a yawn and tried to appear interested.

"All we need to do is link the destruction of a few minor targets to either the cartel or rogue elements in Texas, and the federal government will shut Creed Tucker down in a skinny minute," Elkins continued. "Then it's simple. We let our Navy destroy the submarine; Texas will never legalize marijuana, and we'll be back to the status quo. Both of us will regain our lost revenue, and we'll live happily ever after."

"Then what's the problem, Cory?" Antonio knew exactly what the problem was, but he wanted to hear Elkins spell it out.

"We're supposed to coordinate targeting operations, Antonio. I didn't give you carte blanche to destroy the economy of the United States. The agreement was *minor* targets. Who the hell made the decision to attack the Houston Ship Channel?"

The men heard female voices and then the hollow clink of high heels descending the wooden stairs. They caught the scent of heavy, flowery perfume a second before the women appeared, climbing delicately down the spiral staircase, still topless, and now giggling and slightly drunk from the strawberry daiquiris the bartender had been mixing for them.

"Girls, I'll call you when we need you," said Antonio with a frown.

In a pique, the women made a show of covering their breasts with the striped beach towels they carried, as if punishing the men for their callous lack of attention. They turned abruptly on their heels and walked hurriedly back up the stairs without saying a word. Antonio watched Elkins stare intently at the women.

"I made that decision, Cory. Who else?"

"Oh, I don't know...maybe the same people who sold you the submarine?" replied Elkins.

"You think I'd allow myself to be used as a puppet?" Antonio allowed an edge to creep into his voice and he scowled at Elkins. Salcido was playing a role and toying with the DEA official. He enjoyed negotiating from a position of strength, and nothing could make his position stronger than having his professional "counterpart" on board *High Jinks* ten miles offshore in the Sea of Cortez and over 700 miles from the United States border at Nogales, Arizona. His irritation was feigned, but his lack of concern at Cory Elkins' anger over the attack on the Houston Ship Channel was not. He did not give a fuck. Antonio commanded an empire that rivaled Mexico City for control over vast territory, and he looked on Cory Elkins as a mere government *funcionario*[23].

"No, of course not," answered Elkins.

"Then what's the problem?"

"*No hay ningun problema*[24]," said Elkins quickly in Spanish.

---

[23] bureaucrat
[24] There's no problem at all.

"That's more like it. Now, which girl do you prefer?"

"I'll take the one with the long hair," said Elkins without hesitation.

"Your tastes haven't changed since the last time you were here, I see," laughed Antonio.

***

"What do you mean you've lost control of the operation?" asked D/CIA Ian McGinnis, mouth agape. He looked across the broad desk in his seventh floor office at the DEA administrator and frowned in a distinctly condescending fashion. Ian had little respect for his DEA counterpart, whom he considered little more than a thug in a suit, and he was unable to speak to the man as an equal. He sometimes wondered if Elkins' academic credentials came from an online university. Ian would not accept even the hint of failure, especially when the balance in his bank account was at stake. He found Cory Elkins' passive acceptance of his own impotence pathetic.

A graduate of the Wharton School at the University of Pennsylvania, Ian had made a considerable fortune as a stockbroker at Merrill Lynch during the dot-com boom and later as a venture capitalist and oil speculator. He was a risk-taker and had acquired a reputation for clairvoyance in the investment industry. When Ian began to appear in the

1990s as a regular guest on CNBC to tout the virtues of a particular high-tech start-up, investors had listened and heeded his financial advice like the fanatical followers of a charismatic evangelical preacher.

Despite appearances to the contrary, half a dozen SEC investigations into his relationship with the investment and business TV channel failed to prove allegations of collusion and insider trading. Later, law enforcement interest in Ian's business activities halted abruptly when he began contributing heavily to the campaigns of both political parties. His generous contributions eventually earned him an appointment as ambassador in Beijing where, according to rumor, he sought personal investment opportunities as well as improved trade relations between the United States and China. After four years as ambassador, Ian's reputation and credibility as a foreign policy expert were beyond reproach. When the current democratic president assumed office, Ian's name was already on the short list for nomination as director of the Central Intelligence Agency.

"Speak up, man, are you deaf?" Ian looked at Cory Elkins as if the DEA administrator had lost his mind, and he began to regret their once promising partnership. Ian was a genius at recognizing business opportunities, but an entrepreneur had to pick his people carefully, and Ian had not realized what a spineless opportunist Elkins really was.

Ian did not want to contemplate the possible end game permutations if his latest venture went south. There were other considerations at play as well; things he had not shared with Elkins.

"All I'm saying is that we cannot control Antonio Salcido. He's going to do whatever he wants," admitted Elkins.

"Shit, Cory...that's not exactly what you promised when you proposed this half-ass operation," whispered Ian hoarsely. "I went way out on the limb setting up my side."

"We can still salvage it."

"You mean save our asses, don't you?" Sarcasm dripped from Ian's voice.

"Not at all. Together we have the means to turn this whole thing around on Salcido. But right now we have to plug a couple more possible leaks. Then we turn our attention to that filthy drug dealer."

"What leaks? Have you lost your mind?" asked Ian. "I've stalled the president long enough. Salcido went beyond the terms of our understanding when he targeted the Houston Ship Channel. Jesus, I hate to think of what that disaster's done to the value of my blind trusts, but I've either got to provide some answers to the president, or both our careers are going to end...and rather ignominiously, I would predict."

"There are three more people down in Mexico City who know who's behind the attacks," said Elkins and paused.

Ian looked up sharply from his daily briefing paper.

"You're not proposing to feed them to the sharks too, are you? Two of them are my men, don't forget."

"They're expendable when you get right down to it," replied Elkins. "And they know too much. You and I agreed at the very beginning that we wouldn't let sentimentality get in our way, Ian."

"Well, take care of it and don't bother me with the details. I've got to go to the White House and stall the president for a few more days."

Cory Elkins stood up from his chair and extended his hand.

"I'll take care of the leak."

Ian shook his hand squeamishly but did not bother to say goodbye or even meet Cory's eyes. So far, Ian's performance had been flawless. He was afraid to give away his ebullient mood at the last minute. Things were going exactly as planned.

Chapter 16

As the Volkswagen Passat continued its steady ascent into the mountains, Mako Sloane rolled down the front passenger window of the car and filled his lungs with the cool pristine air that gradually replaced the choking pollution of the capital. The route to Valle de Bravo rose out of the putrid smog of the Mexico City basin and traversed high-mountain passes almost 17,000 feet high. Except for the incongruous presence of palms, yucca, and the occasional vibrantly blooming cactus, Mako could close and open his eyes and imagine for a minute that he was in the Grand Tetons or the Alps.

The thunderstorms in the mountains that typically mushroomed from a few insignificant cumulus clouds each afternoon during the June – September rainy season were much like Mexico itself: deceptive, unpredictable, and shockingly violent. A hot sunny day often surrendered unexpectedly to the onslaught of a torrential downpour with low thick clouds obscuring the horizon and enveloping everyone and everything in an unseasonable cold fog. Mako loved the feral pageantry of the central Mexican volcanic plateau. The cool air made him feel clean and recharged and optimistic about life and human nature. That was usually a fleeting sensation.

After the meeting with Cyrus in the Hotel Nikko, Mako telephoned an old Mexican drinking buddy, who had become the owner of an automobile parts factory in Toluca. His friend was delighted to hear from Mako and only too willing to offer his three-bedroom bungalow in Valle de Bravo to him and his two friends with no questions asked.

The quaint house, its southern-facing façade overgrown by cascading waves of colorful bougainvillea, was located off Calle Bocanegra, a scant fifty yards from a bed & breakfast inn dating back to the eighteenth century when it had been a convent. The house offered privacy within a relatively short drive of Mexico City, and Mako thought it would serve nicely as a temporary safe house.

"So this is Cyrus Tinch?" asked Armando suspiciously once the men were safely ensconced in the house and had deposited their belongings in their bedrooms. "Do all you CIA operatives look so ordinary?"

Armando had not said a word during the entire trip from Mexico City, and for the first time since Mako had met him on Fisherman's Wharf in Monterey, he seemed ill at ease.

"Doesn't the CIA man speak Spanish?" Armando asked Mako, pointing to Cyrus who was pointedly ignoring him.

"Don't pay any attention to him, Cyrus," said Mako. "Armando can't decide if he hates or loves us *gringos*. And I don't think he likes being outnumbered."

Mako caught the wary looks Cyrus and Armando exchanged. They reminded him of two male dogs circling, hair up on their backs, waiting for the other to growl or make the first aggressive move before attacking. Next thing you know they'll be sniffing each other's asses, thought Mako.

"You two get used to each other and make it quick," said Mako. "Armando's got contacts in the cartel, and Cyrus has the CIA's technical infrastructure we're going to need."

"Then why do we need you, Mako?" asked Armando.

"The brains for the operation have to come from somewhere."

A yellow-headed Amazon parrot in a cage hanging from a rafter on the terrace squawked loudly, and the Mazuhua Indian maid who came with the house deftly dropped several pieces of fresh mango through the bars to the cage floor. The parrot jumped down from its perch and greedily pecked at the pieces of fruit, making soft warbling noises. The men heard voices in German outside as a group of tourists strolled down the street from the nearby bed and breakfast inn.

Mako and his two friends sat down at a small round, wrought-iron table on the terrace and relaxed for the first time in days. The rain-cooled breeze ruffled the parrot's feathers and the ozone-laden air carried the promise of more rain. The maid brought them a pitcher of freshly squeezed orange juice and a tray with half a papaya on a plate decorated with thin slices of lime arranged in a circle.

"I'm not comfortable sharing classified information with a former member of the Sinaloa drug cartel," said Cyrus.

Mako rolled his eyes. He realized he had two prima donnas on his hands, and he did not have time for therapy sessions.

"I don't think you have any alternative," said Mako. "Unless you have other sources on the narcotics target, that is. Armando knows Salcido personally, don't forget."

"So what good will that do us if Salcido's trying to kill him? Kind of diminishes his access, doesn't it?"

"Salcido's trying to kill Mako Sloane too, but you don't mind dealing with him, do you?" asked Mako.

"Mako, I *told* you this man's an arrogant asshole. A typical *gringo* if you ask me. What did Soledad see in him anyway?" said Armando in Spanish.

Mako put a restraining hand on Cyrus' shoulder.

"You guys are acting like a couple of adolescents. Come on now. I need both of you, and we need each other. Let's work," said Mako.

He paused and eyed the two men, who self-consciously picked at the papaya and took long draughts of cold orange juice as they studiously avoided looking at each other.

"Listen, if what Cyrus reported about the Ukrainian submarine crew is correct, that might be a lead to follow. In fact, that might be our only lead," said Mako.

"It's only a guess at this point," said Cyrus. "We had advance warning of their arrival in Mexico City and picked them up at the airport with one of our unilateral surveillance teams. They headed towards Veracruz in two rented vans, but we lost them on the outskirts of town. The freighter carrying the submarine was also headed to Veracruz, so I think it's pretty clear that's where they are. Or at least where they were."

Mako looked at Armando and waited.

"Oh, is this where I come in?" Armando asked. "I see how you guys work. Send in the Mexican as cannon fodder when the going gets tough, right?"

"Something like that, Armando," said Mako. "How well do you know Veracruz?"

"Well enough. What do you want me to do?" replied Armando.

"That's more like it. I want you to go to Veracruz and nose around. See whether your contacts know anything about the submarine or about a group of Ukrainians or Russians in town."

"And if Salcido gets wind I'm down there and I don't come back?"

"We'll erect a monument to your memory and recruit someone else to help us. You Mexicans are a dime a dozen after all," said Mako. Out of the corner of his eye, he saw Armando suppress a smile.

***

Bulat Mikoyan sat with his back to the wall in the cramped smoky confines of the dimly lit bar, a short walk from the port and a stone's throw from the Zócalo in Veracruz. Although *El Rinconcito* would never find its way onto Travel Advisor or the Lonely Planet Travel Guide, Bulat did not mind the shabby furnishings in the bar or even the sharp ammonia smell of dried urine emanating from the nearby restroom. He needed a break from the rigorous training schedule and so did the rest of his men.

Five of them sat at an ancient wooden table defaced and crisscrossed by dozens of overlapping circular water stains. The diameters of the faint circles perfectly matched the beer mugs and tequila shot glasses used by generations of waterfront lowlifes, who had sat and drunk at that very table. Half a dozen tattooed Mexicans, wearing backwards baseball caps or bandanas tied around their heads, sat in a semi-circle around Bulat and his co-workers and formed a protective shield between the former Russian submariners and the riffraff in the bar. Handguns of one make or another protruded from under their baggy *guayaberas* in an intentional show of force and a not-so-discreet warning to stay away. Bulat occasionally shot a glance at his cartel babysitters but was so relieved to be out of the suffocating atmosphere of the compound in the port where he and his men lived that he did not mind the presence of chaperones. He felt like a convict on a weekend pass after years in the slammer. He gulped the smoky, oxygen-deprived air that reeked of body odor, cooking onions, and *guajillo* peppers. For the time being, he preferred it to the stench of diesel fuel and lubricating oil.

"Captain, snap out of it!" laughed Bulat's weapons officer, a former Russian navy lieutenant, who lost his chances of ever serving on a submarine again when he chose Ukrainian citizenship over loyalty to the new Russian Federation after the breakup of the Soviet Union in 1991. He too had welcomed the cash and the opportunity to be at sea once more. He nudged Bulat with his elbow. "Stop staring."

Bulat jerked at the unexpected elbow in his side and realized he had been ogling a tall, heavily made-up woman standing at the bar with an oddly square jaw and just the trace of a five o'clock shadow. A black sailor speaking French was at her side kneading her buttocks with his right hand and whispering into her ear. She towered above him and had an uninterested, bored expression on her face but did not remove his hand.

"Is that a man?" asked Bulat, wondering whether he had already drunk too much of the rotgut vodka the Mexican bar sold. The vodka was so bad that Bulat questioned its origin. It tasted like some of the dubious concoctions sold at kiosks in Russia in the 1990s. Some of those beverages bore only the faintest resemblance to vodka, and many contained poisonous doses of methanol.

"I was hoping you could still tell the difference," said the Ukrainian.

"It's been too long. I find myself fantasizing about women even when I'm lecturing on SONAR systems and range finding."

"I hope it hasn't been so long that you'll settle for that transvestite," The Ukrainian nodded his head in the direction of the woman at the bar.

"No, but take a look at that hooker that just walked in," said Bulat, rising up out of his chair to get a better look at the woman who had just entered *El Rinconcito*. She wore a modest white gauzy blouse and a loose-fitting summer skirt with a generic floral pattern. Tall for a Mexican woman, she wore little makeup. Nobody would have mistaken her for a prostitute except for her presence in this particular bar, a favorite watering hole of the dregs of the port district and the Veracruz underworld. A Mexican man of medium height in his mid-thirties had his arm protectively draped over her shoulders as the two wove their way laboriously through the crowd of drinkers. One of the submariners' chaperones waved at the man, who smiled and nodded his head in recognition.

"Look, she's walking this way," said the weapons officer.

Bulat stared hungrily at the woman. She seemed rather unsure of her surroundings despite the confident air of her companion. He greeted several of the crew's chaperones by name, shaking their hands in a ritualistic series of embraces and backslaps. She kept her eyes glued to the floor and avoided eye contact with the dozens of intoxicated seamen who undressed her in their depraved imaginations. Bulat was one of them. She reminded him of his first girlfriend, a tall Armenian beauty several years his senior who had towered above Bulat, but who had been surprised to discover that his diminutive stature had nothing in common with the dimensions of his manhood. She had been a student at the university in Yerevan and had tutored Bulat in Armenian history and culture and whispered her secret desire to see Armenia as an independent country and for Bulat to touch her in ways that he found both exciting and disturbing.

Bulat continued to stare at the prostitute and did not notice her Mexican companion watching him out of the corner of his eye. He continued to speak familiarly with several of the bodyguards, who had procured two additional chairs and were inviting the newcomers to sit down. Although he was in easy earshot of the conversation, Bulat did not understand a word and was startled when one of the crew's chaperones turned to him and motioned him over with a subtle movement of his hand. Bulat stood self-consciously, glanced again at the woman, and walked over to where she stood with her companion and their cartel babysitter.

"Quiero presentarte a un amigo mio,"[25] said Bulat's chaperone.

Bulat looked at the thug with a blank expression and glanced back at the woman. She was more beautiful at close range than he could have imagined. She bore an uncanny resemblance to his first love back in Yerevan. Then her companion spoke, breaking the spell, and addressed Bulat in English, a language he knew well.

"I think he's trying to introduce us. You seem to have taken a fancy to my friend here?" said the man, raising the

---

[25] I'd like to introduce you to a friend of mine.

hem of the woman's cotton dress a good twelve inches and revealing a brown thigh with the muscle tone of a professional dancer. Bulat felt his face flush, but he continued to stare.

"Maybe we can do some business," the man said in English and stuck out his hand in greeting. "My name is Armando."

Chapter 17

It came to Ian McGinnis in a dream. A sudden, almost jarring flash of insight that woke him from a fitful sleep and offered a semblance of clarity and a way out of the hopeless muddle of intrigue into which he had fallen. He sat up suddenly, instantly awake, and looked at the clock on his bedside table. Three o'clock in the morning.

He glanced over at his sleeping wife, her overweight, amorphous body mercifully covered by a thick quilt, and he eased out of bed trying not to wake her. Forty-five minutes later, he sat behind his desk on the seventh floor of CIA headquarters and stared at his computer monitor, reviewing official estimates of Iranian military capabilities.

It might work, he thought. He would need some intelligence reports from the field to support the hypothesis, of course; something for the analysts to use as a basis for the conclusions he would custom order. The intelligence did not have to originate from reliable sources. Colin Powell at the United Nations in 2003 had proved that to the world.

Ian decided to call a meeting of top CIA analysts to sound them out on whether or not the Iranian navy would be capable of deploying one of their Kilo class Russian-made submarines in the Gulf of Mexico and sinking the *Orca* and the *Ostap Bender*. The range of one of those subs was over 7,000 miles after all. He would hint at the existence of a HUMINT source, which pointed to an Iranian plot carried out with the connivance and logistical help of the Venezuelan navy. If the analysts confirmed that it was theoretically possible, he then would request worldwide intelligence tasking on the alleged operation. If the Iraqi WMD debacle was any indication, there would not be a shortage of reports confirming the fallacious hypothesis, and he would brief the president with the CIA's best guess regarding the perpetrator of the attacks: the Islamic Republic of Iran. The Iranians had the motive, and he would invent the smoking gun.

As soon as Congress and the press had a new scapegoat, he would not have to worry about the rumors of a Russia-cartel alliance. His secret would be safe, at least from the inside-the-beltway crowd. Ian wondered what Cory Elkins was doing to patch the leaks in Mexico.

He leaned back in the deep black leather upholstery of his chair, satisfied that he had hit upon a promising strategy. He punched in Bloomberg's website address and peered at the screen on his monitor. The NYMEX Crude Futures price had reached $227 a barrel and was still rising. The Dow Jones Industrial average was already down 55% compared to its value the day before the oil tanker sank in the Houston Ship Channel. Ian chuckled to himself. Timing was everything in the investment game, and it was heartwarming what a little advance warning of impending calamities could do for one's investment portfolio, he thought cynically.

Ian reached into the bottom right drawer of his desk, removed a pint bottle of Hennessey cognac, and poured a half-shot into his cup of Costa Rican fair-trade coffee. Shelling out the extra money for the colorful fair-trade label made him feel progressive and almost virtuous. He sipped the coffee and studied the top news stories of the day.

An article on the skyrocketing price of oil added several degrees to the spreading warmth in his belly. He calculated that the futures price still had legs and decided to sit on his oil-based exchange traded funds for a few more days and hold off on buying more oil futures. At least until he briefed the president on the new threat from Iran.

That could send world oil prices spiraling to the $300 a barrel range. Ian had his money squirreled away in offshore funds, invisible to the prying eyes of the Securities Exchange Commission and the meddling American press corps. Their demands for financial transparency had always struck him as comical. Who would be dumb enough to invest all their capital in the United States? The world economy might be reeling, but Ian's prospects never looked rosier as long as he was able to employ a little poetic license with the agency's intelligence reports. It occurred to him that a strategically placed leak to the *Washington Post* could easily add another five to ten dollars to the price of oil. He would have to consider that option when the price started to flatten out.

***

The CIA's chief of station in Mexico City was a veteran case officer with thirty years of clandestine experience in the shitholes of Africa, Latin America, and South Asia. During the Cold War proxy conflicts of the 1980s, he had deployed in the bush alongside Reagan freedom fighters in Angola, Latin America, and then Afghanistan. He had trained government death squads in Guatemala and El Salvador and witnessed atrocities that no amount of tequila or mescal could erase from his memory. As time passed, the well-defined boundaries between good and evil became blurred and scarcely resembled the distinct moral delineations of his youth. He lived in a permanent hell of his own moral contradictions but knew there was no way out. It was too late for that.

Successive administrations in Washington had been full of wannabe Rambos and politicians whose stark Biblical view of the world regularly led to death on a massive scale. He observed the process and finally realized that nothing ever changed: it was still the messianic policies of nineteenth-century Manifest Destiny but now it was on an international scale. Death was only a slight bump in the road, easily justified and explained away, as long as the victims were not white and did not believe in the Holy Trinity.

He poured himself another cup of coffee and ran the back of his hand over his beard. He hated to shave each morning. Shaving required looking in a mirror and it had been years since the COS liked what he saw in his reflection. The gray in his beard, the sagging flesh in his face. It all reminded him that his physical decay was keeping pace with his loss of faith in the CIA and his own government. His career had once been a source of pride, a daily reminder that the world was at war and that he was in the vanguard of righteousness. Now he was not so sure...or even worse. He was sure that he had been naïve, if not demonstrably delusional.

The moral sleight of hand so necessary for success in his job had crept into his personal life. He had lost his wife and a girlfriend along the way; he drank too much, and now he just longed to be back in a jon boat powered by a twenty-five horsepower Evinrude outboard motor, fishing for speckled trout and red fish and exploring the brackish meandering creeks and rivers near Charleston, South Carolina where he grew up.

He shaved and dressed slowly and considered the countless scenarios that might explain the deafening silence coming out of Langley. Something stank inside the Beltway besides the usual reek of hypocrisy and lies. The United States economy was in a tailspin, and the rest of the world was hurtling rapidly into the same black hole. Who could possibly benefit from such a scenario? The pieces were coming together slowly in his mind, but he still needed answers to key questions. He wondered whether Cyrus Tinch was making any headway. Both of them were risking their careers by defying headquarters, and unless they stumbled upon the answer to this riddle, they both would be looking for a job in the private sector very soon.

The COS tightened his tie and looked at himself in the mirror. He turned his head to either side and squinted at his reflection. He felt the vibration of his secure cell phone in the inside pocket of his navy blue pinstriped suit jacket. He glanced at the caller I.D. and realized it was Cyrus.

"Yeah," he said.

"Hey boss," said the familiar voice. "I ran into an old friend of yours the other day."

"Oh, who's that?"

"Mako Sloane."

"Who?" he asked again, hoping he had heard wrong.

"He's with me now. We're looking for the submarine crew. I hope to have something more in a few days."

He heard the almost inaudible click as Cyrus signed off. Mako Sloane? If Sloane had made contact with Cyrus, the shit was bound to hit the fan if it had not already. He realized that his morning negativism had been prescient. The operation was already in direct violation of a headquarters' directive, and now Mako Sloane had appeared out of thin air. He wondered how things could possibly get any worse.

He inserted the loaded Glock 19 pistol into his Serpa hip holster and adjusted his suit coat. He glanced out of the window and saw the black armored Chevrolet Suburban already waiting on the street beside his apartment building. He hated to rely on a driver and bodyguard, but after the Sinaloa Cartel publicized its contract on Mako Sloane, headquarters had instituted new security precautions. The identity of the COS in Mexico City was known to the station's liaison counterparts in the Mexican government. By definition, that information was available to Antonio Salcido and the Sinaloa drug cartel at the right price.

The COS exited his exclusive Polanco apartment and walked briskly down the short flight of stairs to the sidewalk carrying a light briefcase in his right hand. He was preoccupied with thoughts of Mako Sloane and the thousand and one different ways the operation could go from bad to worse. He barely acknowledged his bodyguard, who clambered out of the Suburban on the passenger side and held the back door open for him. The COS ducked into the vehicle and his bodyguard climbed in next to him and closed the door. The driver turned on the left turn signal and began to pull out into the right lane.

A quarter mile ahead of them on the right side of the street, a lone figure stepped out from behind a newspaper kiosk, dropped to a kneeling position, and placed an RPG-7 on his shoulder. After aiming the rocket propelled grenade launcher at the black Suburban, he pulled the trigger. The force of built-up gasses inside the weapon hurled the grenade from the launch tube at a speed of almost 390 feet per second. When the primer ignited the squib of nitroglycerin powder in the stabilizing pipe, the rocket propulsion system kicked in and boosted the speed of the grenade to almost 900 feet per second. A moment later the suburban exploded and leaped into the air like a breaching whale before crashing to the ground in an orange and black cloud of flame and smoke.

After the warhead detonated, the figure in the street rose from his knees and dropped the RPG tube nonchalantly in the street. He calmly took his seat behind the driver of a small Yamaha dirt bike that sped away, following a maze of narrow alleyways off the main drag until the *ring-ding-ding* of its two-cycle engine could no longer be heard.

Chapter 18

"I had a dream last night."

Armando sat on the terrace of the Valle de Bravo safe house. He relit the marijuana cigarette that lay barely smoldering in a pewter ashtray on the table in front of him. The late afternoon thunderstorm had blown through in a cavorting spasm of wind and rain and left the picturesque town shrouded in a cool, opaque bank of low clouds and fog. The cobblestone street outside glistened with moisture in the eerie late afternoon light, and water stood in the cracks between the uneven stones. Both men had thrown wool serapes around their shoulders to keep out the wet chill. Mako sipped a Cuba Libre from a tall, hand-blown cocktail glass. He picked at the plate of Mexican hors d'oeuvres the maid had prepared.

"I don't doubt that," said Mako. "Considering what you've been drinking and smoking, you're probably dreaming right now."

"An intriguing thought." Armando inhaled deeply. He waited and then exhaled with his mouth closed, the smoke curling out of his nostrils and making his eyes water. "Precisely the point I intended to make."

"Armando, this isn't the usual way I conduct a debriefing. Would it be too much to ask you for a little cooperation?"

"Right now, I find your request to be inopportune. What I saw in my dream was deeply disturbing, and I don't understand the implications. Sometimes I wonder whether dreams are perhaps the thing itself and reality something else entirely."

Mako sliced off a thin piece of mango from a plate of tropical fruit. He looked at Armando and grinned despite himself.

"Sometimes I think it would have been better if you had just killed me back in Monterey instead of subjecting me to your pseudo-intellectual riddles."

Armando ignored Mako and yawned.

"I saw myself asleep and dreaming. Then I stepped into the dream. It was more real than my own life."

"Armando, this is pointless. We have work to do."

"There are more significant issues to contemplate than the violent games and follies of men."

"Oh?" responded Mako. "More significant than the assassination of the top CIA official in Mexico City?"

"That was to be expected," said Armando.

"You knew it was going to happen?"

"Didn't you? I guess you're going to tell me you don't know that Cyrus is next on the list or that Antonio Salcido fed a top DEA official to the sharks last week in Mazatlán?"

Mako looked up sharply from the mango he continued to slice.

"What did you say?"

Mako impaled a slice of the orange mango on a knife, lifted it to his mouth, and delicately removed the fruit from the sharp blade with his teeth.

"There's a cartel contract out on Cyrus."

"I figured that, but what about the DEA official?"

"They say he screamed like a little bitch and begged for his life."

"Armando, cut the shit, will you?" said Mako.

"You mean you really don't know? What is this? Another intelligence failure by the CIA?"

"I haven't had contact with the civilized world in five days," said Mako. "Where would I hear about anything like that?"

"Oh, so now Mexico isn't civilized?"

"What do *you* think? Damn it, Armando, you'd argue with a possum. Just tell me what you know, will you?"

"I don't remember his full name. I remember 'Harvard' but don't know whether it was his first or last name." Armando paused and picked up the joint and lit it again with a plastic Bic lighter.

"Harvard Banks?" asked Mako. "They killed Harvard Banks?"

"Yeah, that was his name. Fed him to the hammerheads off Mazatlán. Which is unusual for Salcido, by the way. He must have been in one of his creative, artistic moods. Normally, he just uses a chain saw and decapitates his victims. Sometimes he tosses them alive into a vat of acid. But that's when he's depressed."

"Where'd you hear this, Armando?"

Thunder rumbled in the distance and then again closer. The ceramic tiles on the roof shook and rattled faintly. Then it was still. Mako waited for Armando to answer.

"It was in a bar near the port in Veracruz. I looked up some old colleagues. Murderers, mostly. One convicted rapist and a pedophile as well. They all work for the cartel now. They like tempting fate. Today they work for Salcido and the Sinaloa Cartel and tomorrow they'll move on to the Zetas or the Gulf Cartel if the price is right. They usually don't live long switching back and forth. But they don't care. Life has little to offer them, and they're curious about the hereafter."

"One of them told you about Banks?" asked Mako.

"Yeah, he was right there on board Salcido's yacht and saw everything."

Mako whistled. Death by shark was not an exit strategy he would have chosen for himself.

"Apparently there was another American on the yacht with Harvard Banks, but my source didn't know who it was," added Armando.

"Another American? You think Banks was double crossed?"

"Yeah, I'd say he was set up," answered Armando.

"But what was he doing there in the first place?"

Mako leaned forward across the table and picked up a pair of stainless steel tongs. He then retrieved several ice cubes from an oblong crystal bowl and deposited them carefully in his drink.

"Who knows?" said Armando. "But you seem surprised. Do you think we Mexicans have a monopoly on treachery?"

"Monopoly? No, but you have an impressive market share."

A car door slammed out on the street in front of the bungalow and they heard the front door open followed by footsteps trotting up the stairs.

"Maybe, we'll hear what the embassy has to say," said Mako. "That sounds like Cyrus."

***

"Pour me a drink." Cyrus threw open the door to the terrace and plopped into a chair beside Mako. He leaned back against the plaid pillow on the back of the chair, stretched his legs, and groaned.

Mako took one look at Cyrus' haggard features and reached for the bottle of 12-year Flor de Caña Nicaraguan rum he had purchased that morning in a local liquor store. He poured two fingers in a glass with no ice and no mixer and handed it to Cyrus who emptied the glass in one gulp and motioned for more. Mako obliged.

"Bad day?" Mako asked.

"Not really, just nerves. A couple of times I thought I was being followed. Then I wasn't sure. I'm starting to see ghosts out there."

"What's the news from the embassy? Armando here tells me Harvard Banks was murdered last week in Mazatlán."

Cyrus looked quickly at Armando who sat calmly observing the two Americans.

"Murdered? Really?"

Mako nodded his head.

"DEA reported him missing. That's all," said Cyrus. "Did they find his body?"

"Probably not much left to find," commented Mako.

"What?" asked Cyrus.

"Sharks," said Armando.

Cyrus looked at Mako for clarification.

"Armando says Salcido fed him to the sharks off Mazatlán last week. Said another American was present, but he doesn't know who it was," said Mako.

"So, this isn't a joke?"

Mako shook his head.

"No joke," responded Armando. "And you're probably next."

"Yeah, it would make sense. First the attempt on Soledad, then Harvard, and now the COS. Everyone who knew about the Russian connection. I'm bound to be next."

"If you're lucky, they might let you select the manner of your own death," said Armando. "Don't choose the chainsaw. It's not elegant. Your corpse deserves something more refined and memorable. Like maybe hanging from a bridge in Nuevo Laredo with a bullet in the back of your head."

"Armando, do you know where Soledad got her information?" asked Mako. "I mean another source besides her boss?"

"Her source?" Armando repeated the question.

"That's right. Whoever it was, he's probably on their list too," said Mako.

"I've been on their list ever since you met me, Mako," said Armando.

Mako sipped his Cuba Libre and studied Armando's enigmatic expression.

"You were one of Soledad's sources?"

Armando nodded his head.

"The main one," he said quietly.

"Why the hell didn't you tell us that before?" asked Cyrus.

"You didn't ask," replied Armando.

Cyrus glanced at Mako, who raised his arms in a gesture of exasperation.

"They've crossed the red line by killing the COS, you know," said Cyrus. "The embassy's battened down the hatches. A team of FBI investigators arrived this morning, and the ambassador is meeting with the Mexican president this evening."

"What good is that supposed to do?" asked Armando. "That'll just give Salcido more targets. He sunk a Coast Guard cutter and an oil tanker in the Houston Ship Channel. Do you think he gives a shit about what your embassy can do? Or the Mexican government?"

Cyrus held out his glass and Mako obligingly reached for the bottle of Flor de Caña and poured another drink.

"Go easy on that," Mako said.

Cyrus dismissed Mako's warning with a wave of his hand.

"No, I'm sorry. They can't just kill a top U.S. official in Mexico and get away with it. It's an unwritten law."

"Don't be so sure," said Mako. "That might have been true back in the 1980s. You remember what happened to Caro Quintero after the Camarena murder? We forced the Mexicans to get off their asses and act. But times have changed. There are no unwritten laws any more. No gentlemen's agreements. The Mexican government has lost control. They've got a full-scale criminal insurgency on their hands. They crack down on the cartels, and the cartels ratchet up the violence. It's a vicious circle."

"So what else did you find out?" Cyrus asked, turning to Armando.

"You walked in on the debriefing," said Mako. "Armando just told me about Banks."

"Hey, by the way, doesn't the CIA pay its agents?" asked Armando. "I haven't seen any money yet. Aren't I on a retainer?"

"Cut the shit, Armando," said Mako. "Tell us what you found out in Veracruz."

"Oh, you mean about how I set up the Russian submarine captain with an old hooker girlfriend of mine?"

"You found the submarine captain?" asked Mako.

Both he and Cyrus put down their drinks and stared at Armando with their mouths open in surprise.

"Isn't this what you CIA types call 'recruiting an access agent'? Not bad for a dime-a-dozen Mexican, eh Mako?"

"Not bad at all," agreed Mako. "Keep talking."

"Yeah, turns out he's Armenian. My friend says he hates the Russians but needs the money they're paying him. But she doesn't know how much more she can take. She says he's horny as a goat, and he's hung like a bull elephant."

Chapter 19

"Ian, what the hell took you so long to get over here? I need some answers!" said the president.

Despite the cool, temperature-controlled atmosphere in the situation room, located in the basement of the West Wing of the White House, the president was percolating in his own sweat. He had loosened his red and blue striped tie and unbuttoned the top button of his heavily starched white shirt, but perspiration soaked through the summer-weight cotton. Beads of sweat perched precariously on his forehead and glistened in the bright artificial light.

"I brought you into the administration precisely because you hadn't been a government puke your entire career. I expected a more timely and proactive response to a national security crisis!"

"Mr. President..." Ian pulled a thick briefing paper from his Riomaggiore briefcase, the stylish distressed Tuscany leather blurring the boundary between chic and frumpy.

"The Dow Jones has lost 61% of its market value in 10 days!" the president interrupted. "The price of oil is over $225 and still rising, and the republicans are calling for my impeachment because I can't tell them who's attacking us!"

"Yes sir. I know." Ian nodded his head without looking at the president and separated the one-page executive summary from the body of the report.

"The Department of Defense has no idea who's sinking the ships, and even your CIA has given me nothing but cover-your-ass platitudes."

"I do have a startling piece of intelligence here," Ian said, but the president interrupted him again.

"I also want the CIA to look into the reports that the Mexican drug cartels and those yahoos down in Texas had something to do with the sinking of the Coast Guard cutter," suddenly demanded the president. "Sons o' bitches want to legalize drugs. They're pleading states' rights and telling us to go fuck ourselves. And now the press is on it. It's got to be just another conspiracy theory, but we have to respond."

"Strictly speaking, Mr. President, that's not the CIA's bailiwick. Our charter won't allow us to investigate domestic security issues. That's for the FBI." Ian looked at the president with surprise.

"Besides," he continued, "in our opinion..."

"Listen," the president interrupted. "The FBI can't tell its ass from a hole in the wall. Never could. If they ever stop pressuring young Muslims to become jihadists and then busting them when they agree to go along with the FBI's own sting operation, they wouldn't have any domestic terrorism cases at all. So, don't tell me the CIA doesn't have a mandate. We make our own mandates around here. I want your best guess on this within 48 hours."

"Yes sir."

"Now what the hell do you know, Ian? Who sunk the *Orca* and blocked the Houston Ship Channel?"

Ian took a deep breath. He had practiced his lines and his delivery. He knew this president did not like to be burdened with details. The commander-in-chief liked it short and to the point, which was just as well because Ian had only a bare-bones conspiracy theory, the kind neo-conservative talk show hosts like to banter around the air waves without overly concerning themselves with verisimilitude or facts.

"Everything points to the Iranians, sir," said Ian. "We don't have the smoking gun yet, but we have three independent HUMINT sources that have provided information on an Iranian-Venezuelan joint operation. Too much corroborating intelligence to ignore."

"Ian, are you fucking with me?" the president asked. "You're trying to tell me that two third world countries have the balls to run a joint operation against the world's only superpower? That they're sinking ships off our coast and wrecking out economy….with a half-ass military capability and beyond-the-pale radical governments?"

"Mr. President, the Iranians have a couple of Kilo-class submarines they got from the Russians. Those babies have a range of 7,000 miles. We think Venezuela is letting them use Puerto Cabello to refuel, rearm, and conduct maintenance operations. That's where the Venezuelan navy's based. It's about a three-hour drive west of Caracas."

"Do you have any overhead photography to back up those allegations?"

The president scowled and Ian saw skepticism written all over his face.

"I'm not about to take military action based on a couple of unconfirmed reports from your sources, Ian," the president said. "That might have worked back in 2003 when the White House custom-ordered its intel and your people cooked their reports to deliver what Bush and Cheney wanted. But times have changed."

"Mr. President, let me leave this report with you. Our best analysts took a look at all available reporting from both HUMINT and technical sources. They've come up with a pretty compelling case implicating Iran based on motives, naval exercises involving their submarines, and their strategic alliance with Venezuela. We're still working on it, but where there's smoke, there's usually fire, especially with Venezuela and Iran."

"Ian, what about the rumors of a Russian alliance with the cartel?" asked the president. "Why haven't you mentioned anything about that?"

"Just rumors, sir. Nothing to it. In my opinion, the spooks at the Russian desk are exaggerating the threat to regain turf and budget."

The president reached for his coffee cup stenciled with a cartoon depiction of the democratic donkey and blew on the piping hot liquid. He took a long gurgling sip. He put the cup down and studied the party's logo.

"You know, Ian, this donkey's been associated with the Democratic Party since 1828 when Andrew Jackson's opponents tried to label him a jackass." He paused and stared at Ian. "Don't try to make one out of me. If I find out the CIA has been withholding information from the president, I'll have your ass in a sling. Understood?"

"Yes, Mr. President," replied Ian.

"Well, I need more details before I can respond in any meaningful way to the attacks. You disappoint me, Ian. In the meantime, though, get together with the secretary of defense and come up with some contingency plans on the outside chance your CIA has it right this time."

***

"The captain says they're moving the submarine up the coast; from Veracruz to a new facility they've built at the Laguna Verde nuclear power plant. About a hundred kilometers north of the Veracruz international airport," Armando said.

"Why would they do that?" asked Mako.

Cyrus sat at his laptop computer with a Google Earth image of the Mexican Caribbean coast on the screen. Armando stood to the side and traced the route with his finger north from the port along the Veracruz – Poza Rica highway towards Laguna Verde.

"Security considerations," answered Armando. "The captain says the Russians want to pull the training crew out. They're worried about leaks and about potential political fallout, but he says the Mexicans aren't ready to take over yet."

"What Russians?" asked Mako.

"Someone in Mexico City," Armando replied. "The captain goes to Mexico City every couple of weeks to meet with his Russian contact."

"I wonder who the hell that is," said Cyrus.

"Probably the SVR Rezident at the Russian embassy," Mako speculated.

"That would be Vladimir Kazakov. Met him at the Consular Club meeting at the Maria Isabel Sheraton Hotel once. He's old-school. A relic from Soviet times," said Cyrus.

"That makes him even more formidable," said Mako. "The old KGB holdovers are hard-core as hell."

"Anyway, Salcido paid off the head of the Mexican Electrical Commission, and his people leased a trailing suction dredger to deepen the channel. It leads to an enclosed dry dock where they plan to keep the submarine between operations," Armando said. "Once the submarine submerges in Veracruz, it won't surface again until it's enters the dry dock."

"Talkative captain," commented Mako.

"He's lonely," said Armando. "Like you, Mako."

"I don't go spilling my guts to whores."

"Nothing wrong with whores, Mako," said Armando. "Might be the only honest women out there," he added. "No agenda except to fuck you for your money. But at least they're up front about it."

"So what's your commo plan with the whore? How do you contact her?" asked Cyrus.

"I'd rather you refer to my friend with a little more respect," said Armando.

The yellow-headed Amazon parrot shrieked and hopped from one wooden perch in its cage to another and grabbed the bars with its beak for leverage. The acrobatic efforts of the bird caused the cage to swing gently back and forth on the fraying string, which wrapped several times around a wooden rafter high in the enclosed terrace where the men sat. The Indian maid walked onto the terrace with a tray of *taquitos* made with spicy baby goat meat.

"Con permiso," she mumbled softly as she squeezed her ample backside through the maze of chairs.

"Suyo," responded Mako politely as the men fell silent, chewing the tender *cabrito* with relish.

"So how should I refer to her?" asked Cyrus.

"Her name is Inmaculada," said Armando.

"La Inmaculada Concepción?" asked Cyrus.

"Yeah, that's it," replied Armando.

"The Immaculate Conception. Great name for a whore," stated Cyrus dryly without looking up from his *taquito*.

"What is it about you *norteamericanos*?" asked Armando, turning to Mako for an answer. "You CIA *cabrones* are no more virtuous than the whore you mock. At least she is up front and sincere in her transaction. Cyrus, you, on the other hand, would sell out your own mother, who is probably a whore anyway."

Cyrus ignored the comment and instead held out his glass for a refill. Mako poured the last of the Flor de Caña, which Cyrus emptied immediately as if it were a physiological necessity.

"What else?" asked Mako.

"The Armenian's looking for a way out," replied Armando.

"He wants to defect?"

"Maybe. Isn't this how you people work? The access agent identifies vulnerability, and then one of you shows up like Jesus Christ himself and promises salvation and everlasting life in return for the target's cooperation?"

"You have a low opinion of your new friends, Armando," ventured Cyrus.

"I'm not sure what your definition of a friend is," replied Armando. "But I've read a few CIA training manuals. I know how you work."

"Did the captain say what the next target is?" asked Mako, trying to redirect the conversation.

"Finally, we get to the most important point. I think you were supposed to start the briefing with a question about immediate threats to U.S. security, weren't you?" asked Armando. "At least that's what your manual says. Yes he did, as a matter of fact..."

They felt it a fraction of a second before they heard it. The earsplitting crash of the explosion and the flash of the fireball outside stunned the men even as the entire house seemed to lift off its foundation and slam back to the ground, causing fissures to appear in the concrete block walls and breaking every window facing the street. The shock wave sucked the air out of the men's lungs and their ears popped and then rang painfully. Damp, cool air rushed in through the broken glass of the windows and somewhere outside a fire burned and cast angry shadows on the walls.

The men froze momentarily and stared in shock at one another. Blood ran from Armando's nose. The parrot lay motionless on the bottom of its cage. They heard a woman scream and a man shouted in Spanish. Then they ran, stumbling and tripping over to their weapons and took cover against the wall facing the street. They could already hear short bursts of automatic weapons fire coming from somewhere nearby as they doused the lights in the house and sought cover away from the windows. Bullets pinged off the far wall, chipping irregular gouges in the plaster and propelling small bits of concrete at random around the room like shrapnel from a fragmentation grenade.

"That was a car bomb," yelled Armando.

"Looks like you had some company after all, Cyrus," said Mako. "Where the hell did you get your surveillance detection training?"

"Shit," mumbled Cyrus. He wiped at the blood on his forehead that trickled from a superficial wound above his eyebrow.

Mako crawled to the empty window frame overlooking the street and slowly raised himself to his knees. He peered out of the window and jerked his head back as several shots rang out and bullets peppered the outside wall of the house next to where the window used to be.

"I see at least two of them hiding behind the Bimbo bread van out there," he said. "There're also a couple of bodies on the street. Either collateral damage or they blew up a few of their own people by mistake."

"I've got to get Soledad," mumbled Cyrus. "They're going to get her sooner or later if I don't."

"Forget Soledad! She's safe for the moment. Think about yourself right now, or you'll never be of any help to her," said Armando. "Can you guys shoot?"

He pointed to their Kalashnikovs and nodded towards the street.

"Yeah, what you got in mind?" asked Mako.

Armando was already low crawling towards the stairs with his AK-47 cradled in his arms in front of him. He turned toward the Americans and called out in a hoarse whisper.

"I'll distract them. When you hear my voice, count to five and then open up with everything you have."

Mako and Cyrus checked their magazines and moved the selector lever on the AKs to the fire position. They crouched, ready to move to the open window as soon as they heard Armando's voice.

"I hope we can trust that Mexican," whispered Cyrus.

"You can," said Mako. "But he wonders the same about you."

They heard the metallic clank of the dead bolt sliding open on the front door and then a series of high-pitched creaks as Armando jerked open the massive, hardwood double door that had been damaged in the explosion.

"*Están muertos los gringos!*"[26] he called out.

"One, two, three, four, five...let's go!" whispered Mako.

The two Americans rose to their feet at the corners of the two windows that faced the street and saw three Mexicans who had come out from behind the cars parked on the opposite side. The assassins held their weapons over their heads in celebration, not expecting to become targets of the hail of gunfire that unexpectedly erupted from the shattered second-story windows where tendrils of smoke from the explosion partially obscured the figures of Mako and Cyrus and their Kalashnikovs. That was the last mistake the *sicarios*[27] made, and not one they could easily remedy. The Mexicans crumpled to the ground, their torsos crisscrossed with bullet wounds. Mako saw Armando run across the street and administer the *coup de grâce* to one of their attackers whose legs still twitched.

Two minutes later the three men hurriedly threw themselves into the VW Passat, and Cyrus slammed the sedan into first gear and stomped on the accelerator. The vehicle lurched forward and sped away from the idyllic setting, which had morphed into a hellish kill zone.

---

[26] The gringos are dead!
[27] assassins

"Their car bomb must have exploded prematurely," said Armando. "The ones who were shooting were in the second car. The body parts belonged to the first one."

"That was close," exclaimed Cyrus. "Where to now, Mako?"

"Just drive towards Toluca. I hope you did better in your defensive driving course at the Farm than you did in your surveillance detection classes."

"We'll need to get a new car in Toluca. They obviously know what I'm driving," said Cyrus.

"*Puta madre!*" exclaimed Armando. How did you assholes ever win the Cold War?"

"I'm not sure we did," replied Mako.

Chapter 20

Governor Creed Tucker's dusty white pickup truck headed south from Austin along I-35 at a snail's pace. The truck crabbed slightly to the right, a memento left by his son Matlock, who years ago thought driving a pickup would be just like driving the family's John Deere tractor. Creed and his son had gotten over the accident, but the pickup still limped in obvious discomfort. Creed was not the type to give up on a vehicle over a minor cosmetic deficiency, though, and he continued to drive the old truck over the protests of his wife and gubernatorial staff in Austin.

Two black Chevy Suburbans with tinted windows bracketed the pickup, one in front and one in back, while a steady stream of eighteen-wheelers and the rest of the Laredo-bound traffic sped by in the left lane. Passengers in the vehicles flying past the slow-moving security detail glanced at the split-second, blurred images of the government-issued SUVs surrounding the old pickup and wondered briefly about the identity of the old cowboy inside the truck.

Nobody slowed down to admire the scenery. The Brush Country north of the Rio Grande River with its mesquite trees and cactus-infested wastelands did not have much to offer tourists unless you counted the maimed corpses of the skunks, armadillos, and possums littering the highway.

Four men in limp, sweat-soaked white shirts, Wrangler jeans, and western hats sat motionless in each vehicle, looking like badass relics from a past nobody remembered. The small motorcade took the exit off the interstate to the service road five miles south of Cotulla and then turned onto the hard-packed gravel track that led to the Broken "T" Land & Cattle Company. The two SUVs slowed down, and two Department of Public Safety officers staffing the air-conditioned guard shack at the entrance to the ranch waved them through.

"Is he here yet?" Creed called out as his pickup truck rumbled over the cattle guard and slowly rolled past the security post.

"Arrived fifteen minutes ago," replied one of the guards. "He's alone. No security, no aides, no nothin'."

That was unusual, thought Creed. Ian McGinnis ought to know better than most people that the Brush Country was rapidly degenerating into a no-man's land. The Mexican drug cartels were brazenly setting up roadblocks, stopping one or two cars at a time, robbing and intimidating U.S. citizens, and then disappearing into the vast nothingness of the country like a raiding party of Comanches melting away into the night. It was foolhardy to move about the region without considerable and visible firepower. The Texas National Guard patrolled the highways but had yet to put a dent into the cartel's new aggressive tactics. The federal agencies were not helping, and Creed suspected they were following instructions from a hostile administration in Washington that had decided to let Texas sink or swim on its own, with the preference apparently going to "sink".

McGinnis would be a prize catch for the drug cartel, Creed thought. Wouldn't they love to kidnap and ransom the director of the Central Intelligence Agency? Or maybe just decapitate him with a chain saw and put the video up on one of the internet narco blog sites.

Creed parked his truck in front of ranch headquarters and saw his wife Guadalupe waiting for him on the screen porch. She nodded her head in the direction of the house, and Creed knew he would find Ian inside.

"Is Brazzle here too?" Creed spoke in a low voice as he walked slowly up the creaking and warped wooden steps and kissed his wife on the cheek.

"He's down by the barn looking at a colt," she answered in Spanish. "He didn't want to be alone with the CIA man."

"Don't blame him."

"You don't trust him either, do you?" asked Guadalupe, switching back to English.

"Not as far as I can spit," whispered Creed as he opened the screen door to the porch and walked into the house. He took off his western hat and hung it on a deer antler hat rack on the wall.

"Would you mind calling Brazzle in from the barn? He's going to want to hear this conversation."

Guadalupe handed her husband a cup of hot coffee and walked briskly out the door and towards the barn. Creed watched her as she walked away. He reluctantly turned and strode through the kitchen towards the living room. He smelled cigar smoke and frowned. Don't tell me that Ivy-League sonofabitch helped himself to my cigars, he thought.

Creed entered the living room and caught sight of Ian McGinnis reclining on the leather couch, his feet propped up on the coffee table and smoking one of Creed's Montecristo 75th Aniversario cigars. Creed recognized the full-bodied aroma from the blend of Nicaraguan and Honduran tobaccos long before he saw the cigar in Ian's hand and its characteristic ring band with the Montecristo logo: a triangle of six swords surrounding a fleur-de-lis. Creed frowned at the sight of McGinnis enjoying Tucker hospitality, which he had yet to offer.

"Ian," Creed said gruffly in greeting and nodded his head. He walked over to the fireplace mantel under a magnificent bison skull mounted high on the wall without bothering to shake Ian's hand. He stood there with his back to the CIA director and retrieved a cigar from the kiln-dried Spanish cedar humidor on the mantel. He took a wooden match from a small cardboard box and struck the match head on the heel of his boot. He waited for the sulfur to burn off, then held the tip of the cigar about three inches away from the flame, and slowly rotated it. As the tip began to ignite, Creed puffed on the cigar and continued rotating it around the flame.

"What are you doing?" asked Ian.

"Toasting the foot," replied Creed as he held a match to the outside of the tip and rotated the cigar to evenly toast the edge.

"Toasting the what?" asked Ian.

"Don't they teach you cigar etiquette up there at Langley?" asked Creed. "If you don't toast the binder and wrapper, the filler will burn faster. You don't want that."

"Now watch," Creed instructed. "I'm lighting the filler."

He lit another, longer wooden match, held it about one-half inch from the cigar, and then puffed. When the suction pressure released, a surge of flame shot from the tip of the cigar.

"There. Now you've learned something. Your trip to Texas was not in vain."

"I certainly hope not, Creed," said Ian. "Although I do feel like I crossed into enemy territory when I got out of the plane at DFW. All those 'Don't Mess with Texas' signs have a different meaning nowadays, don't they?"

"Look, we're pretty much under siege these days, aren't we? The administration has ratcheted up the pressure against Texas. The threats are loud and clear."

"Threats?" asked Ian.

"Yea, like hints that Washington will cut off federal aid if we legalize marijuana in Texas," said Creed.

"Oh, that! That's not a threat. That's a fucking promise."

"Well, Ian, that's the whole problem, don't you see?" Washington cannot dictate to the states, especially not to Texas," said Creed.

Ian snorted and put out his cigar in an ashtray on the coffee table. A lazy tendril of smoke rose slowly from the crushed cigar.

"What can I do for you, Ian?" asked Creed, feigning politeness. "How about some cognac to go with that cigar you just snuffed out like an ignorant Philistine? Cigars are meant to die a noble death of their own accord."

"What's in that oval-shaped bottle?" asked Ian, ignoring Creed's remark. He pointed to the liquor cabinet against the wall adjacent to a window that looked out into the round pen and corrals by the barn.

Both men heard heavy footsteps approaching from the screen porch and turned to see a tall, lanky man about sixty years old wearing a stained, misshapen cowboy hat, red-checkered long-sleeve shirt, and dusty cowboy boots. His spurs clanked loudly on the Saltillo tile, and he strode slowly into the room without removing his hat.

"I thought this was going to be a private meeting, Creed." Ian turned to face James Brazzle and averted his eyes from the hostile stare that greeted him.

"This is James Brazzle, director of the People's Intelligence and Security Service. Whatever you have to tell me, James needs to know," said Creed. "That bottle, by the way, contains 18-year old Flor de Caña rum. It'll give any fine cognac a run for its money. It's got a full-bodied palate with dark chocolate and brown spice flavors."

Ian looked up at Creed with his eyebrows arched.

"What'd you do? Read that in an advertising brochure?" asked Ian.

Creed laughed for the first time since he caught sight of Ian smoking one of his favorite cigars.

"No. I don't even drink the stuff. I'm just repeating what Mako Sloane told me."

"Mako Sloane?" asked Ian. "You know the Department of Justice is preparing to indict that character, don't you?"

"What the hell for?" asked James, the first words he had uttered since he entered the room.

"They'll find something," said Ian. He grinned.

"If it weren't for Mako Sloane, the Mexican drug cartels would be running the show down here in South Texas," said Creed. "You and I both know that. Indicting Mako would just be another administration tactic to pressure us."

"He'll be indicted, sure as hell. So will anybody else who was with him when his team raided that cartel safe house and the vice-president mysteriously ended up on the receiving end of thirteen 9 mm rounds[28]," said Ian.

"Are you prepared to indict the governor of Texas as well?" interrupted James. "He was there too, you know."

Ian did not answer.

"State your business, McGinnis," Creed said. "We've got work to do."

Ian strolled over to the bar and poured himself three fingers of Flor de Caña without asking permission of his host. James Brazzle moved in between Creed and the CIA director just in case. He had known Creed since they were kids and was altogether too familiar with his short fuse. He also knew how it would look if Creed were to beat the shit out of the president's envoy in his own house.

---

[28] TEXMEX by Clabe Taylor, Legacy Publishers, 2012.

"Gentlemen, the president wants to know if you people had anything to do with the sinking of the *Orca*. I assured him you weren't that stupid. It's possible I may have been hasty with my judgment."

"Ian, I'm not sure why you're the one asking the question instead of the director of the FBI, but it doesn't really matter. I'd tell either of you to go fuck yourself."

"That's your answer?" Ian asked.

"It is," said Creed. "If you don't know by now who's responsible for the *Orca*, you're running a piss-poor intelligence organization."

"Oh, so you know?"

Ian's tone of voice changed dramatically. His sudden interest in what Creed might or might not know seemed genuine. He looked first at Creed and then at James Brazzle. He put down the brandy snifter and took a step in Creed's direction. Creed and James Brazzle exchanged glances.

"Well, we've got some ideas, but we were hoping to hear the gospel truth from you, Ian. You *are* the head of the Central Intelligence Agency, aren't you?" responded Creed.

"We've tasked our HUMINT and technical sources for answers. You can bet on that," replied Ian.

"And?" asked Brazzle.

Ian paused, picked up the snifter, and sipped the dark rum before continuing.

"And we think it's the damned Iranians. Venezuela and the Chavistas are involved too," he added.

Silence met Ian's claim. Creed stared at him as he shifted uncomfortably from one foot to another. Ian turned around, returned to the bar and downed the remaining rum in the sifter.

"I'll pass on your answer verbatim to the president. I doubt he'll be amused," said Ian.

Creed accompanied the CIA director outside to his rented Lexus and reluctantly shook his hand.

"Tell the president to look somewhere else for a scapegoat," Creed said in parting.

"Creed, let it go. You're out of your league and you're treading on too many feet. Why pick a fight with both the drug cartels and the United States government? The Mexicans won't let you get away with it and neither will we." Ian put the automatic transmission in "D" and eased his rental car down the gravel road towards the interstate.

Creed returned to the living room where James Brazzle was sipping the Nicaraguan rum with a broad grin on his face. He glanced up when Creed walked in the room.

"Iranians," he said. "With the help of the late Hugo Chavez no less."

"And that's the director of the Central Intelligence Agency!" said Creed. "Let's call Mako. He could use a laugh about now, I imagine. Iran.....do you believe that shit?"

Chapter 21

Ian McGinnis slammed on his brakes to avoid hitting the vagrant who staggered into the center of the interstate access road in front of the rented Lexus. The man had a scraggly beard and wore military-style fatigues tucked into combat boots. He was bareheaded, and his hair was long and unkempt. Ian thought he looked Hispanic.

The Lexus skidded along the asphalt, fishtailed slightly, and came to a shuddering stop only a few feet from the vagrant who stood calmly watching the car approach. He swayed slightly from side to side with glassy eyes and stared blankly at the Lexus. Ian recognized the type from the streets of southeast D.C. and shook his head in disgust. He was certain the man was either drunk or high on drugs. He rolled up his window, locked the door and waited for the man to get out of his way.

Grinning, the homeless man held up his hands in front of the Lexus like Moses commanding the waters in the Red Sea to part. Ian tapped the horn politely, but the vagrant remained motionless as if he were waiting on a stage manager's belated cue.

The deep-throated growl of diesel engines in the distance caused Ian to glance at the rear view mirror. He saw several SUVs approaching at high speed from the north, and he honked his horn more insistently for the vagrant to move. As Ian watched, the vagrant's slouched shoulders suddenly straightened, and he sprinted athletically around the car to the driver's door. He reached for the door handle with one hand and pounded on Ian's window with his other fist. Ian belatedly realized that the man was a decoy, and that he had driven into a trap.

For five crucial seconds, though, fear paralyzed Ian, and he did nothing. Finally, he grabbed at the gearshift lever in panic and tried to throw the car into drive, but the first SUV had already careened around the Lexus, flinging gravel as it lurched to a stop and blocked the road in front of him. The second vehicle skidded to a stop behind Ian, and its bumper rammed the Lexus and jerked Ian's head back. He threw the car into reverse and stomped on the accelerator, but except for the sound of steel scraping steel and the smell of burning rubber on the hardtop, Ian's desperate maneuver accomplished nothing.

The homeless man pulled a large handgun out of the inside of his fatigues and emptied an entire thirteen-round magazine of armor-piercing cartridges into the locking mechanism of the car door. He jerked the door open, and Ian felt the man's hands on his shirt, ripping the expensive cotton twill fabric and pulling and dragging him onto the hot asphalt surface of the access road as other car doors slammed and voices cursed in Spanish. Ian saw several figures with their faces covered by black balaclavas running towards him, and he felt his arms roughly pulled behind his back and then the cold steel of a pair of handcuffs closing painfully over his wrists. Then one of the men yanked a ski mask over his head and he saw nothing more.

***

They gagged him and stuffed his six-foot frame into the trunk of a Ford Taurus that pulled up just as one of the thugs delivered a right hook to Ian's rib cage to discourage further struggle. The trunk slammed, and the change in air pressure hurt Ian's ears. His knees pressed into his chest, and after about thirty minutes into the ride, his arthritic joints began to ache. After what seemed like an eternity, he heard shouts in Spanish and loud *ranchera* music as the SUV stopped briefly and then continued on its way to the accompaniment of sporadic gunfire and triumphant *gritos*. Ian knew they had crossed into Mexico.

The shooting pain in his knees and back made him sick to his stomach. It originated somewhere below the back of his cranium and shot down his spine like pulses of electric current, through his pelvis, hamstrings, and into his knees in unpredictable bursts of white-hot agony. Nausea welled up inside Ian, and he vomited until his stomach was empty and his belly ached from retching. He lay in his own filth, sobbing silently and wondering when they would kill him and not caring whether they did or not.

They drove all night, stopping once to let Ian shit on the side of a highway with saguaro cactus in the Sonoran Desert looming eerily in the faint moonlight on either side of the road like leering voyeurs. Ian's extremities were without sensation. He barely felt his kidnappers drag his body out of the car or the kicks that punished his legs and back when he was unable to stand on his own. They drug him to the side of the road, and Ian half lay and half squatted five yards from the car, illuminated by the driver's flashlight like some frightened nocturnal creature caught in an unspeakable indiscretion. Three gunmen stood guard and pointed their AK-47s at Ian as he tried in vain to defecate. He wondered whether they would execute him on the side of the road, and he braced himself for the impact of the 7.62 mm rounds that never came. Then he was back in the trunk with blinding pain and debilitating fear blocking all rational thought.

Towards dawn, a maddening attack of claustrophobia overwhelmed him and he screamed and kicked the side of the trunk in a hopeless effort to free himself from the confinement of what he feared would become his coffin. He shouted and cursed until his throat hurt and he gasped in a hoarse whisper. He felt the car slow abruptly, and he heard the crunch of gravel as the vehicle pulled to the shoulder. The trunk opened and two of his captors took turns pummeling his body with fists and rubber hoses.

"Callate, pendejo![29]*"*

They taunted Ian and beat him until he lay in the trunk whimpering, tears of pain and self-pity muddying the dirt that covered his gaunt, bloody features. The trunk slammed and the car resumed its interminable trek towards a denouement that Ian did not care to contemplate.

Fifteen hours after he stopped for the vagrant, Ian felt the vehicle turn off the main highway and slow perceptibly. Ian bounced around in the trunk from side to side, and he groaned in semi-conscious misery. When the car stopped yet again and the trunk opened, Ian closed his eyes at the blinding tropical sun. He sucked in the fresh air gratefully but braced himself for the beating he knew would follow.

The voice in unaccented English was unexpected, and Ian caught his breath and dared to hope that he might yet survive the ordeal, and that it might all prove to have been a horrid mistake: a case of mistaken identity. Then he heard his name.

***

---

[29] Shut up, asshole!

The governor's security detachment heard the explosion, and they saw black smoke rising into the air a mile to the south of their guard shack. Two of the DPS officers grabbed their weapons, climbed into a black Suburban, and accelerated rapidly in the direction of the smoke. When they arrived at the scene a scant ninety seconds later, they saw a late model Lexus in flames with the driver-side door wide open in the middle of the interstate access road. The security officers gave the burning vehicle a wide berth as they circled it on foot looking for a body they expected to find, but there was nothing.

Back at the ranch, Creed took the phone call from his chief of security and slammed his fist on the bar. He turned grim-faced to James Brazzle, who stood beside him mixing another drink.

"Hold off on the booze, James. Looks like Ian McGinnis just got himself kidnapped a mile down the road."

"That stupid motherfucker!" said Brazzle. He set the glass of Coca-Cola down on the bar and drained the glass of Flor de Caña straight.

***

"Mr. McGinnis, Welcome to Culiacan. I trust you've had a comfortable trip?"

"Who a-a-a-are you?" stammered Ian. He lay on his side in the burning gravel driveway and looked at the pair of fashionably weathered Docksiders in front of his face. He raised his head painfully and saw a pair of neatly pressed khaki trousers with a fresh crease down each leg and a pink Ralph Lauren polo shirt. Then he lost consciousness.

When he came to, he was naked and a pressurized stream of cold water cascaded off his lily-white back and pimply buttocks. The water stung, and he curled up in fetal position and wrapped his arms around his head to protect his face and eyes from the water. Someone turned off the hose, and Ian turned his head toward a murmuring of voices in Spanish. Four men armed with AK-47s flanked a well-dressed Mexican about 40 years old. Two on either side. The bodyguards watched Ian and smirked. Ian knew they were his tormentors, and he suddenly wanted to kill another human being for the first time in his life. Ian saw one of the gunmen approach and he closed his eyes and cringed.

"*Toma[30]*," the man said.

Ian saw him toss a colorful beach towel on the ground beside him and then step back. Ian clasped the towel to his chest, covered his face, and for some reason thought of his mother and sobbed.

---

[30] Take it.

"Please forgive the primitive shower conditions, Mr. McGinnis."

There it was again. Someone was speaking English. Ian raised himself to his knees and covered his nakedness with the towel. He looked at the Mexican who spoke. The man affected the studiously casual yet cliquish look of old money in the young American South. He might have just stepped out of his golf club on a Sunday afternoon after a gin and tonic at the nineteenth hole bar.

"Someone is waiting to see you," the voice said. "Let's get you cleaned up and dressed. You must be famished after your trip."

Chapter 22

"If you don't like the Russians, why do you work for them?" asked Inmaculada.

She and Bulat lay together in a double bed under limp, stained sheets in a musty third-story hotel suite just outside the port of Veracruz. It was one of Bulat's last nights in town, and he had persuaded his cartel babysitter to let him visit Inmaculada one more time before he and the training crew shipped out for Laguna Verde the following week. They both knew it was a gross violation of operational security for Bulat to leave the compound, much less alone and to visit a prostitute, but at this point, the rules were more of an inconvenience than a real prohibition. Anyway, neither man expected to live long enough to suffer the repercussions of his indiscretions. Despite the language barrier, the two had become friends, and if one could make life easier for the other, even just for a few hours, they were not going to let rules get in the way.

Bulat had seen Inmaculada regularly since the night they met at *El Rinconcito* when her pimp, a Mexican who introduced himself as Armando, leased her on an exclusive basis to the Armenian submarine captain. Bulat had become infatuated with her even though he knew she was a prostitute. She looked Armenian to Bulat, and sometimes he unconsciously addressed her in his native language and was vaguely surprised and disappointed when she failed to understand him.

The window air conditioning unit in the hotel room labored to keep the temperature comfortable, something it accomplished with only marginal success, but they dared not open the window. It was hot and sticky outside and the air was still. Mosquitoes swarmed around stagnant pools of water that collected in the streets and stopped-up gutters. Given the chance, the insects would pour through the window like so many blood-sucking vampires looking for their daily protein fix. A ceiling fan clanked loudly, and its warped wooden blades moved the thick humid air just enough to render the tropical heat and humidity tolerable.

They spoke English together, and Inmaculada's fluency and extensive vocabulary impressed Bulat each time they spoke. He realized that English was a professional necessity given her occupation and her international clientele. Thinking about all the men she had been with sometimes made him jealous, and he chided himself for his adolescent insecurity.

"Why?" he repeated her question.

"Yes, why?" she asked again. "You say the Russians are racists and that they oppressed your people and even suppressed the culture and language of Armenia. Yet you do their bidding and you take their money."

"There are many things about life in Russia you don't understand," said Bulat as he took a lock of her thick black hair between his fingers and carefully pulled it away from her face. He ran the back of his hand slowly down the side of her cheek.

"I've met Russians and they didn't seem any better or worse to me than most men. You're all pigs, you know."

Bulat laughed but inwardly bristled at the thought of Inmaculada with another man, much less a Russian. His dislike of Russians had intensified since he began working with Vladimir Kazakov from the Russian embassy. What an arrogant bastard the SVR Rezident was! But the Russian Foreign Intelligence Service in Mexico City was one thing, and the top Kremlin leadership quite another. Bulat found it hard to believe that the Russian president could have sanctioned this kamikaze operation involving a Ukrainian-made attack submarine and a partnership with a Mexican drug cartel. How far Russia had fallen since the breakup of the USSR in 1991!

Sure, he understood that Russia would benefit from increased oil prices and that it would be a boon to its embattled economy, which after all depended heavily on energy prices. It would also strengthen the political standing of the president. The increased revenue flow would enable him to introduce social programs, which might placate the population and ease the wave of rising dissent in Russia. But at the risk of war with the United States? It made no sense, but then Russians rarely did.

"Why do you hate them so?" asked Inmaculada.

"You wouldn't understand," Bulat answered. "You haven't had to live in the shadow of an uncultured bully your whole life and bow your head and bite your tongue and accept your role as a second-class citizen."

"Oh really?" she said. "And what about the *gringos*?"

Bulat looked up, surprised at her response.

"I hadn't considered that," he said. "But there's more. Before 1991, Armenia was part of the Soviet Union along with fourteen other republics except everyone knew that Russia was the only one that counted. As kids, we had to learn their language, their history, and their culture. The Russians discouraged or even made it impossible for us to learn about our own country. They always occupied the top positions in Yerevan, and we Armenians knew that unless we kissed their asses, our own careers would never prosper."

Inmaculada sat up and propped herself up on a pillow. She intentionally let the sheet fall off her shoulder to reveal most of one breast. She looked down at herself and adjusted the sheet so that Bulat could see the edge of her dark nipple.

Bulat smiled.

"You tire of our conversation? I know you well. You distract me when you think I'm getting morose or homesick for my country."

"I only want to please you. Maybe that's how we Latinas differ from the women in your country."

"No doubt," Bulat agreed. He devoured her with his eyes and tugged gently at the sheet, which dropped further to reveal her entire nipple and the full roundness of her breast.

"But I digress." He tried to look away from her body.

"My country was part of the Russian Empire before the Revolution, and in 1918 we became part of the USSR...and I've been a whore to the Russians my whole life."

"Then perhaps we have something in common," said Inmaculada.

Bulat laughed in spite of himself. He was becoming increasingly alarmed over his presence in Mexico and his participation in the Russians' clandestine mission. He had a premonition that the operation would not end well. Then there was the risk he was running with his liaison with Inmaculada. Sometimes he imagined how Vladimir would react were he to discover that Bulat, far from being the ideological and moral conscience of the training crew, had himself violated most of the security instructions he had received from the Russian embassy and even added a few of his own invention. So far, it had been blind luck that had kept news of his dalliance from reaching the desk of the SVR Rezident in Mexico City. Bulat knew that could only last so long. The narcos were far less disciplined than his own men and were likely to talk if questioned. He could only imagine what the repercussions of his indiscretions would be.

"Why don't you do something about it?" asked Inmaculada.

"It's too late. I'm in over my head," said Bulat. "Besides, if I quit now, my family in Russia will starve. The Russians won't pay me what they owe, and they'll see to it I never get another job. They might even kill me."

Inmaculada dipped her right shoulder and exposed her other breast. She placed her hand on Bulat's rock-hard stomach and caressed him with the back of her fingers.

He continued. "It probably doesn't matter." he said. "I doubt if any of us have much longer to live."

"It doesn't have to be like that, *mi amor*," she said. "I have a friend who can help you."

***

"Let's continue where we left off, Armando," suggested Mako. "Do you know what the next target is?"

"I know it's going to be a big one...and maybe the last mission," said Armando. "But that's all."

Cyrus gradually increased his speed as the VW Passat wound its way out of the mountains down from Valle de Bravo and hit the flatter ground on the approaches to Toluca. The men had managed to sleep a few hours in the car when Cyrus turned onto an old logging road and parked about fifty yards from the highway shortly after midnight. They still stifled the occasional yawn, but the sun was already high in the eastern sky towards the mountains around Mexico City, and traffic heading into Toluca was getting heavier by the minute.

"Why do you say that?" Mako asked.

"The Armenian doesn't think he'll live through the next mission," said Armando.

"Where's does that information come from?" Mako asked.

"From the horse's mouth. I called my friend while I was taking a shit in the woods last night."

"You talked with the whore last night?" asked Cyrus.

"*Ay caray!*" exclaimed Armando. "Here we go again. That 'whore', as you call her, is about to arrange your introduction to the Armenian submarine captain. Don't you think she deserves a little more respect?"

"Is he ready to meet with us?" asked Mako.

"Getting close, I think. I'd say it's time to move our base of operations to Veracruz to be ready when Inmaculada gives the go-ahead."

Cyrus looked at Mako and shook his head.

"Not me. I have to get Soledad out of that hospital before the cartel gets her. I'll meet you in Veracruz in a couple of days."

"Alright," said Mako. "But at very least ditch this car before somebody recognizes it and manages to kill you this time. And try not to bring anyone tagging along behind you to Veracruz."

"Yeah, sorry about that," replied Cyrus."

Armando took a pen from his pocket and a scrap of paper from his wallet. He scribbled something and handed the paper to Cyrus.

"Here's the address of a place that'll be safe for Soledad. It's in Tlaxcala, a few hours from Mexico City. You can see La Malinche volcano from the house. Ask for Juan Ignacio and say I sent you. He won't ask any questions."

"To the airport?" asked Cyrus, glancing over at Mako.

"Yeah, let me make some reservations first," replied Mako, taking his cell phone out of his pocket and speed dialing a number.

"*Tranquilo,*" said Armando. "I already made our reservations...we leave in two hours."

"Hijole," said Cyrus. "You made *two* phones calls last night?"

"Yeah, I was constipated," said Armando.

Chapter 23

Ian McGinnis looked at himself in the mirror. The cuts and bruises were still there, and his nose was swollen and probably broken, but at least he had been able to wash off the blood, dirt, and pieces of dried vomit that had stuck to his face. The shower returned a semblance of humanity to Ian.

He was still frightened and disoriented. He knew his captors must be drug traffickers, and he suspected he was in the Mexican state of Sinaloa, judging by the light blue license plates he saw on an SUV in the compound. Beyond that, what had happened to him was still a jumbled clutter of nightmarish images, and he was still sorting out the pieces. Ian wondered if Creed Tucker had sold him downriver. He knew the old rancher-turned-governor despised him. Or maybe this was Cory Elkins' way of getting rid of another "leak" just like he had disposed of Harvard Banks. That made more sense than anything else, thought Ian and involuntarily shivered. He heard a loud knock on the bathroom door.

"Mr. McGinnis, please, you're keeping our guest waiting."

The voice belonged to the Docksiders and pink Polo shirt. Who is this guy? Ian wondered. He cracked open the bathroom door and peered out.

"Now that's more like it," said the Mexican. "You clean up real nice, Ian. Are you ready for our little diplomatic reception?"

"Who the fuck are you?" asked Ian.

"Ian, please. Don't be rude. After all, you and I have several mutual friends. You don't recognize me from my 201 file?"

"What the hell are you talking about?"

Ian stared at the man and the truth began to sink in. He did bear a resemblance to somebody whose photo had recently crossed his desk, but Ian was having trouble making the connection. He knew he was not going to like the answer, though, when he found out.

"Antonio Salcido," the Mexican said, removing any doubt Ian may have still had. He extended his hand. *"A sus ordenes*[31]*."*

A fleeting shadow of recognition passed over Ian's features and he scowled and struggled to maintain his composure. He felt an almost physical jolt from the revelation.

---

[31] At your service.

"I recently entertained several colleagues of yours on my yacht," Salcido said. "Perhaps we can take a short cruise later." He laughed and withdrew his hand.

Ian could do nothing more than stare at the Mexican's Polo shirt and the putter he carried ostentatiously in his right hand.

"But I digress. Shall we?" Salcido motioned Ian forward with an exaggerated wave of his hand and a bow.

Ian did not reply but stepped trance-like out of the room and walked with jerky robotic strides down a hallway lined with rustic benches and carpeted with long Oaxacan runners. He moved towards the sound of flamenco guitar music in the next room like an insect following its genetically coded instructions to fly towards self-immolation on the white-hot surface of an incandescent light bulb.

He entered a large room, the walls painted a rustic and textured pale yellow with orange feathering. The mounted heads of mule deer and elk peered down from the walls, and well-oiled hunting rifles hung from elegant wooden racks. A guitarist sat on a stool next to a black Yamaha baby grand piano and played a plaintive song by Camarón de la Isla while a cadaverous man with a scraggly beard sat next to him and alternately clapped his hands rhythmically and sang in the haunting, often unintelligible syllables of Spanish flamenco. Ian stood transfixed, listening to the music.

He barely noticed the figure of a short stocky man standing motionless under the mounted head of a massive bull elk. He was mostly bald and wore a white dress shirt open at the collar and baggy black slacks. Ian heard footsteps behind him and saw Antonio Salcido pass by and approach the man under the mounted elk. He whispered something in his ear and both of them turned to look at Ian.

"Ian, may I introduce you to Vladimir Kazakov from the Russian embassy?" Salcido executed an exaggerated bow and laughed. "I imagine the two of you will want to chat in private."

***

"I think your friend's going to get himself killed," said Armando. "He's out of his league down here."

The two men arrived in Veracruz earlier that evening on the flight from Toluca. Mako tipped the bellhop, who bowed obsequiously on his way out of the room. Mako threw his leather shoulder bag on the hotel bed and stretched his back, arms raised towards the ceiling. Then he walked over to the minibar, opened the tiny refrigerator, and took out a 50 ml bottle of Bacardi light rum and a can of Coca Cola.

"Where are the limes when you need them? What kind of a country is this anyway?"

"Did you hear what I said about your friend?" Armando repeated his question.

"Yeah, I heard you. To tell the truth, I'm more worried about him getting us killed. That's the new CIA for you. The old warhorses are gone. Nobody left to teach proper tradecraft to the youngsters."

"I'm not so sure about you either," said Armando. "Why the hell do you pick a hotel like the Fiesta Americana? Is this your idea of lying low; being inconspicuous, as you always say? There're plenty of hotels nobody's ever heard of near the port."

Mako mixed a rum and coke in a short glass without ice and drank greedily. He plopped down in the armchair next to the window with his drink in one hand and propped up his legs on an ottoman upholstered in a generic Native American pattern. He looked out the sixth floor window down at the swimming pool below and the vacationing tourists.

"Well, sometimes the best place to hide is in a crowd. Lots of *gringos* and lots of Mexicans here," replied Mako. "I think we fit in pretty well."

Mako's cell phone vibrated.

"*Bueno,*" he answered. He motioned for Armando to be quiet.

"Mako, is that you? Where the hell are you? Why haven't you called?"

James Brazzle's voice was strained, and Mako knew immediately that something was not quite right on the north side of the Rio Grande. He normally avoided conversations on his new cell phone despite the sophisticated encryption software, but he knew he had no choice this time.

"Just checked into a hotel room in Veracruz, James. Is something wrong up there?"

"Veracruz? What the hell are you doing down there?" Brazzle asked.

"My job. You *did* hire me to get to the bottom of all this, didn't you?"

"Yeah, but I expect you to check in every now and then and keep me posted."

Mako noted the tension in his voice, something very uncharacteristic in the usually taciturn James Brazzle.

"Mako, something's happened up here. I need you to put out some feelers as soon as possible," Brazzle continued.

Armando had turned on the television and was watching a soccer game between Chivas and Las Águilas. Mako motioned for him to turn the volume down. Armando rolled his eyes but lowered the volume and moved closer to the small flat screen television so he could hear the game.

"Ian McGinnis dropped in earlier today for a chat with Creed," Brazzle began. "Drove down from Austin all by himself."

"Go on," Mako said. "Sounds interesting already."

"Way too interesting. First he told us who the CIA thinks is responsible for the attacks in the Gulf."

"Oh? Something we didn't know?"

"Yeah, if you believe an Iranian sub sunk the *Orca,*" said Brazzle.

"An Iranian sub? That his idea of a joke?"

"Yeah, Ian is cranking out disinformation just like the old KGB," said Brazzle. "According to his line of bullshit, the Iranian hardliners are working with Hugo Chavez' successor in some asinine conspiracy against the U.S. He claims they're using the Venezuelan navy base at Puerto Cabello."

"So what's his angle?" Mako asked. "We know he doesn't believe it, but there's got to be a reason why he's slinging that crap around. Ian's an asshole, but he's not an idiot."

"That is one man's opinion."

Armando was now listening intently to Mako's side of the telephone conversation and he turned off the television.

"I wish that was all the news I had," Brazzle continued. "But here's the kicker. Someone ambushed McGinnis' car on the access road to I-35 when he left the ranch. When our people got there, Ian's car was on fire...but he was gone."

"Gone?"

"We think one of the cartels kidnapped him," said Brazzle.

"Jesus, kidnapped the director of the Central Intelligence Agency?" Mako said, looking over at Armando, who was mixing a drink for himself.

"See if you can find anything out. We think they took him to Mexico."

Mako heard a click as Brazzle signed off. He threw down the rest of his drink, walked over to the minibar, and took out another 50 ml bottle of rum.

"Guess I'm supposed to find out where your CIA director is, right?" asked Armando.

"You're clairvoyant today," said Mako. "Must be the Barcardi."

"No, just getting used to you *gringos*. You guys would fuck up a wet dream, wouldn't you?"

***

"I'll come back in a few minutes," Salcido said. He snapped his fingers and waved his hand towards the door of the courtyard. The musicians and waiters put down their instruments and trays and obediently followed him out of the room.

Vladimir turned his back on Ian and walked slowly across the room to a dark mahogany bar with a brass foot rail running the length of the bar about six inches above the tiled floor. The heels of his black dress shoes clicked softly in the empty room. Ian stood transfixed and stared at his new acquaintance.

The Russian moved behind the bar and removed a bottle of Stolichnaya vodka from the cabinet against the wall. He held the bottle up to the light and peered at the label.

"A bit of a cliché, don't you think?" he asked in heavily accented English. "Ask someone to name a Russian vodka, and nine times out of ten they'll say Stolichnaya. But it's not bad. I can't deny that."

He set two water glasses on the bar and filled each of them halfway.

"These Mexicans don't know enough to keep vodka chilled," he said in disgust.

He thrust one of the glasses in Ian's direction.

"Drink," he said.

Ian had not moved and he continued to stare at the Russian.

"Drink, I said," Vladimir repeated.

Ian walked machinelike to the bar and took the vodka-filled glass in his right hand. Vladimir clinked glasses with him and emptied his glass in one gulp, *zalpom*. Ian reluctantly did the same and almost gagged as the vodka burned his throat and made his eyes tear. Vladimir filled the glasses again.

"Who are you?" asked Ian.

"Drink," said Vladimir and tossed back the second glassful of vodka.

Ian did the same. He choked, coughed, and looked up at Vladimir with glassy eyes.

"I'm Vladimir Kazakov," said the Russian.

"I heard that much," said Ian, "but who is Vladimir Kazakov?"

Vladimir ignored the question, picked up a beef taco in a soft shell, and sniffed at it squeamishly.

"I apologize for the lack of suitable hors d'oeuvres to go with our vodka. These Mexicans are absolutely barbaric; dark-skinned savages, really, don't you think?" Vladimir smiled with a mouth full of old Soviet-style stainless steel teeth but still did not answer Ian's question.

"Am I a prisoner?" asked Ian. He continued to shudder at the lingering aftertaste of the vodka.

"A prisoner? Don't be silly. You're free to go, of course. I doubt you'd get very far, though. Antonio's men would love to use you for target practice."

Vladimir poured another round of vodka and offered the glass to Ian who shook his head.

"Drink, Ian. What's the matter, don't you respect me?" said Vladimir and laughed. "That could be unhealthy."

Ian reluctantly took the glass half-filled with Stolichnaya. Vladimir held his glass high with one arm held behind his back in an almost military posture.

"Ian, let's drink to history," he said and emptied his glass.

Ian suddenly put his drink on the bar and shook his head.

"Stop it. I can't drink anymore. What do you want with me?" he asked.

"Watch your manners, Ian," said Vladimir. "You're a long ways from Langley."

"You can't kidnap the director of the Central Intelligence Agency and get away with it! I don't care *who* you are."

Vlaldimir put his empty glass on the bar and pointed his finger at Ian.

"Listen to me. Your title and credentials do not impress us. Understand? We just picked you up from under the nose of the governor of Texas. The next time you ignore our signal for a meeting, I'll have you picked up on the streets of Georgetown. Only my Chechen colleagues won't be quite as congenial as my Mexican friends have been!"

Chapter 24

Three hundred yards of glistening black asphalt and a forty-acre pasture of freshly cut Coastal Bermuda lay just beyond the massive Austin-rock entrance to Throckmorton Acres. The vice president's ranch was located ten miles south of Weatherford, Texas, a half hour's drive west of Fort Worth in the middle of cutting horse country. A green John Deere tractor pulled a hay baler over neatly arranged winrows, and occasionally gave birth to a perfectly formed round bale weighing close to 1,000 pounds. Creed tapped the brakes of his old Chevy pickup and slowed to a halt in front of the Secret Service checkpoint.

"State your business, sir," said a plainclothes agent at the security booth. He adjusted his earpiece and peered into the cab of Creed's beat-up pickup with his right hand on the butt of his handgun.

"Name's Creed Tucker. I have an appointment with the vice president."

"Oh, I'm so sorry. My apologies, governor," said the agent, clearly embarrassed at not having recognized the governor of Texas. "I'm afraid I have to ask to see your identification, though. Procedures, you know."

Creed looked at the agent as if he were crazy but handed over his Texas driver's license for examination.

While he waited, he pulled out a plastic pouch of Red Man, tore open the top, and placed a pinch of the leafy chewing tobacco between his cheek and gums. He saw horses in the distance and wondered idly whether Rick Throckmorton knew how to ride. He doubted it. The agent returned the driver's license, and Creed nodded to him and drove on towards Throckmorton's house.

The vice president had called him the night before and requested a face-to-face meeting. Creed was surprised but agreed to drive up from Cotulla even though his animosity towards Throckmorton had increased in a geometric progression since the cocky sonofabitch traded in his governor's mansion in Austin for the vice presidency and Number One Observatory Circle in Washington, D.C. As soon as he crossed the beltway, the man's loyalty towards his home state seemed to disappear, and in true chameleon fashion, Throckmorton unabashedly joined the anti-Texas lobby that was screaming for Creed's head. What can you expect from a graduate of the University of Texas? Fucking teasip.

About a hundred yards from the vice president's mansion, a secret service roadblock stopped Creed's truck while a team of explosives experts wearing bomb disposal suits and aided by a pair of Labrador Retriever sniffer dogs meticulously examined the truck's chassis and engine compartment. Creed was not offended. He knew that

Throckmorton was paranoid and obsessed with his own security. To put it bluntly, Rick Throckmorton was scared of his own shadow. He had nightmares about assassination attempts by the Mexican drug cartels, Islamic terrorists, and even his own enemies in Texas, of which there were plenty.

Creed also was not surprised that Vice President Throckmorton made him wait twenty minutes before acknowledging his presence. He had been like that even as governor. An advisor finally made his appearance and escorted Creed to an elegantly appointed library with floor to ceiling bookshelves on one wall and countless portraits of Throckmorton posing with prominent U.S. politicians and world leaders on the opposite wall. Creed even noticed an enlargement of the famous photograph of Lyndon Baines Johnson holding a Beagle off the ground by its ears.

"The vice president will be with you shortly, governor," said the aide and left Creed alone in the library.

Creed looked idly around the spacious room and glanced at a copy of the *Washington Post* that lay on the top of Throckmorton's expansive desk.

"CONFRONTATION BREWING IN TEXAS!" stated the headline. Creed did not have time to look at the body of the article before he heard his name called out in Throckmorton's affected Texas drawl.

"Howdy, Creed!" he said and slapped Creed on the back. Creed cringed inwardly but extended his hand and greeted the vice president with mumbled banalities.

Creed held up the newspaper and pointed to the headline.

"I assume this is what you wanted to talk about?"

"You don't mince words, do you? I don't think you've changed a bit since we first met, Creed. You may be governor now, but you're still all rawhide and barbed wire, aren't you?"

"If it ain't broke, don't fix it," replied Creed and smiled in spite of himself.

Throckmorton motioned to a leather chair in front of his desk, and Creed sat down gratefully, the air hissing out of the cushioned seat. He leaned back, took off his Resistol cowboy hat, and placed it in his lap. He winced at a sharp pain in his lower back and grimaced. He had been checking one of the young colts his son-in-law was training when the horse spooked at a black plastic garbage bag blowing across the pasture. The unexpected deviation from the gentle lope had tweaked Creed's back, something that would not have bothered him twenty years ago.

Nobody suggested, though, that he take it easy or even hinted that the irascible old rancher-turned-governor was aging. That would be a mistake, and nobody would think of calling Creed's attention to that truth. You would have about as much success if you suggested he take up yoga or enroll in a Pilates exercise class.

"Alright, I'll get straight to the point," said Throckmorton. "The president doesn't think you're a team player," he said.

"Sounds like a compliment to me," replied Creed.

"Don't be a fool, Creed. You stood up to the drug cartels last year,[32] and these Texas rednecks loved the melodrama. You got to star in your own soap opera. That's what got you elected. But don't think you can defy Washington this time and get away with it."

"Why not, Rick?" asked Creed. "We both did, or have you forgotten?"

"No, I haven't. But the vice presidency has given me a different perspective. I can see the big picture now. Your thinking is parochial and narrow-minded."

"In other words, your people want the drug war to continue, don't they?" asked Creed.

"Don't be ridiculous," said Throckmorton. "We want it to end, and we'll do whatever it takes to win it."

"You lost it years ago."

"The statistics tell a different story."

---

[32] See TEXMEX by Clabe Taylor, 2012

"It's just another industry to you," Creed stated. "Jobs for your constituents and prisons full of blacks and Mexicans buy a lot of votes... ain't that right?"

Throckmorton laughed. "Sounds like you've been smoking some of that shit yourself."

"Me? asked Creed. "Hardly, but history is on our side, Rick. This whole thing is going to end just like alcohol prohibition did in 1933. The momentum is building. Look at Colorado and Washington."

"Listen to yourself, Creed. You sound like a damned Bolshevik."

Creed snorted. He crossed his legs and absentmindedly poked at the dried cow manure on the sole of his boot with a ballpoint pin.

"We're going to start cutting federal aid, you know," said the vice president.

Creed clenched his jaw but said nothing. He knew the administration was planning to tighten the screws. The Texas treasury was the most obvious target.

"And don't give me any of your anti-government bullshit about how Texas can stand on its own. I was governor for three years and know how much federal aid Texas gets from Washington. Want to hear the figure?"

Creed spit into his omnipresent Styrofoam cup, a gesture that expressed his thoughts with uncanny accuracy.

"About fifty billion, this year," said Creed, not waiting for the vice-president to rub it in. "So?"

"So do the math, Creed."

"You plan to do that to the rest of the states that follow suit?" asked Creed. He leaned forward and pulled his Wranglers down over his cowboy boots.

"Only if we have to," replied the vice president. "Read the constitution, Creed. Federal law trumps state law."

"The constitution also gives you feds responsibility for defending our national sovereignty."

"And?"

"And you're doing a piss poor job of it," said Creed. "I've got Mexican drug cartels firing mortars into South Texas, and Washington won't lift a finger to help. Not to mention the great CIA has no idea who's been sinking ships in the Gulf of Mexico right off our coast, or who's thrown our economy into a tailspin."

Throckmorton shuffled through a stack of documents and pulled a manila folder from the bottom. He handed it to Creed.

"This is for your eyes only," he said. "You are not authorized to reveal its contents to anyone."

Creed pulled out a pair of twelve-dollar Walmart reading glasses and put them on before taking the folder from Throckmorton. He opened it, skimmed the two-paragraph executive summary and looked up wide-eyed at the vice president. He tossed the folder back on the desk, folded his collapsible glasses and put them back in his shirt pocket.

"We heard this from Ian McGinnis himself. About a half hour before he disappeared," said Creed as he stood up to leave. "It was bullshit then and it doesn't smell any better now just 'cause it's on paper."

"It's the best information the president has, Creed," said Throckmorton. "But if a Mexican drug cartel can kidnap the CIA director a half mile from the governor's ranch, I'd say you're losing control of your state."

"Is that your plan?" Creed put on his hat and pulled the brim low over his eyes. "Looking for an excuse to intervene?"

"Congress wants answers, Creed."

"Well, answer them. Tell them Ian McGinnis is a damned fool and that he's lying to the president about the attacks on our shipping lanes."

The vice president's intercom buzzed softly.

"Rick, the Mexican foreign minister is here," said a husky female voice.

"I'll be right there," said Throckmorton and turned back to Creed. "If you know anything about this, I need to hear about it."

"I should know more in a few days. Mako Sloane's in Mexico working on it."

"Sloane? I should have known he'd be right in the middle of things. You two are as thick as flies, aren't you? The attorney general wants to indict Sloane, you know," said Throckmorton.

"For what?"

"They say he crossed the line, Creed."

"And you believe them?"

"Congress wants his ass on a plate," said Throckmorton. "He does have a reputation, you know."

"You do too, Rick," said Creed. "And you're living up to it."

"Creed, it's one thing for the potheads in Colorado and Washington to legalize marijuana, but Texas has a long border with Mexico. We're not about to let you get away with this," declared the vice president. "Any message for the president?"

Throckmorton ignored Creed's last remark and reached out to shake his hand. Creed stared squeamishly at the vice president's manicured fingernails and reluctantly took his hand. Mesmerized and deep in thought, he turned slowly on his heels and took two steps towards the door. Throckmorton stood and stared at the back of his wrinkled blue-checkered shirt.

"Creed, what shall I tell the president?" he called out as Creed opened the door to leave.

"Same thing I told Ian McGinnis," said Creed. "Tell him to go fuck himself."

Chapter 25

"What are you planning to do with me?" asked Ian. The vodka buzz exacerbated his already debilitating headache, and he was still wobbly on his feet from the ordeal in the trunk of his kidnappers' car. Ian could barely concentrate on his conversation with the stocky Russian although he instinctively knew his life likely depended on his answers. He did not fully understand the Russian's presence in Salcido's house or his hostility. Ian wanted to grab him by the shoulders, shake him, and scream that they both wanted the same thing. He did not, though. He was too frightened, and he was not sure what organization the Russian represented. Maybe he was just another thug...like Antonio Salcido. A drug trafficker and a murderer cloaked in a deceptive aura of legitimacy. Russian embassy? That could mean many things these days. The Russian government was practically a criminal organization. At least that was what his analysts told him.

Vladimir poured himself yet another vodka, emptied his glass with an abrupt backwards jerk of his head and then slammed the glass down on top of the bar. Ian jumped at the sound. Vladimir suppressed a belch and reached for the plate of Mexican appetizers on the bar. He picked up a piece of sliced jícama with spicy crabmeat spread evenly on top. The Russian seemed unaffected by the shots of vodka despite his prodigious efforts to deplete Salcido's inventory of Stolichnaya. Other than a flushed face he appeared perfectly sober.

"It's up to you, Ian," said Vladimir, his smile suddenly disappearing as his eyes narrowed. The muscles on the sides of his jaws alternately tensed and relaxed. "You have several choices."

Vladimir picked up a small bell on top of the bar and rang it. The shrill chime still echoed in the spacious room when one of Salcido's lieutenants walked briskly through the door and snapped to attention in military fashion. He stood expectantly but said nothing.

"It's time for the entertainment," said Vladimir in accented Spanish, his voice devoid of emotion. The lieutenant promptly turned on his heels in a perfectly executed about-face and exited the room. Ian heard a door slam and heard the Mexican barking orders out in the courtyard like a drill sergeant.

"What is it you people say in English?" asked Vladimir. "A picture is worth a thousand words?"

They both waited in silence for a few minutes and then Vladimir's cell phone rang. He answered, listened for several seconds, and then signed off.

"Come to the window, Ian," Vladimir said as he stood and motioned for Ian to follow.

As Ian approached the window, Vladimir opened the wooden shutters, which served to keep out the harsh light and the midday tropical heat. Ian looked out into the sun-drenched courtyard and saw a disheveled man with his hands tied behind his back kneeling in front of Salcido himself. The man's face was bruised and swollen and his guayabera shirt was ripped and hung from his shoulders in shreds. Ian could see he was weeping. The lieutenant stood behind the man with a pistol aimed at the back of his head. Salcido glanced towards the window where Ian and Vladimir stood. He nodded his head, motioned with his hand to his lieutenant, and then stepped quickly away from the two figures. Ian turned his head away a fraction of a second before the shot rang out.

"Choice number one," said Vladimir.

"You wouldn't dare kill the director of the Central Intelligence Agency," Ian said but somehow his voice lacked conviction. They had kidnapped him off a public highway in South Texas. What was there to stop them from murdering him here in Mexico? Ian began to panic, and his mind ran through the possible ways this scenario might end. He did not care for any of them.

"In that case you have another option," suggested Vladimir. He removed his cell phone from his right trouser pocket and speed-dialed a number.

"La segunda opción,[33]" he said into the phone as he stared at Ian.

Salcido's lieutenant led a second battered and filthy prisoner to the courtyard and forced him to kneel beside the first victim, who lay prostate and unmoving on the salmon colored tile, his head lying in an ever-expanding pool of dark blood. Then the lieutenant waved his arm, and an obese Mexican in light blue hospital scrubs carrying a chain saw strode purposefully into the courtyard and stopped directly behind the kneeling prisoner. As Ian watched, the man yanked the starter rope, and the chainsaw chugged into action, enveloping the man in a small cloud of bluish smoke. Too rich a gas-oil mixture, Ian idly thought to himself, but then felt goose bumps run down his back and arms as he realized what he was about to witness.

"Stop, I get the picture!" shouted Ian.

"Don't you understand who you're dealing with?" whispered Vladimir. "These people don't play by your fucking rules. They shit in the milk of your mother." He grabbed Ian by his shirt collar and pushed him against the wall. A shout from the courtyard blocked out the rest of his words. Ian saw Vladimir's mouth moving but heard nothing except the howl of the chainsaw and a high-pitched scream,

---

[33] The second option.

which cut off abruptly a fraction of a second later. The chainsaw coughed and died. Then it was deathly still.

"What's the third choice?" asked Ian.

"You play by our rules."

***

"We found him!" said James Brazzle excitedly as he rushed past the startled secretary in the governor's reception room and burst into Creed's private office.

"Found who?" asked a startled Creed Tucker, spilling coffee over his copy of the *Austin-American Statesman*.

"Ian McGinnis, that's who!" Brazzle was panting from the exertion of his sprint up the stairs to Creed's office from the underground parking garage.

"Where was the sonofabitch? At a Mexican whorehouse?" Creed stood up quickly from his expansive mahogany desk, which stood under a majestic lithograph depicting the American victory at the Battle of Chapultepec.

"He just showed up at the U.S. Customs crossing in Laredo. A little worse for the wear but waving his American passport and happy as hell to be back in Texas," replied Brazzle. "It'll be on all the evening news shows."

"Where the hell was he for the last forty-eight hours?" asked Creed.

Brazzle tossed his western hat on a leather sofa on one side of the governor's office and sat down in a chair in front of Creed's desk.

"Your guess is as good as mine. He wouldn't say. Just kept cussing you and promising to make your life miserable. Blames you for gettin' kidnapped. Says if you can't keep the cartels from snatching U.S. officials off the street practically in sight of the governor's home, you should be impeached."

"He might be right," said Creed. "Where is he now?"

"On his way with Vice President Throckmorton to DFW. They're flying back to D.C. in Air Force Two later this afternoon."

Creed stood up and began pacing back and forth across his office. Brazzle sat and watched him. Neither said a word for several minutes, but Brazzle knew better than to interrupt Creed's ruminating.

"I almost think this whole thing was setup to make us look bad," Creed finally said. "Now the administration has that much more ammunition to justify any drastic action they might take against us."

"You wouldn't say that if you had seen Ian down in Laredo," said Brazzle.

"Oh?"

"Somebody beat the crap of him, Creed. He started crying like a baby when he saw me and hugged me like we were long-lost brothers."

"That doesn't sound like the cocksure sonofabitch we saw at my ranch a couple of days ago," said Creed.

"That's what I mean. My contacts on the Mexican side reported a rumor that some big-shot had been kidnapped by one of the cartels, but they thought it was some more bad blood between the Zetas and the Sinaloa Federation. Now we know it was McGinnis."

"But then he got away…." commented Creed.

"Yeah, that's what doesn't make any sense," agreed Brazzle. "You can't tell me that Ian McGinnis has the street sense to escape from his captors in the heart of Mexico and find his way back to the border in one piece."

"I doubt it," said Creed. "But I know one thing…"

He reached into his pouch of Red Man for a pinch of chewing tobacco, leaned back in his swivel chair, and stuffed his open mouth.

"What's that?" asked Brazzle.

"If we don't come up with some details on this cartel submarine and give our own report to the president damned soon, it'll be too late.

"You know something I don't?" asked Brazzle.

"I know that Throckmorton showed me an official CIA report naming Iran and Venezuela as the culprits behind the sinking of the *Orca* and the oil tanker. I also know that the president's approval ratings have dropped to 23% and that he's under tremendous pressure to do something," said Creed.

"Uh-oh," replied Brazzle. "I think I know where you're going with this. Shades of Iraq - 2003?"

"Yep, don't you know it. The president called a press conference for tomorrow morning. Probably hold it right after he meets with McGinnis. I think they're going to take action based on the CIA report. The president doesn't think he can stall the American people any longer. At least that's what he says."

Creed spit into his Styrofoam cup, and James sipped a cup of steaming coffee the governor's secretary brought into the office and placed carefully on a leather coaster on Creed's desk.

"Action against whom? Us or Iran?" asked Brazzle.

"Probably both," said Creed. "On top of everything else, there are nine states planning to legalize marijuana in the next six months. The DEA and the president are frantic. I think they plan to make us an example to deter the others."

Creed waved his index finger at Brazzle.

"James, I appointed you head of the People's Intelligence and Security Service for a reason. I need some answers. Quick!"

"We're almost there, Creed. Mako thinks he'll have something big for us in the next day or so. I talked to him this morning. Told him about finding Ian."

"Did he know anything about it?" asked Creed.

"Yeah, he confirmed it was Salcido's people. Mako thinks Ian's working both sides of the fence."

"But why?" asked Creed.

Chapter 26

"It's time," said Armando, walking into the Fiesta Americana hotel room where Mako had been waiting for over three hours.

"Jesus, I thought you'd defected back to the cartel," said Mako only half in jest. The Armenian captain is ready to talk now?"

Armando laughed. He plopped down on the sofa in the suite, opened the minibar, and took out a cold beer.

"I guess you could call it that. He needed some convincing, though."

"I hope you didn't threaten him." Mako knew coercion was practically the worst way to recruit an agent, but he was using Armando as an access agent, and he would not have complete control of the operation until he met the target himself. Armando often had his own ideas about doing things and took direction about as well as George Armstrong Custer.

"I told him the Americans knew all about both him and the submarine, and that he basically had two choices: to die here in Mexico or retire in the United States and play golf at a country club in Florida."

"Did he make the right choice?" asked Mako although he already knew what the answer would be.

"Yeah, except he asked for Southern California," replied Armando.

"He might have to settle for the Texas Hill Country. I don't have much cachet in Washington these days."

Armando chuckled.

Ten minutes later, he and Mako hailed a taxi in front of the hotel. They took a circuitous route through downtown Veracruz and then back towards the port. They switched cars several times before striking out on foot about ten blocks from the hotel where Armando said the Armenian captain and Inmaculada were waiting.

"I'd rather the girl not be present during the conversation," said Mako.

"No choice on that one. The girl set up the meeting, and the captain wants her to be there. Period. He's nervous."

"Yeah, I guess I don't blame him," commented Mako.

The hotel was located just outside the port of Veracruz. It was a ramshackle old building that should have been condemned a quarter century ago by the city authorities. Chunks of stucco were missing from the façade and deep cracks were visible in the outer walls. Mako hated to think what the rooms looked or smelled like.

He saw Armando hand the hotel clerk a wad of peso bills, and the two men walked straight to the stairwell and headed up to the third floor. The elevators had not been in working order for ten years according to Armando. Mako touched the 9 mm Browning stuck in the back of his jeans. It gave him little comfort. He knew that if this were a setup, the cartel assassins would have assault rifles at the very least. Not that he did not trust Armando, but he knew the game they were playing.

Armando knocked on the door of the room while Mako stood to the side in the corridor, his back flat against the wall and the 9 mm pointed at the door. The door opened almost immediately, and Mako saw an exotically beautiful Mexican woman with sad eyes briefly embrace Armando. Mako saw her glance at him. She nodded but then saw his gun.

"You won't need that," she said softly in Spanish. "He's ready to cooperate."

Mako followed Armando into the room and saw a dark-complexioned man of short stature with a black moustache sitting on the corner of the bed with both hands on his knees. He looked Mexican, and for a minute Mako was afraid they had been duped. Then the man stood up, smiled, and approached Mako with his hand extended.

"Mikoyan...Bulat," he introduced himself. "I sorry for English. It not so good."

"Let's speak Russian, then," suggested Mako and switched languages. Bulat looked at him, eyes wide with surprise but gratefully answered in Russian.

"What is it you want from me?" he began.

The girl sat down on the bed next to the Armenian and draped her arm protectively around his shoulders. Armando poured shots of vodka from a half-empty bottle that stood on the windowsill into three paper cups he found in the bathroom.

"Bulat, please forgive me for being blunt, but I don't want a thing from you. Inmaculada said you needed help. From what I've heard, that's an understatement."

Mako pulled a chair close to the bed where Bulat sat and stared first at him and then at the girl.

"What do you know about me?" asked Bulat.

"I know you're the captain of a Ukrainian-made submarine owned by the Sinaloa Federation that has sunk ships in U.S. waters and killed American citizens," replied Mako grimly. "That makes you a pirate, and those are capital crimes."

"Who are you?" asked Bulat. He shifted uneasily on the bed and removed the girl's arm from his shoulders.

"My name's Mako Sloane."

"Never heard of you," replied Bulat.

"Ask your boss from the Russian embassy. He'll know me."

"I don't know what you're talking about."

"Bulat, listen to me," said Mako. "You're in a shitload of trouble. I suggest you drop your tough-guy act and let us help each other."

The Armenian tossed back his glass of vodka and signaled Armando for more. Mako put his glass down without drinking and waited.

"Can you offer me asylum?" Bulat finally asked.

"Maybe. It depends on what you have to tell me," replied Mako. "Are you the captain of the submarine?"

"Yes," answered Bulat.

"Were you responsible for sinking a Coast Guard Cutter and an oil tanker in the Gulf of Mexico?"

Bulat nodded his head in silence.

"Who gives you instructions?" Mako placed a tiny recording device on the bed and turned it on. He knew Bulat would not object.

"The Russian SVR Rezident in Mexico City," Bulat said nervously. "We meet once every two weeks at the Russian embassy." He stood up and began to pace back and forth across the bedroom.

"They'll kill me if they find out I've spoken with you," he said. "I must have guarantees that you will relocate me to the United States."

"Sit down," said Mako. He motioned to the bed with his free hand and drank his glass of vodka with the other.

Bulat sat down again beside Inmaculada. Mako saw that his hands trembled.

"I can tell you that if you cooperate fully and don't conceal any information from me, the United States government will offer you asylum, a significant sum of money, and protection. But until you provide that information, and until I am satisfied that it's the truth, there can be no guarantees."

Mako knew he was going out on a limb, especially since the director of the Central Intelligence Agency was working hard to convince the president that Iran was behind the attacks. Going against the CIA would be risky. Mako knew McGinnis had his own agenda and for some reason was concealing the truth. How much the president trusted him was the unknown factor in the equation. Mako was sailing in uncharted waters, but that was something he had done his entire career.

Armando filled up the three glasses again, and the men drank once more. Bulat was perspiring, and he looked at Inmaculada like a frightened puppy.

"And if I refuse?" asked Bulat, puffing himself up like a bantam rooster.

"Then I wouldn't give ten cents for your life," replied Mako. "The Americans will be looking for you because they'll know what you've done, and the Russians will too because they'll know you've talked to the Americans. The drug traffickers would get you first, though. No doubt about it."

"Then you give me no choice," said Bulat and reached into his briefcase with his right hand. Mako yanked his Browning from the back of his jeans, and Armando advanced quickly on Bulat with the longest knife Mako had ever seen.

"Stop!" cried Inmaculada. "He's unarmed!"

Bulat pulled a leather-bound notebook out of his briefcase and handed it to Mako. He looked at the muzzle of Mako's 9 mm pointed at his forehead but seemed almost disinterested.

"Here's my deck log. I think you'll find it interesting."

***

Less than twenty-four hours later, James Brazzle stood apart from the usual gaggle of Iranian, Pakistani, and Nigerian chauffeurs waiting at DFW's international arrivals exit. When Mako finally emerged from the baggage claim and customs area, Brazzle walked forward and the two men embraced briefly.

"I've got a car just outside at the curb," he said. "Even got a driver. With a security clearance."

"Damn, you've come up in the world since I last saw you down in South Texas."

"Frankly, I'd rather be back there branding calves," said Brazzle. "I miss the smell of cow manure on a hot summer afternoon."

"Me too," Mako said laughing.

The men were silent as the driver took the north exit out of the airport and followed signs to Hwy 121 South.

"It's good to be back in Texas," said Mako. "Got to admit, though, I hate the ride into Forth Worth. Wall-to-wall suburban sprawl makes my guts knot up. Existential fucking despair and the song never gets sung. Thoreau would shit his pants."

"Yeah, I don't like it much more than you do. South Texas may not be pretty, but at least we don't have to stand in line to get from one place to another."

"Where're you taking me, James?" asked Mako.

"Creed has a suite at the Worthington in Fort Worth. He's waiting for us. I hope you have proof of what you told me on the phone."

"I've got it."

They were quiet as the driver weaved in and out of the heavy traffic and merged into the right lanes at the I-35 intersection with the Fort Worth skyline looming less than a mile ahead.

"Tell the driver to go west on I-30 and keep going," said Mako suddenly.

"What the hell for?" asked Brazzle.

"I think we got company," said Mako laconically.

"You've grown eyes in the back of your head or something?"

He started to turn around to look out the back window, but Mako elbowed him painfully in the ribs.

"No, but I've been watching the rear view mirror. Like you and your driver should have been doing."

"In Texas?" Brazzle asked. "Come on."

Mako's silence told Brazzle all he needed to know.

"You heard the man," Brazzle said to the driver who nodded in response.

The limousine swerved abruptly onto the I-30 exit. A few seconds later Mako peered into the limo's rearview mirror and thought he saw a black SUV several cars behind them do the same thing. The driver confirmed his suspicions.

"The gentleman is correct," said the driver. "At least one, maybe two."

"Those motherfuckers," whispered Mako.

"Mako, don't get a wild hair up your ass. This is Texas, not Mexico. We're not going to do anything to these guys, understand?"

"That's your call, James," said Mako. "At least we know the score now."

Brazzle tapped the driver on the shoulder.

"Pull into the gas station at the Bryant Irvin Street exit, and then we'll head back into town."

"Make it look natural," said Mako.

The limousine pulled into a gas station off the freeway, and the driver casually refueled. Mako and Brazzle stepped out of the car and stretched.

"They're parked down the road. Two SUVs," said Mako.

"Yeah, I see 'em," replied James. "Wonder who the hell they are."

"McGinnis' people, I'd say. Do you believe it? The damned CIA working the streets of Fort Worth, Texas!"

Five minutes later the limousine turned back on the interstate heading east, took the Cherry Street exit, and wove its way through downtown Fort Worth towards the Worthington.

"Doesn't this limo have a bar?" asked Mako.

"Plenty of time for that later," answered Brazzle. "I want you sober for the meeting with Creed. Do you realize the implications of what you told me on the phone?"

"That's why I need a drink," answered Mako as the driver pulled into the hotel's underground garage. "Christ! And they said the Cold War was over."

Chapter 27

"Cold War hell!" said Brazzle as the elevator door shut. "Things could heat up pretty quickly if Washington doesn't play its cards right."

"Washington play its cards right?" asked Mako sarcastically.

"Yeah, not much of a chance of that, is there?

Both men laughed as their elevator bounced to a stop on the twelfth floor. Two uniformed hotel security guards were waiting outside in the corridor. They quizzed Brazzle and Mako before allowing them to move down the corridor towards the governor's suite where the two CIA veterans passed through the gauntlet of Creed's own security screen.

"Jesus," said Mako. "You'd think Creed was someone important," he said, but the joke fell flat.

"There're almost as many people want to kill Creed as you," said Brazzle. "And he doesn't take it as a compliment like you do."

There were more bodyguards inside the entrance to the suite. One of them held up his hand for them to stop, but then Creed's grizzled visage appeared behind him.

"It's alright, boys. These are the friendlies we've been waiting on," said Creed. "You can leave us alone now."

The guards nodded and quietly closed the door to the hotel suite as they left. Creed took two steps forward and shook hands with his old friends without saying a word. He walked back to the bar at the far wall of the small living room and pointed to a bottle of 12-year old Flor de Caña.

"I knew you were coming," he said. A hint of a smile flickered across his face but disappeared almost immediately. Mako wondered if he had imagined it.

"Only if you'll join us," said Mako.

"Oh, what the hell. I was trying to give up drinking. Guadalupe's been on my ass about it, but these are extenuating circumstances, right?"

"That's one way to put it," said Mako.

"I'll have one too," Brazzle said. "Anything to dull this gnawing sense of impending doom."

"Let me get that," said Mako. He sat three glasses in a row on the bar and started to slice a lime.

"We had company in from DFW," Brazzle said.

"You were followed?" asked Creed.

Brazzle nodded his head.

"It could be Ian McGinnis. He might have Mako on a watch list," he said.

Creed cursed under his breath.

"That sonofabitch isn't supposed to operate inside U.S. territory," he said.

"The CIA isn't supposed to do a lot of things," said Mako. "That's never stopped 'em before. Why should it now?"

"Anything from Washington today?" asked Brazzle.

"Sit down," Creed suggested. "You better have that drink before you hear this."

"That bad?" asked Brazzle.

Creed did not bother to answer.

"Let's have it then," said Mako. "The drink can wait."

Mako dropped the knife and it clattered on the polished wood surface of the bar. He wiped the lime juice from his hands on the legs of his faded Wranglers and leaned backwards on the bar.

Creed lifted himself onto a tall cowhide stool and spun around with his back to the bar. Mako had never seen Creed without a pair of spurs on his boots and only once or twice without a cowboy hat. He had not realized the recently elected governor of Texas was going bald.

"Here's the long and short of it," said Creed. "Ian McGinnis has convinced the president that an Iranian submarine sunk the Coast Guard cutter and the oil tanker. The administration is preparing a military strike in retaliation."

He paused to let the news sink in. Neither man showed any emotion. Brazzle's raised eyebrow was the only indication he had even heard the news. Mako was stone-faced, and his facial expression had not changed.

"The president even bought the line about logistical help from the Venezuelan government. Hugo Chavez casts a long shadow, even in death. Personally, I believe the director of the CIA faked overhead photography of the Venezuelan navy base at Puerto Cabello to prove his case."

Mako whistled. "How the hell did he do that?"

"Or why?" added Brazzle.

"We think he got hold of satellite coverage from the 2008 visit by the Russian fleet to Venezuela. He doctored the dates, removed any identifying features from the photography, and claims the images were recorded six weeks ago. There's a Russian Kilo class submarine in the photo, and McGinnis is screaming that it's Iranian. The smoking gun, he says. Claims that's what sunk the *Orca* and killed Americans."

Mako finally poured himself a drink. He looked out of the window at downtown Fort Worth and Sundance Square. He had no idea things had gotten this out of hand and wondered if his meeting with the Armenian submarine captain had been too late.

"Where'd your information come from?" Brazzle asked.

"The vice president called me this morning. Even Throckmorton smells a rat and wanted to compare notes," replied Creed.

"What'd you tell him?" Brazzle asked.

"I told him all three of us would fly to Washington this evening and prove to him that Ian McGinnis and the CIA are full of shit, and that the Iranians had nothing to do with this. Am I wrong?"

Mako emptied his glass and reached for the bottle to pour another.

"No, you're not. That's the problem."

"Drink up then," said Creed. "I've got a private jet waiting for us at the airport. We'll have dinner in Georgetown tonight."

Mako exchanged glances with Brazzle and finished mixing his drink.

"You make that trip without me, Creed," he said. "I've briefed James, and here's all the proof you need."

He reached into his shoulder bag and drew out the leather-bound deck log the Armenian captain had given to him.

"Don't let that out your hands and don't show it to Ian McGinnis," he said. "That's a death sentence for my agent if his notebook gets in the wrong hands."

"Mako, I want you there to brief Throckmorton. He knows and trusts you," said Creed.

"No way! I hear McGinnis told you they have a warrant out for my arrest," said Mako.

"I think he was bluffing," said Creed.

"Do you?" asked Mako. "You're willing to play Russian roulette with my freedom?"

"You work for me, dammit. I'm not going let anyone arrest you," said Creed. He slid off the stool and walked over to a chair next to the window where his suit jacket lay neatly folded. He reached into the inside pocket and cursed softly again. "Where the hell's my Red Man?"

"Don't let this governor thing go to your head, Creed," said Mako. "As soon as you cross the Sabine River, you no longer call the shots. The president is not going to listen to you unless it's an election year, and the CIA never will. They'll do whatever they want."

"He might be right, Creed," said Brazzle. "Whoever followed us from the airport wasn't interested in me. If you ask me, Ian McGinnis is hiding something big. He knows about the Mexican connection, and he's afraid Mako's on to him."

"So what do you propose?" Creed turned to Mako, who had drained his glass and was mixing another drink.

"I've got to get back to Mexico," said Mako. "The Armenian captain is moving the submarine up the coast to Laguna Verde to a new facility they just finished building.

I'll need to stall him for a while since we've got no commitment from Washington to let him defect."

"What about that CIA officer from the Mexico City station who was helping you?" asked Brazzle.

"His name is Cyrus Tinch," answered Mako. "We can still count on his help. He should be waiting for me in Veracruz when I get back. He's a good man, but not much of a case officer. No street smarts at all. On top of everything else, he fell in love with his agent. The one the cartel tried to blow up in front of the attorney general's office."

"Really?" laughed Brazzle.

"She's a Latin beauty. I don't blame him," said Mako.

He squeezed a lime into two healthy ounces of Flor de Caña, poured in the same amount of Coke and handed the glass to the governor of Texas.

"Thanks," said Creed. He placed the cocktail on the bar without drinking. "Mako, we need to know what Ian McGinnis is up to," said Creed.

"Come on now," answered Mako. "I can't conjure up angels."

"Well, you're as close as we have to anything with divine powers down there in Mexico," said Creed.

"I feel sorry for you then," said Mako and laughed.

"Look, here's the deal," said Creed. "Brazzle and I both think that Ian is mucking around in

Mexico...freelancing. It has something to do with the coast guard cutter and the submarine. It's also possible Ian ordered the murder of the head DEA analyst. The one that disappeared in Mazatlán. What was his name?"

"Harvard Banks," said Brazzle.

"Yeah, he's the one that Cyrus Tinch briefed on the cartel alliance with the Russians," said Mako.

"Anyway," said Creed, "we think it's all somehow connected."

"I do too, and what about the DEA administrator, Cory Elkins?" asked Mako.

"What about him?" responded Brazzle.

"I wish we could put him under surveillance. My bet is that he and Ian McGinnis are working together," said Mako.

Creed picked up the leather notebook Mako had placed on the bar.

"Well, we can't," he said. "So let's not worry about it for now. You say this is the smoking gun?"

Creed held the notebook up and studied it, slowly leafing through the pages.

"Damn thing's in Russian!" he said.

"Yeah, they don't speak much English in the Russian navy," said Mako.

The men fell silent and sipped their drinks. Finally, Brazzle broke the silence.

"You be careful down there in Mexico. That place is the incarnation of evil," he said.

Mako shook his head and laughed.

"Maybe you got your geography mixed up," he said. "At least in Mexico you know who the bad guys are. It's different in Washington. Damn viper's nest if you ask me. You men watch your backs. Don't trust anyone, even Throckmorton."

Chapter 28

Cory Elkins was scared although he would be the last to admit it. Fear was not something he admired when he saw it in others, and he was not about to accept the possibility that he was subject to the foibles of lesser men.

However, things were not going according to plan. That much he would admit. Normally, a few bumps in the road would not bother him. As head of the DEA, Cory dealt with minor catastrophes on a daily basis. But this time his problems went far beyond the day-to-day operational gaffes and corruption scandals he usually encountered. Cory was mired in deep shit and he knew it.

He slammed the telephone receiver down in frustration. Why was the CIA director refusing to take his calls? They were colleagues, after all. Almost partners. He reached into the bottom right drawer of his desk at DEA headquarters and took out a pint of Wild Turkey. He opened the bottle and recklessly splashed a half ounce into his coffee cup. These days alcohol seemed to be the only thing capable of taking his mind off the specter of the personal Armageddon that shadowed him wherever he went.

To add insult to injury, the plan originally had been Cory's idea, and it was a brilliant one. At least until Ian McGinnis got his hands on it. Cory had foreseen the danger posed by Colorado and Washington and their referendums to legalize marijuana. He had used his authority and expertise to lobby against the initiatives, but the potheads and liberal kooks in Colorado and the Pacific Northwest had voted in favor of legalization. The inaction of the federal government when confronted with such outrageous challenges to its authority, Cory thought, was unforgivable and cowardly. What ever happened to the rule of law?

When the new governor of Texas announced his intention to follow suit, Cory knew he could not let it happen. Texas, after all, had an almost 2,000-mile long border with Mexico. The implications of legalization in a border state like Texas for the War on Drugs were something he could not ignore. This was his rice bowl, and nobody was going to break it.

Cory viewed the CIA as a natural ally, and he had found a willing partner in Ian McGinnis. But at Ian's insistence the limited scope of Cory's plan had mushroomed into a vast international conspiracy. Cory thought it risky and foolhardy. He should have anticipated that the CIA director would want to take charge and run the operation himself. The man was an ambitious, egotistical ass and had no scruples about trampling whoever got in his way. Contacting the Russians had been his idea, and that was when things had begun to unravel.

Cory looked at the old-fashioned electric clock on his office wall. It was time to leave for Dulles if he wanted to make his flight to Mexico City. He had decided to confront Salcido personally despite the man's mercurial personality and uncontrollable temper. Ian McGinnis was taking the operation in the wrong direction. Salcido would understand. He and Cory were both in the same business, after all.

Cory hurriedly threw a few articles of clothing from a closet into a leather shoulder bag. He buzzed his secretary, and she stuck her head in his office a few seconds later.

"I'm ready to go," he announced.

"The car's downstairs waiting for you," she said with a smile.

At least he still commanded respect and called the shots in his own agency, Cory thought bitterly and jogged briskly down the stairs to the front door of DEA's Arlington, Virginia headquarters building. He walked instead of taking the elevator, hoping the exercise might help clear his head, but nagging doubts continued to swirl and torment. Why was he suddenly out of the loop? Had Ian lost his mind? Did he think he could just turn his back on Cory at this point? With what he knew?

Cory had done his bit. He had been the point man, the one who had natural access to the cartel leadership. When it became necessary to plug a few leaks that threatened the security of the operation, Cory outsourced the job to Antonio Salcido, who carried out his end of the bargain with typical sadistic ingenuity. Everyone suspected the Mexican drug cartels were behind Harvard's disappearance and the brazen assassination of the CIA chief of station in Mexico City. Cory appreciated the irony of that truth. He smiled at the memory as he stepped into the waiting car.

Cory glanced at the driver and did not recognize him.

"Where's Mr. Cunningham?" he asked, wondering where his usual driver was.

"*Está muy enfermo*[34]," said the replacement driver, turning around and smiling at Cory.

Cory bristled at the driver's answer in Spanish. He always insisted that even his Hispanic agents speak English with each other in the office. It was an unwritten rule and everyone knew it. Cory opened his mouth to admonish the driver when he noticed blood on the dashboard and saw the 9 mm Glock in the driver's left hand pointing at his face. Cory stared in detached fascination at the 6-inch suppressor attached to the end of the barrel.

"*Que le vaya bien,*"[35] said the driver an instant before squeezing the trigger.

---

[34] He's very sick.
[35] Good luck to you – Spanish.

***

Mako looked out the window of the El Expreso bus as it barreled down I-35 south towards Laredo. It was familiar country. Somehow, the flat inhospitable landscape of barbed wire, mesquite, prickly pear cactus, and the occasional windmill made sense to him. The passengers on the bus were almost all Hispanic, and the lilt of their quiet murmurings in Spanish was comforting and practically serene. The women unwrapped pork and beef tamales and spooned pinto beans into small plastic containers and fed their men and children. The pungent smell of spicy meat and corn tortillas permeated the bus while tinny norteña music emanated from someone's transistor radio. Mako took a pewter flask from his travel bag and unscrewed the top.

"Salud," he said to the elderly Mexican man who sat beside him. The old man crinkled his face into a wrinkly smile and nodded his head as Mako drank straight from the flask. Mako offered to pour some into the old man's Jarritos bottle, but the *viejo* just grinned and covered the top of the bottle with a gnarly, veined hand.

"No, muchas gracias," he said.

It was dusk when the bus arrived in Laredo. Mako knew the town well, but he did not intend to stay the night. A chartered plane waited for him across the border at the

Nuevo Laredo airport for the two-hour flight to Veracruz. He took a taxi to the Hamilton Hotel, where the South Texas headquarters of the People's Intelligence and Security Service was located. Mako picked up a new set of alias documentation from Brazzle's secretary, who stammered and averted her eyes in Mako's presence.

He slept most of the flight to Veracruz and even dozed during the short taxi ride to the Fiesta Americana. He surprised Armando who was not expecting him till the next day. A plump, dark-skinned beauty, who could not have been more than sixteen years old, rolled naked out of bed and dressed hurriedly. Armando thrust a handful of bills into her outstretched palm and send her packing with an affectionate wallop on her generous buttocks.

"Sorry for interrupting, friend," said Mako.

"*No hay cuidado[36],*" said Armando. "I'll see her tomorrow night anyway."

"You know how to pick them, don't you? That ass will be still be jiggling when you pick her up tomorrow."

"Your coarseness offends me," said Armando. "She's a student at the university. I was helping her to understand Octavio Paz."

"I suspect you were helping her to understand the Kama Sutra," said Mako. "Any news from Bulat?"

---

[36] No worries

"Yeah. He's in Mexico City, meeting with the Russian. Be back tomorrow. He's got a case of cold feet but knows it's too late to back out. He's afraid you took what you wanted and won't come through with your end of the bargain."

"That might be closer to the truth than he knows."

Mako walked over to the window and opened the door to the balcony. The hot sticky night air slowly replaced the cool clamminess of air conditioning in the tropics.

"This room smells like a whorehouse. I'm surprised the management let you in with that prostitute."

"Next time announce your arrival in advance," replied Armando. "Stop pretending you're some kind of super spook. We both know the truth. I could have killed you in Monterey."

Mako knew he was right, but was loathe to give Armando the satisfaction by admitting it. He had let his guard down on that fishing pier and literally would have been cooling his heels in a Salinas, California morgue waiting for the police to identify him, had Armando not decided to befriend Mako and escape from his cartel masters.

"You killed him, didn't you?" suddenly asked Armando.

"Killed who?"

"Don't play games with me, Mako. You expect me to believe it was just a coincidence?"

"Armando, what the hell are you talking about?"

"I'm talking about Señor Elkins, of course. You go to Washington and the man dies."

"Cory Elkins is dead?"

Armando nodded his head.

"I wasn't even in Washington, but go on," said Mako, still not knowing whether to take Armando seriously.

"They found his body in the backseat of his own DEA car this morning with his brains splattered all over the upholstery. Apparently, it was quite a mess. You should read the newspapers."

Mako felt like he had been kicked in the solar plexus by a horse. A dozen conspiracy scenarios careened through his brain like an avalanche but then crystallized into one frightening possibility. He grabbed his encrypted cell phone and dialed James Brazzle's number but there was no answer. Maybe they're flying back to Texas already, Mako thought, but he was afraid that was wishful thinking. Dammit, he had warned both of them about flying to Washington.

Hell, Mexico was a cakewalk in comparison. The difference was that the White House allowed its killers to cloak their atrocities in the Star Spangled Banner and Jesus Christ. Nobody could argue with patriotism and religion, could they? Mexico, on the other hand, was rotting from within. The stench of its own moral putrefaction was too obvious to ignore, and nobody pretended it wasn't there. But the smell up in Washington was just as bad. That was why Mako had removed himself from that milieu a decade ago. He had a sensitive nose and a conscience that gave him no peace.

"So it wasn't you?" asked Armando.

Mako shook his head.

"Then who?"

"If I had to take a guess, I'd say it was Ian McGinnis."

"The director of the Central Intelligence Agency ordering the killing of the head of DEA?" asked Armando. "Sounds pretty wild."

"He's desperate. Probably didn't think he had a choice."

"Why do you think he's even involved?" asked Armando.

"Because all the evidence points to Salcido's people orchestrating his kidnapping in South Texas and then taking him to Culiacán. Then Ian shows up at the border two days later still in one piece. That makes no sense. I think somebody sent him back. That's the only reason he's still alive."

"But who?" asked Armando.

"There're only two possibilities. The Russians or Antonio Salcido."

"Salcido wouldn't have let him go. It must have been the Russians," said Armando.

Chapter 29

"You look nervous today," said Vladimir Kazakov as he looked across his embassy desk at the diminutive Armenian.

There was something in the former naval captain's demeanor that bothered him. The Armenian avoided his eyes, and he seemed preoccupied, almost as if he were embarrassed about something. His voice sounded strained and unnatural.

Vladimir thought himself a shrewd judge of character, even though most of the people he dealt with singularly lacked anything that remotely resembled that intangible quality. Bulat was different. He had backbone, integrity, and *cojones*[37] to spare, and that's why the difference was so noticeable.

"I *am* nervous," Bulat answered. "And if you're not, you're as crazy as those narcos are."

"We've done this before, don't forget," objected Vladimir. "Twice, as a matter of fact."

"Yeah, but each time I take that submarine into the Gulf, our risk increases tenfold. The Americans have more submarine detection ships and aircraft deployed in the Gulf

---

[37] balls

of Mexico right now than Russia has in its entire navy," said Bulat. "They're looking for us."

"But they don't know who or what we are. According to my sources, they think the Iranians sunk those ships."

"You *do* know what the sentence for piracy is, don't you?" Bulat continued. "And we're talking about a country that won't hesitate to swoop down here to Mexico and kidnap both of us. Right out of our fucking beds. Then they'll haul us across the border, and after they execute us, their newspapers will write about the fair trial we got. The hypocritical bastards."

"That's only if we fail," said Vladimir grimly. "If we succeed, Russia will take care of us. We'll be heroes."

"Sure, I remember how Russia rewarded me for thirty years of dedicated service to the motherland," retorted Bulat.

Vladimir was taken aback by the edge in his voice. Before the breakup of the USSR, a sarcastic statement like that from an intelligence operative abroad would not have been tolerated. Vladimir would have ordered the offender's immediate return to Moscow for a thorough counterintelligence investigation by the watchdogs of the KGB's Second Chief Directorate. This was the new Russia, though, and things had changed.

The two leaned over a map of the Gulf of Mexico that covered the entire surface of Vladimir's desk. Color-coded circles and squares dotted the map and were especially dense along the coastline from Texas to Mississippi. Vladimir decided to concentrate on their mission and deal with his nagging doubts about the Armenian captain later. They were both under a lot of stress, he told himself.

"Look here, Bulat. These orange circles are oil platforms. They're easy targets, ripe for the plucking, but not important enough for us to risk you or the submarine."

Bulat nodded his head and followed Vladimir's finger as it moved up along the Texas coast, into Louisiana, and then across to Mississippi. The Russian's immaculately manicured finger stopped at the Port of Pascagoula and began tapping. His nail made a hollow, hammering sound on the laminated map.

"Now this is a different story. Big oil refinery right here. Run by Chevron. Security is lax. Just like before we sank the Coast Guard Cutter and the oil tanker. The Americans have no strategic imagination. That's why they haven't had any decent chess players since Bobby Fischer. With all the naval resources they have, they're only defending the Texas coast. *Kakiye duraki!*[38]"

"Wait," Bulat pointed to the map. "Look how far the refinery sits back from the water. The submarine could only do limited damage to the refinery itself. Maybe set a

---

[38] Russian - What fools!

storage tank or two on fire, but we'd have to surface to even do that. It's too risky."

"No, that's not the target. You think I'm an idiot?" asked Vladimir.

Bulat just shrugged in response.

"See these tankers unloading? There's a pipeline that runs from the pier to the terminal. Your target will be the docked foreign oil tankers that are waiting to unload. Most of the oil refined here comes from Mexico and South America. We want that to stop."

He looked up and smiled. "Too much time has passed since the Houston Ship Channel mission. The price of oil is dropping. We need to reverse that trend."

He laughed.

"This time we'll need to refuel to get back," Bulat objected.

"There won't be any need to refuel. You're not coming back; at least not to Mexico. It's time to pull out. I see now that the Mexicans will never be able to operate the sub. That was wishful thinking on Moscow's part. I should have listened to you."

"It was obvious from the beginning. These Mexicans are animals," said Bulat with disgust.

"Apparently not all of them," Vladimir said. He did not think there was any reason to give away his sources or reveal everything he knew. He had learned about Bulat's obsession with the exotically beautiful prostitute in Veracruz. In the back of his mind, he wondered if Bulat's nervousness today had anything to do with her.

Bulat looked at him but was silent. Vladimir shrugged his shoulders.

"We're both men," he said. "I understand. As long as you carry out your missions, Moscow will never hear a word about what you do in your spare time. You can trust me."

Again, Bulat did not reply.

"You'll scuttle the sub here," Vladimir said and wrote the coordinates in magic marker on the map and circled the spot. "A Russian freighter coming out of Veracruz will pick you up. We'll reimburse Salcido later for the loss of his submarine."

"When do we leave?" asked Bulat.

"In seventy-two hours. We're monitoring the American satellites. You will have a 90-minute window to leave Laguna Verde and submerge. I'll call with the exact time."

Vladimir stood up from his chair, signaling that the meeting was over. He gave Bulat a perfunctory embrace and handed him a large envelope bulging with hundred-dollar bills. "A bonus for the crew," he said. "Tell them the motherland is proud of her warriors."

Vladimir knew the money was not from Moscow. The Russian government was notorious for taking its operatives for granted and discarding them once they had served their purpose. He wondered whether the Americans were any different. The money was from the Sinaloa Cartel, a personal gift from Antonio Salcido. He, at least, knew how to reward loyalty. And punish treachery as well.

***

Bulat did not intend to let the SVR sucker him into another sneak attack on the United States' oil industry infrastructure. That much he knew. He was not the type to commit suicide or lead his men to certain death in the name of a megalomaniac in the Kremlin. For what? At first, he had been grateful to get off the unemployment rolls in Russia and was happy to be back at sea. No amount of money, however, could justify the risk he was taking, and no amount of vodka or Armenian cognac could salve his conscience. One way or the other, he was going to make a run for it and take Inmaculada with him. He had not asked her yet, but Bulat knew she would come. This would be their only chance. He had three days to make his move.

His decision to provide information about the submarine and the Russian role in the operation to the tall American had been rash, but it was his only way out. He liked what he saw in the American's eyes, and it made him dare to hope. Bulat assumed the man worked for the CIA.

Whether that made him any more moral or trustworthy than Russia's own SVR officers, Bulat did not know. He was not naïve enough to believe in the virtue of one country's intelligence service over another's. But he did know his own country's history, and it was soaked in the blood of millions of its own citizens. That alone argued in favor of the American.

There was hardly a Russian family that had not lost at least one relative in the basements of Lubyanka and Butyrka or in the corrective labor camps of Vorkuta, Norilsk, and Magadan during the purges of the 1930s. Bulat's own family had been no exception. Some of the victims were rehabilitated posthumously after Khrushchev's famous speech at the 20th CPSU[39] conference in 1956, but most lay in unmarked graves in Northeastern Siberia.

Bulat was a well-read man even though the books he devoured at the university were the ones that had passed through the censorship filter of the regime's ideological gatekeepers and could not boast of any degree of objectivity. If they did not meet the ideological demands of the communist dialectic, Bulat had not seen them. He knew the United States also had a history that shrieked violence and brutality, but to his mind, there was a difference between the insanity of Stalin and Beriya and the

---

[39] CPSU – Communist Party of the Soviet Union

ruthlessness of the Americans. There was also a difference in the scale of the killing. That set the Americans apart in Bulat's eyes and made their murders almost forgivable.

In his view, the historic sins of the Americans were also ameliorated by a level of personal freedom and affluence the average Russian could not even imagine. Bulat had seen in the early 1990s how a taste of democracy in Russia quickly degenerated into chaos and near anarchy. Maybe Russians were not capable of the self-restraint necessary for a nation to exercise its personal freedoms, he thought. Maybe the old communists, nostalgic for the past, had it right when they claimed that Russians required an iron fist to rule them. But he was sick of that iron fist and the collective cowardice of a people that willingly submitted to one authoritarian government after another.

Bulat looked out of the window of the Embraer 145 as it began its descent into Veracruz after the short flight from the Distrito Federal. He hoped he had read the American correctly. If not, he and Inmaculada were doomed. His would be a quick and violent death while Inmaculada would be consumed by the slow rot of her profession.

Bulat did not plan to join the crew in Laguna Verde. He would use some of the money Vladimir gave him to bribe his cartel babysitter and stall his departure from Veracruz. He would spend the night with Inmaculada at the same hotel near the port in Veracruz and steel himself for the meeting tomorrow with the American, who would come with the answers he needed. If he had no answers, Bulat would kill him.

Chapter 30

Hotel rooms always made Mako feel claustrophobic. The waiting and doing nothing made it worse. He eased his body through the narrow doorway leading to the balcony of the Fiesta Americana hotel room and collided with a wall of stifling tropical humidity. The dank, artificially cooled air in the room behind him gushed outside, and Mako quickly closed the door. The bottle of cold beer in his left hand sweated and dripped as he tilted his head back and took a long draught. His gut knotted in worry, and sleep would not come.

He told himself there was no logical connection between the assassination of Cory Elkins and the lack of news from James Brazzle and Governor Creed Tucker. He knew he was rationalizing, though, and the uncertainty gnawed at him. Mako was convinced that Elkins was murdered to keep him quiet, and he recognized the signs of a professional hit. Silence carried a price tag, and Mako had a feeling that the people behind the killing did not have to count pennies. What was there to prevent the assassins from taking out the governor of Texas and the director of his personal intelligence service as well? The information they carried to Washington was no less explosive than what Cory Elkins could have known. It was not what some people within the administration wanted to hear. It contradicted the narrative of the moment and threatened the raconteurs of the party line.

Mako had told Brazzle and the governor back at the Worthington Hotel that Washington was more dangerous than they realized. They paid him no mind. Why do Americans believe that benighted third-world countries have a monopoly on political murders-for-hire, he wondered? Don't they realize that more sleaze goes down in a one-mile radius around Capitol Hill than in most entire countries?

He sifted through what he knew about the operation and the murky maneuvering of whoever was killing to cover his tracks. It was a deadly and desperate game of chess, the beginning of the end game. But who were the players? The cartel, the Russians, a penetration of the U.S. government? They would all have their reasons to commit murder to pursue an agenda or to protect their own interests.

Mako knew it was happening. He was aware of the accumulating body count but was mostly in the dark on the details. He hated it when his adversaries knew more than he did. All signs pointed to the involvement of Ian McGinnis, director of the Central Intelligence Agency, but to Mako's eye, Ian did not have the street smarts or the *cojones* to put this thing together. There had to be others. Maybe a puppet master or ghostwriter to pull Ian's strings or feed him lines.

Soledad Castillo, who had first broken the story of the cartel's submarine, was still recovering from serious wounds after an attempt on her life. The COS in Mexico City had been assassinated by unknown assailants, but it took little imagination to guess who the culprits were. The only two DEA officials who knew about the joint Russian-Sinaloa Cartel operation were dead, murdered in particularly brutal fashion. Finally, a team of cartel killers had narrowly missed eliminating Soledad's handler Cyrus Tinch in an attack on the safe house in Valle de Bravo. Mako and Armando came within an inch of becoming unintentional collateral damage in that exchange of shrapnel and lead. All the victims and would-be victims had one thing in common, though. They all knew about the Russia-cartel alliance and the submarine. And they were all dead or in hiding.

Now the governor of Texas had taken James Brazzle and blithely walked straight into the viper pit with proof of Russian involvement in the attacks on the United States Coast Guard Cutter and the Houston Ship Channel. To make it worse, Mako's agent had provided that proof. Mako knew he should not have given them the Armenian captain's deck log. Damn it! Why wasn't Brazzle answering his phone?

Mako punched the number into his encrypted cell phone yet again, and again the call went straight to voice mail. Mako stepped back into the hotel room and shivered in the cold air belching from an archaic air conditioning unit that hummed so loudly the men had to raise their voices to be heard.

"Nothing on CNN?" he asked.

"Not a thing," answered Armando. "What are we waiting to hear?"

"I'm not sure. Something might have happened to James Brazzle and the governor," Mako replied. "If it has, it'll mean we're up against something much bigger than we anticipated."

"Too big for the great Mako Sloane?" asked Armando. He raised his eyebrows and looked at Mako.

"You heard me." Mako did not feel like putting up with Armando's usual ironic bantering, and he did not want to share all of his suspicions with his sidekick. No use worrying him yet. Mako splashed cold water on his face and lay down on the queen-sized bed nearest the window and the air conditioning unit.

Mako's experience in running clandestine operations spanned a career of thirty years, minus the seven he spent in the joint, but that was ancient history. He knew that when you ran an agent, your biggest fear was that the enemy might have penetrated your own organization. You could vouch for yourself and maybe a few colleagues that you had worked with for years, but even that could be iffy.

You promised your agent security and made outlandish claims to him, promising to compartmentalize his betrayal. In the final analysis, though, your own security and the safety of your agent might depend on some desk-bound bureaucrat in Washington who had access to your closed-channel cables, but who might be looking for an easy way to pay off his mortgage or just to get rich. Mako had gotten out of that game years ago. He now worked informally on a fat retainer and only for the state of Texas. He no longer sent cables back to Washington or even Austin for that matter.

The governor had flown to Washington to share Mako's report with an administration that appeared not to know its ass from a hole in the wall. The naiveté of that decision and the knowledge that he could have done more to stop it haunted Mako.

He dozed off and slept fitfully. Shadowy figures wearing black balaclavas pursued him through a maze of back alleys and parking lots full of Soviet-vintage black Volgas and nondescript beige and white Zhigulis. Shots echoed in the still night of the dream and ricocheted off metal garbage cans in deserted alleys, narrowly missing him. He pulled his handgun from a shoulder holster and tried to shoot back, but the trigger mechanism stuck and the gun refused to fire no matter how hard he squeezed. Two bullets slammed into his torso, and he fell to the ground, watching his attackers close in. Strangely, he felt no pain, just annoyance over his malfunctioning handgun. One of his assailants grabbed him by the shoulder and turned him over, preparing to deliver the coups de grâce with a Glock 9 mm pressing against his temple. He awoke, breathing heavily and found Armando shaking him gently.

"You're dreaming," said Armando. "Wake up. You might want to see this."

Mako sat up like a shot and tried to focus his sleep-heavy eyes on the television screen. He saw a blurry image of satellite photography and saw the caption below the screen in capital letters.

"PUERTO CABELLO, VENEZUELA."

He heard the words *"misil de crucero*[40]*"* and began to focus on the images of destruction on the screen. A local Venezuelan television feed augmented the fuzzy satellite images on a split screen, and Mako saw buildings in flames, ambulances and stretchers, and several naval frigates in the distance, one of which was on fire. He heard the panicked voice of the Venezuelan reporter in the background shouting something about *"provocación"* and *"imperialistas"*, and knew that the president of the United States either did not get the message from the governor of Texas or had not believed it. As he watched the news

---

[40] cruise missile

report, wild-eyed and incredulous, a huge flash illuminated the screen followed by a loud boom, and then the television screen went blank.

"What the hell was that?" asked Armando.

"I'd say we just lobbed another cruise missile into the port," Mako replied. "That'll teach Venezuela to mind her own business. This is the sequel to the invasion of Iraq. Lower budget, though, thank goodness."

"Are you telling me the Americans think Venezuela attacked the Houston Ship Channel and sunk a U.S. Coast Guard Cutter?" asked Armando.

"No, someone convinced them Iran did, and that Venezuela is providing logistical support."

"That's the best your CIA could come up with?"

"It's not my CIA," replied Mako. "They apparently didn't want to hear our version."

Mako stood up to gobble some ibuprofen for a headache that promised to keep him up the rest of the night, and he almost missed the news headlines scrolling by at the bottom of the television screen.

"Private jet of Texas Governor Creed Tucker Reported Missing."

***

Mako finally managed to fall asleep for an hour shortly before sunrise. He awoke to the smell of coffee Armando had brewed and heard doors slamming in the corridor just outside the room. Before he opened his eyes, he grimaced from a headache that seemed to have taken up permanent residence behind his eyeballs. His temples pulsated with pain. He groaned as he recalled the CNN report of the night before. He reached for his cell phone and quick-dialed his contact number for James Brazzle. Voice mail again. Could James and Creed really be dead? The governor had always seemed indestructible, so permanent.

"Turn on CNN, will you?" asked Mako.

"Already did while you were asleep. They found the wreckage."

"They what?" Mako's mind refused to process the news. He rejected it out of hand. That was not the way stories ended. These were the good guys.

"The governor's plane crashed in the mountains in West Virginia. They spotted the wreckage from the air, but there's no sign of survivors. A search and rescue team on the ground is trying to reach the plane. It's rough country, though."

Mako lay back in bed and gratefully sipped the hot coffee Armando poured for him. He tried to gather his thoughts. The coffee helped.

"Any mention of foul play?" Mako tried to control his breathing for the sake of appearances.

"Not much reporting on the crash at all," said Armando. "The cruise missile strike on Puerto Cabello is grabbing all the headlines."

"And?" asked Mako.

"You can imagine what a barrage of your cruise missiles can do to a small port. Dozens of casualties. One frigate severely damaged. A shipyard destroyed."

"At least we can do something right."

"Well, Venezuela's going nuts, rejecting the *gringos'* accusations. They've invited a team of international inspectors to look for evidence of the Iranian submarine. Iran's called for a meeting of the U.N. Security Council. Both countries are talking about an oil embargo against the United States. Oil futures are up to $300 and still rising."

"That'll make someone happy," said Mako.

"That could be the key to the whole puzzle," said Armando.

Mako looked at him in surprise and had to smile despite the ominous news.

"Armando, you're probably right. That would narrow the list of suspects considerably, wouldn't it?"

Armando tossed Mako his boots and Wranglers.

"Let's worry about that another time. Bulat's waiting for you."

Chapter 31

Mako went through the motions. That was all he could do, given the calamitous news of the night before which he still had not managed to digest or catalog. At this point in his career, though, surveillance detection precautions were second nature. The taxi changes, the unexpected stops to buy a newspaper, a cup of coffee, a cold drink; he did everything an experienced case officer would do except he did it all in a stupor.

When they arrived at the hotel where Bulat always stayed, everything seemed familiar, and that was reassuring to Mako. He had to think less. The same unwashed clerk sat behind the same antique wood counter, and a familiar abacus lay incongruously next to a desktop computer. Mako saw Armando thrust a wad of peso bills into the clerk's hand as he had done before and saw the clerk's oily smile. He saw the same *"Fuera de Servicio"* sign hung by a knotted string on the elevator door, and they climbed the flight of creaking stairs to the third floor as they had last time. He saw the same walls with the same crooked lines of peeling discoloration running down from the ceiling, serpentine traces of leaking water pipes from decades past. He noticed nothing out of the ordinary until they approached Bulat's door. Mako saw that it was slightly ajar.

That was different and in his business different was not good.

Both he and Armando drew their handguns, and they stood in the corridor on either side of the door. Mako nodded to Armando and eased the door open slowly. The door creaked on rusty hinges as it scraped across a colorful Oaxacan runner on the floor. There was no sound from within, and at Mako's signal, Armando followed him as both men sprinted across the threshold. Mako dove to the floor on the left and came up with his gun panning across his side of the room looking for potential targets. Armando did the same on the right side, but there was nothing. Nothing moving at least.

Bulat sat motionless on the couch facing them with a vacant look in his eyes and his mouth agape. An electric cord was wrapped around his neck. His head tilted unnaturally to one side, and Mako knew he was dead. The two men stood stunned and silent for several seconds. Mako felt lightheaded but not from the sight of death, which he had seen all too often. An unpleasant prickling of his scalp and a tightening in his throat reminded him that any illusion of order in the world was just that.

He sensed they were not alone in the hotel room, and in that instant he knew they had walked into a trap. He was poised to dive again for the floor and absentmindedly wondered how many shooters he and Armando would be facing. Then he heard a voice.

"You didn't think I would let this cockroach betray me, did you?"

Mako kept his handgun at his side and turned his head slowly towards the voice. He warned Armando with his free hand not to make a sudden move. The Russian-accented English came from a bald, stocky man dressed in dark slacks and a white shirt open at the neck. He held an AK-47 pointed at Mako's chest. Mako noted he was left-handed, unusual for a Russian.

"Please drop your weapons," the man said politely.

Mako knew it would be futile to resist with the barrel of the AK-47 aimed at his chest from a distance of fifteen feet. He dropped his gun, and Armando did the same.

"Kick them towards the door," commanded the Russian.

Mako kicked his gun away in anger and heard Armando's piece slide across the wood floor and crash against the open door.

"*Otlichno*[41]," said the Russian. "I guess we'll have no further need for this then. He removed the magazine from the Kalashnikov, laid it on the kitchen table, and then propped the AK-47 against one of the chairs.

---

[41] Excellent - Russian

"*¿Dónde está Inmaculada?*" asked Armando.

"*Tranquilo,*" replied the Russian. "She's tied up in the bedroom. We don't kill innocent women."

"I take it you're from the Russian embassy?" Mako said, his senses still on alert, wondering if anyone else was in the hotel room. "Vladimir Kazakov, if I'm not mistaken?"

"*A sus ordenes*[42]," said Vladimir. "Your reputation precedes you, Mr. Sloane. Delighted to meet you. I only regret the circumstances."

"A little abrupt with the captain, weren't you?" asked Mako nodding in the direction of Bulat's corpse.

"You would have done the same thing. He betrayed me personally as well as his country. I don't tolerate that."

"Washington already knows about your submarine," said Mako. "You're a little late with your kangaroo court retribution."

"Really? Is that why you just destroyed Puerto Cabello in Venezuela with cruise missiles?" Vladimir laughed. "Don't play games with me, Mako. And don't underestimate me."

"What do you want?" Mako said.

"The same thing everybody wants; world peace, a loving family, grandkids, a secure retirement. I've always wanted to learn to play golf, by the way."

---

[42] At your service

"And more specifically?" Mako asked.

"I want to take the captain's place."

Mako glanced out of the corner of his eye at the handguns lying on the floor near the door and the Kalashnikov propped up against the chair. He knew there was one bullet still in the chamber of the AK-47. After a quick calculation, Mako rejected the possibility of lunging for one of the guns. A 7.62 mm round fired at a muzzle velocity of 2,350 feet per second at point blank range could do more damage than he was willing to risk.

"Looks to me like you're doing everything possible to ruin any prospects for world peace, and I'm not sure I can help you with the rest of your agenda."

"That's where you're wrong, Mako. I'm not a beggar grabbing at your sleeve and pleading for alms as you walk by in a third-world bazaar," said Vladimir. "I have something to offer in return."

"You're the man with the Kalashnikov. Keep talking."

"Captain Mikoyan, I'm sure, told you everything he knew. You already squeezed him dry and were coming back today to tell him he had to wait a few more days for his one-way ticket to the United States. Isn't that right? Where was he going to live; Florida or Southern California?"

Mako stood still and listened. The man knew a lot. Much more than he should have.

"It's harder than it used to be to get Washington's approval for a defection, isn't it? Especially when Washington doesn't want to hear what your defector has to say. As a matter of fact, I know what you can't possibly know, Mako. I know there is someone in Washington who will kill and kill and kill so your president never hears the truth. He won't do it himself, of course. No, he wouldn't want to bloody his manicured fingernails or soil his starched white shirts. He'll hire others to do his dirty work. Wouldn't you like to know who that is?"

"I know who it is. It's Ian McGinnis. You'll have to do better than that to impress me," Mako was bluffing, but it was time to put the theory to the test.

Vladimir slammed the palm of his hand on the table, and the Kalashnikov started to fall. He reached down and caught the weapon before it hit the ground. He whipped it up and held the butt against his abdomen with the barrel once again pointing at Mako's chest.

"Oh, I can do better than that, Mako."

He punctuated his sentences with emphatic slashes through the air with the muzzle of the Kalashnikov. Mako watched him carefully, worried that he was losing control.

"I can give you recordings of telephone conversations with Ian, and I can give you video of our personal meetings in Mazatlán. I'm sure you heard something of his adventures in Mexico, didn't you?"

"I heard a little," said Mako.

"Well, did you hear that Ian proposed this whole operation three years ago? Did you hear about his stock holdings in Rosneft and Gazprom? How about his offshore accounts and his oil-based securities? Didn't you ever stop to think what effect skyrocketing oil prices might have on Russia's coffers or on the personal fortunes of an investor with inside information? How much more inside can you get than the director of the Central Intelligence Agency?"

Both men were silent and stared at each other as Vladimir caught his breath. He put down the Kalashnikov again, and Mako inwardly breathed a sigh of relief. He hated the prospect of being gunned down by the Russian SVR Rezident in a low-rent Veracruz hotel suite. He knew he would have to be careful with his reply.

"What else do you know?" asked Mako.

"Slow down," laughed Vladimir. "I've already proved my bona-fides, haven't I?"

"Let's just say I'm intrigued."

"Then you'll love this. We knew your boss was flying to Washington with the governor. We knew they were carrying the captain's log book."

"How the hell did you know that?" asked Mako.

"McGinnis was intercepting all of your phone calls. NSA was tapping the personal phone calls of the governor of Texas at the unofficial request of the CIA. And you Americans think you're free!"

"And the governor's plane?" asked Mako.

"This is where the quid pro quo begins," said Vladimir. "I want immunity and asylum guarantees before I say anything else."

"I usually don't make those kinds of guarantees to someone who has a 7.62 mm cartridge still chambered in an AK-47 within easy reach," said Mako.

Vladimir reached down and picked up the Kalashnikov. He ejected the remaining cartridge in the chamber and tossed it to Mako.

"Satisfied?"

"That's good for starters," said Mako. "Now what about the governor's plane?"

"First things first, Mako. I'll tell you that when we cross the Texas border."

Mako looked at Armando, who was staring past Vladimir into the hallway that led to the small bedroom in the back of the tiny suite. Mako heard rapid footsteps and turned towards the sound just in time to hear a deafening roar and see a Vladimir's forehead disappear in a fountain of spurting blood and brain matter. His falling body revealed Inmaculada standing behind him still pointing an FN 5.7 pistol with both hands at the back of Vladimir's head. Or more precisely, where it used to be.

Chapter 32

Mako wished Armando had not shot the clerk on the way out of the hotel. Violence has to have a purpose, or else it is mere self-indulgence, he always thought. The man was unarmed after all and appeared none too pleased when three bullets from Armando's Glock 9 mm thudded into the left quadrant of his chest in a tight pattern. Armando, of course, had a different way of looking at the incident.

"That *pendejo* double-crossed us. He knew the Russian was up there in the room waiting. He probably took money to keep quiet," he said. "And then he took my money in exchange for the key. Just like Judas Iscariot taking thirty pieces of silver to betray Jesus."

"Oh, so now you're Jesus, huh? Look, we can always explain why there are two dead Russians in the hotel room, but a dead Mexican on top of everything else could complicate things," said Mako as he stood on the curb with his arm wrapped protectively around Inmaculada with Armando trying to wave down a series of uncooperative taxis.

"He shouldn't have fucked with us. It's that simple. But it's not a problem. We're in Mexico. You should trust me. I've taken care of you so far in this country, haven't I?"

Police sirens were wailing in the distance when they finally hailed a cooperative taxi.

"Or maybe I've taken care of you," mumbled Mako as they climbed into the VW bug taxi.

"You worry too much, *viejo*," said Armando.

"Do I? This script is starting to read like a Shakespearian tragedy. Pretty soon, I'll be holding your skull in my hands and saying, 'Alas, poor Armando, I knew him.'"

"Or maybe I'll be holding your skull in my hands soon and saying, 'Alas, poor Mako, *qué pendejo era'*."[43]

Normally Mako would have laughed, but the operation had unraveled, perhaps irretrievably. When they got back to the Fiesta Americana, he took a long pull straight from the bottle of Flor de Caña and turned on CNN. In five minutes, he found out all he needed to know. A search and rescue team had reached the wreckage of the Texas governor's private jet in the West Virginia mountains. Four bodies had been recovered, but the remains were burned beyond recognition. It would take several days for DNA testing to confirm the identity of the victims. In the meantime, there had been no communication from either the governor or the head of his personal intelligence

---

[43] What an asshole he was - Spanish

service. To Mako it seemed pretty obvious what had happened.

"We're all dressed up with nowhere to go," declared Mako after several more pulls on the bottle.

"What's that supposed to mean?" asked Armando.

Inmaculada had not said a word since their unexpected reunion. She sat on the easy chair in the corner of the hotel room and stared at the wall. Mako offered her a rum on the rocks and she took the glass silently in her hand and drained the contents. Mako refilled her glass, looked into her eyes, and realized how painfully beautiful she was.

"It means we have the family jewels but can't do anything with them," said Mako, his eyes riveted on Inmaculada.

"Say it in Spanish," said Armando. "You're not making sense in English right now."

Mako continued to stare at Inmaculada. He could well imagine what she was feeling. Last hopes for redemption dashed in a brief orgy of death. Not too far from his own state of mind. He glanced backed at Armando.

"It means that we have information that could bring down the American government and possibly cause a shooting war between the United States and Russia, but there's nobody we can tell without joining the ranks of the recently departed."

"Don't you think you're being a little over-dramatic?" asked Armando. "Get a grip on yourself, Mako, or I'll have to find myself a new superhero to follow around and save from himself."

"How long before the cartel finds out what happened?"

"They'll know before nightfall," answered Armando turning serious. "We need to be on the road as soon as possible."

"Let's wait another hour," said Mako. "Cyrus is supposed to meet us here."

"*Perfecto!* He'll probably drag along another crew of cartel *sicarios* to finish the job they botched in Valle de Bravo," snapped Armando.

"Cyrus is our last connection to the U.S. government. He might know something beyond what CNN is reporting."

Armando sat back and roared with laughter. "That'll be the day!"

"We'll see," answered Mako. He stood up and approached Inmaculada. He took her hand, and she followed him out to the balcony where they stood together for fifteen minutes without speaking. Inmaculada's presence gave him strength. He sensed it but could not have explained or rationalized what he was feeling. Mako had spent most of his life ignoring or suppressing his personal feelings. That was probably what had kept him alive this long in a business that did not forgive personal weakness. Right now, though, he needed her. As pathetic as he realized it might sound, she gave him purpose, a reason for continuing when little else remained.

The door to the balcony slid open. Armando stuck his head out and hissed, "Someone's knocking at the door."

Mako whispered to Inmaculada to stay on the balcony until he came back. He and Armando drew their handguns and flanked the entrance door. Mako stepped halfway into the bathroom, and Armando squeezed as far as he could into the closet on the other side of the narrow entranceway. Mako nodded to Armando.

¿Quién es?" Mako called out.

"Mako, it's Cyrus," said the voice.

Armando opened the door slowly, his Glock extended in front of him. Cyrus saw the gun before he saw Armando and visibly paled.

"Hey, you don't need that!" hissed Cyrus through his teeth.

"We did last time you showed up," responded Armando.

"Nobody followed me this time," insisted Cyrus.

Armando smirked. "That'd be a first."

"Come on in," said Mako. "Armando, put the damn gun away."

Armando shoved the Glock down the back of his jeans with a scowl and stepped away from the door. Mako followed him with his eyes and just shook his head. He motioned for Cyrus to come in, and then he closed the door behind him.

"How much do you know?" Mako asked.

"More than I'd like to," answered Cyrus.

"The governor?"

"Yeah, I heard it on the radio."

"There's more," said Mako.

Cyrus arched his eyebrows but said nothing.

"The Armenian submarine captain is dead. So is the SVR Rezident."

"How the...?" started to ask Cyrus.

"I'll fill you in on the details later. Where's your car?"

"Two blocks down the street in a parking lot."

"The one across from the bank?" asked Mako.

Cyrus nodded his head.

"You two head out right now. Inmaculada and I'll meet you there in five minutes," said Mako.

"Where're we going?" asked Cyrus.

"Haven't decided yet. We'll discuss that on the way out of town."

Less than fifteen minutes later, Mako weaved through the crowded streets of Veracruz in Cyrus' rented Chevrolet Tahoe, deftly maneuvering around jaywalking pedestrians and vendors on the sides of the streets with their fast food stands on wheels. Cyrus sat in the passenger seat and Armando shared the back seat with Inmaculada. Nobody had spoken since Mako eased out of the parking lot into the stop-and-go traffic.

Within a half hour the steady stream of vehicles leaving Veracruz began to thin out, and the Tahoe picked up speed as Mako followed the highway signs towards Mexico City via Highway 150.

"Mako, when we pass the Poza Rica highway intersection, look for a place to pull off. I need to get something out of the back," said Cyrus.

A few minutes later, Mako braked and exited onto a dirt road that led to a white stucco farmhouse in the distance. A stand of palm trees broke up the monotony of the flat coastal plain and its low-lying scrub vegetation. Mako stopped the car behind a clump of trees that shielded the car from the highway and he turned to Cyrus.

"Well?" he said. "Let's see what you have back there that's so important."

Cyrus got out of the car and walked around to the back of the SUV. He opened the rear door, and Mako heard the rustling of a blanket and the clank of steel on steel. He looked in the rear view mirror and saw Cyrus walk back around the car carrying something. He leaned across the front seat and opened the door wide for Cyrus, who stood with a long bundle cradled in his arms.

"I could only get two of these, but I thought they might come in handy," he said.

"What the hell is that?" asked Mako.

"You've never seen the Fire Serpent?" Cyrus pulled the blanket back from the weapons he carried. "This is the FX-05 Xiuhcoatl, Mexico's version of the Heckler & Koch HK G36. It's not really the same, but close enough that the Germans thought of suing for patent infringement. Anyway, I thought we needed the fire power."

"Where'd you come up with these, *gringo*?" asked Armando.

"Can't reveal my sources," said Cyrus, only half joking. He handed Armando one of the assault rifles along with a 30-round box magazine.

"Hmm, maybe I underestimated you after all," Armando said and took the weapon from Cyrus' extended arms, caressing the titanium frame and adjusting the butt stock. "Let's kill someone," he suggested.

"Sounds good to me," said Mako as he eased the Tahoe back on the highway and accelerated rapidly. "Got anyone in mind?"

Chapter 33

Ian McGinnis understood the cryptic text message on his private cell phone immediately. The news came as a surprise, but it was far from unwelcome. The man, after all, had subjected him to unspeakable humiliation. The threats he made against Ian's life had been graphic and unambiguous, but now the arrogant bastard was lying in a state of permanent rigor mortis on a stainless steel slab in a Veracruz, Mexico morgue. Justice at times was indeed poetic. The Russian embassy had yet to claim the body according to the message Antonio Salcido sent. The death of the submarine captain in addition was just an added bonus, like a shiny toy in the bottom of a box of Cheerios. The Armenian would have had to die eventually anyway, Ian reasoned.

So, the Russian prick thought he could call the shots? Fuck that. Ian leaned back in his chair and pumped his fist in the air. Vladimir obviously had forgotten who the Big Dog was. Things had changed since the Cold War, and it was time for the Russians to accept reality. They were a second-class power and a pawn in Ian's game of chess, not the other way around. The end game was progressing nicely, and only a few moves remained until Ian could relax and announce, "checkmate". It was hard not to gloat.

Ian had utilized the assets and credibility of his own CIA to help him debunk the rumor of Russia's role in the crisis. A trail leading to Russia would inevitably point in his direction too. That was the Achilles Heel of the entire operation. He knew the SVR now would be eager to squelch any suspicion of a Russian alliance with the Sinaloa Cartel. He could imagine the closed channel cables whizzing back and forth between Moscow and the Russian embassy in Mexico City. They would want to scuttle the submarine and recall the crew as soon as possible. Ian had no objection. He had accomplished his mission and covered most of his tracks.

The shit storm over the cruise missile strike against Puerto Cabello was subsiding and after a week barely rippled the water. The debate still simmered on the Sunday morning talk shows and in the United Nations General Assembly, but talking heads and third world autocrats were of little consequence to Ian or the rest of the administration.

Ian had done what he needed to do to protect himself. He had diverted attention from the real culprits, and the president had silenced his own critics with decisive action. The fact that U.S. cruise missiles had targeted an innocent country just added to the comic relief in Ian's opinion. He loved the irony of the plot he had conceived. Ian knew America well and was gambling on its short attention span.

Americans thrived on non-stop action, and they loved Hollywood melodrama with a tear-jerking soundtrack. Now that the stock market was recovering and the price of oil was moving steadily south, the fickle electorate and the news media were ready to move on to the next major scandal or national crisis.

With the unidentifiable remains of the governor of Texas and the head of the People's Intelligence and Security Service taking up shelf space in a government forensic laboratory, there were only two thorns remaining in Ian's side, Antonio Salcido and Mako Sloane. The Mexican drug lord had turned into an ally of sorts and helped Ian get rid of Cory Akins, a potential source of inconvenient leaks. That had gone a long way to smooth out their differences, and Ian was not the kind to hold a grudge. But he knew Salcido had to go eventually. The man simply knew too much. Ian wondered how Antonio would respond to an invitation to go fishing in the Florida Keys? Would that be too obvious?

Mako Sloane, on the other hand, presented a different set of challenges. First, he would be difficult to locate. With the crash of the governor's jet, Ian was sure that Sloane would have put two and two together and gone to ground, and probably not in the United States. Maybe Salcido could do one last favor for him. Mako had to be in Mexico, Ian thought, and if he was, he was a dead man.

Ian was at the top of his game. He had taken Cory Elkin's parochial operation designed to keep Texas in the War on Drugs and turned it into the greatest get-rich scheme since the pillaging of Tenochtitlan and Cusco by Cortez and Pizarro. Ian could not even begin to estimate his net worth after the roller-coaster run-up of oil prices. Energy was where the real money lay. Everything else was chump change. Ian had pulled off one of the greatest foreign policy frauds of all time. He wished he could share his success with someone, but that was impossible, of course.

As he left CIA Headquarters and drove home to his sprawling suburban home in McLean, Ian felt an unaccustomed stirring in his loins. He grinned as he imagined how surprised his wife would be at his sudden interest in her rapidly fading charms. He could not remember the last time they had enjoyed each other's company, much less had sex. He was amused at the sudden detour his thoughts had taken. Danger and success were certainly aphrodisiacs. He just wished there was a more deserving target for his sudden amorous intentions than his frumpy wife of thirty-five years with her sagging buttocks and varicose veins.

***

"Anything new?" asked Mako as Cyrus slid the cell phone back into the zippered pocket of his navy-blue windbreaker. He threw the jacket over his shoulders and shivered. The air had turned cool as the highway snaked out of the tropical coastal plain and gradually rose into the rugged Mexican highlands.

"Only what the news networks are reporting. DNA testing was inconclusive. My secretary says the governor is still officially listed as missing and presumed dead."

Mako shook his head in disbelief. He refused to believe the tough old rancher-turned-politician could be dead. Creed Tucker was synonymous with Texas, almost geological in his ideological consistency and his physical presence. Even harder to fathom was James Brazzle. He was too smart not to have taken the necessary security precautions to keep the two men alive. But James differed from Mako in the way the two men looked at the world. Despite abundant evidence to the contrary, James continued to believe in the essentially benevolent character of the U.S. government. Mako, on the other hand, had stopped believing in fairy tales long ago, and he, at least for the time being, was still alive.

"What's going on at the embassy, Cyrus?" asked Mako.

"My secretary doesn't know much. But you know the drill: full damage-control mode. All of Latin America is outraged at the cruise missile strike on Puerto Cabello. For them it's nothing more than déjà vu. More Yankee aggression. The ambassador and his staff are spending most of their time in meetings with the Mexican government, lying through their teeth, of course, explaining why we had to attack Venezuela."

"And the station?" asked Mako.

"The new COS has everybody out polling our agents for intelligence that would corroborate the Iran/Venezuela connection," answered Cyrus.

"That's ass-backwards as usual," said Mako. "You don't reach a conclusion and then request intelligence to backstop your theory. That's like the FBI when they decide someone is guilty of a crime and then tailor the evidence to support a conviction."

Cyrus nodded his head in agreement.

"You'd think we would have learned something from the bogus intelligence we flogged right before the Iraq invasion in 2003," he said.

"Oh, and learn from history?" Mako just shook his head at the thought. What do you know about the new COS by the way?"

"Only that Ian McGinnis personally picked him. No wonder he's parroting the party line."

"No reporting on the Russians or the cartel?" asked Mako.

"Not a whisper. It's like the fairy tale about the Emperor's New Clothes. Everyone is saying Ian's bullshit smells like roses."

"Bolshevik discipline in the CIA," mumbled Mako. "At least until Ian goes down, and then the rats will fight each other to get off the sinking ship and try to prove they knew the truth all along."

"Are you sure he's going down?" asked Cyrus.

"I'll make sure of it," said Mako grimly.

Armando leaned forward and put his hand on Mako's shoulder.

"Slow down, *viejo*. What's that up ahead?"

"Is that a roadblock?" asked Cyrus, reaching down and taking hold of the Fire Serpent assault rifle on the floor in front of his seat.

"If it is," said Mako, "I guarantee you it's not official."

Mako looked ahead and saw a column of cars and trucks stopped in front of a makeshift barrier, a log resting on two large flat rocks blocking the right lane. Several uniformed federal police officers were examining the identification papers of the drivers as armed men in street clothes peered into the interior of the cars before letting the vehicles trickle around the left side of the barrier.

"They're looking for someone," said Mako. "I wonder who?"

"Christ, that was fast!" exclaimed Cyrus. "We've only been on the road for two hours."

"The cartel doesn't have to wait for a presidential finding or approval from a Congressional oversight committee," said Mako. "Still, I agree. They're damned efficient."

The Tahoe crept forward as the police officers continued to direct traffic.

"We may have to shoot our way out of this one," said Mako.

"Here we go again," whispered Armando.

"I'd take the safety off the Fire Serpent now if I were you," said Cyrus, turning to the back seat and addressing Armando. His voice was slightly hoarse with tension. "It tends to stick occasionally."

Armando nodded and clicked the safety to the "off" position and double-checked it. He covered the assault rifle with Inmaculada's shawl. Mako reached across to the glove compartment, removed his Browning 9 mm pistol, and laid it in his lap.

"If you have a choice, take out the ones in civilian clothes first," suggested Armando. "And don't drive away till we get them all. We don't want any phone calls made, or we'll just run into another roadblock a few kilometers down the road."

"Inmaculada, lie down on the floor!" instructed Mako as one uniformed police officer and a thuggish gunman in civilian clothes approached the car. Two others by the roadblock waved the car in front of them around the makeshift barrier and then slowly walked back to join their two companions who were about to inspect the Tahoe. Mako rolled down his window as the uniformed officer approached.

"*Sus documentos, por favor[44],*" said the police officer to Mako as his partner in civilian clothes peered through the back window at Armando. Inmadulada lay on the floor with a blanket draped over her.

"Are you Americans?" asked the officer in Spanish as he looked at Mako and Cyrus and compared their faces to photographs that he held in his hand. "Let me see your passports, please."

"Here's my identification," said Mako in Spanish. He raised the 9 mm pistol and pointed it at the policeman's face. A fraction of a second later the man's face disappeared in a shower of blood and bone matter as the 9 mm thundered once in the confined space of the car. Mako saw the man's body collapse Gumby-like to the ground as a deafening burst of gunfire erupted almost simultaneously from the back seat of the Tahoe and made his ears ring.

---

[44] Your ID, please.

The thug in civilian clothes flew backwards, surprise etched on his frozen features. He fell to the ground, eyes wide as a crimson stain spread rapidly across the front of his Dallas Cowboys grey and blue sweatshirt.

The other two gunmen began to sprint towards the Tahoe at the sound of shots. Both Armando and Cyrus leaped out of opposite sides of the SUV and fired bursts of 5.56 mm rounds at the approaching men. They were just bringing their AK-47s to bear when the first rounds from Cyrus' Fire Serpent found their target. The top of the uniformed policeman's head disappeared as he spun clumsily to the left, his AK-47 firing erratically into the air. His armed companion continued running towards the Tahoe for a few more steps before three rounds from Armando's weapon crashed into his abdomen, stopping him in mid-stride, shredding his liver and ripping apart his small intestine.

Both men dropped to the ground, and for a few seconds nothing could be heard except tires squealing and horns blowing as cars arrived at the roadblock, screeched to a stop, and reversed course, fishtailing and narrowly avoiding collisions with other fleeing vehicles.

"There were only four of them?" shouted Mako as his head swiveled back and forth looking for more targets.

"This was just the advance team. Probably more on the way by now," answered Armando as he walked slowly towards one of the gunman, who lay writhing on the ground, clutching his belly and trying instinctively to push pale, veined intestines back into his abdominal cavity.

Mako looked back at Inmaculada, who was climbing onto the back seat from the floor of the Tahoe where she had been hiding. A single shot from Armando's Fire Serpent rang out, and Mako jumped involuntarily. He watched as his friend strolled nonchalantly back to the Tahoe as if he had just put down a horse with a broken leg.

"We should stay off the main roads now," said Armando. "And let's not even think about going to Mexico City. The area around your embassy will be swarming with Salcido's people."

"How about Juan Ignacio's house?" suggested Cyrus. "Where Soledad is staying."

"That'll work for a day or two," said Armando. "Until we hear what our fearless leader decides."

"He's already decided," said Mako and gunned the Tahoe around the improvised roadblock.

Chapter 34

Mako Sloane rolled his borrowed pickup truck to a stop in front of an old cattle guard that had seen better days. The hole in the ground beneath the runner pipes was so clogged with dirt and debris that the rusted-out contraption no longer served as a deterrent to wandering livestock. A jerry-rigged panel gate on the other side of the cattle guard was tied shut, the fragile structure held in place by foot-long lengths of baling wire wrapped around the thin aluminum and stapled to wooden fence posts at either end. It had rained earlier in the morning, and the air was still moist and cool. The breeze was brisk from the north, and fleecy clouds raced across the leaden sky on their way to Mexico.

There were fresh boot prints in the moist sand on either side of the cattle guard. Someone had crossed through the gate since it rained. That much was clear. Tire tracks beyond the makeshift gate led downhill along a dirt lane towards a house half-hidden by a cluster of scrub cedar and live oak.

Mako climbed gingerly out of the truck, carefully avoiding the puddled water that had collected in the ruts of the uneven dirt road. He reached both hands high over his head and stretched. The ride from Laredo to Bandera,

Texas had taken less than three hours, but his knees ached and his hamstrings knotted, something that would not have happened even a year ago. Mako would be the first to admit he was getting long in the tooth, certainly for his particular line of work.

A half mile back on Farm-to-Market Road 470, Mako had passed the remains of a large feral hog that lay across the broken white line in the middle of the highway. By the size of its head, Mako figured the pig must have weighed close to 300 pounds before scavengers began to feast on the dead beast. Over the next mile and a half of country road Mako saw in quick succession two dead raccoons, a skunk, an armadillo, and a half buzzard-eaten yellow dog whose left ear flapped apocalyptically in the *whoosh* of a passing eighteen-wheeler. Unforgiving country. One ill-conceived move and there could be hell to pay. Sounds familiar, he thought.

Mako untwisted the baling wire and walked the gate open. He got back in his truck and checked landmarks one last time before driving through the narrow opening. He glanced at his odometer. Fifteen point three miles from the Bandera city limits sign. White mailbox on the north side of the road. Steer skull nailed to the cross beam of the "П"-shaped entranceway that towered above the gate. He nodded his head in silent confirmation and eased the pickup over the cattle guard, drove through the gate, and got out.

He closed the panel behind him and twisted the baling wire tight. If something went wrong, he might have to ram the gate open on his way out, but the lessons of youth are persistent. He had spent too much time as a kid rounding up errant livestock ever to leave a pasture gate open.

Mako followed the serpentine dirt road as it dropped precipitously into the valley below. Two ugly brown & gray mottled dogs met his truck even before the house came into view. They ran on either side of the pickup, snarling and barking and jumping up to stand briefly on spindly hind legs to get a look at the occupant of the vehicle. Mako did not recognize either dog, and that worried him. A few seconds later, a one-story clapboard house came into view. It was as dilapidated and unkempt as the rest of the ranch appeared to be. The house was the color of gray barn wood, and the lap siding folded upwards into a warped curlicue. The front porch listed unabashedly to the right. The railing had broken away from the corner post on the far side and lay forlornly on the ground.

There was no sign of life in the house. No lights were on, and Mako could see no movement through the half-closed venetian blinds. He glimpsed the white tailgate of a pickup truck in an old aluminum storage shed about fifty yards from the house under two towering live oaks trees and knew someone was watching.

The dogs continued to harass the truck, and Mako sat waiting for the owner to come out and call them off but nobody came. He thought about backing up quietly and returning to Laredo. He could not do that, of course. This was the only lead he had. Still, the feeling of being a target for unseen and possibly disagreeable men made him uneasy.

Mako finally opened the door of the pickup and slid out. He lashed out with his boot at one of the dogs that lunged at him and caught the animal squarely on its chin. Jaws snapped together with a loud click and the dog yelped. It backed off and cowered although it continued to bark and growl, the short hair bristling on its back. The other dog made several threatening lunges at Mako, but it too retreated, lips back and yellowed teeth bared.

"You didn't have to kick my dog."

Mako turned at the sound of the voice and saw an elderly man dressed in blue overalls and an old Purina Mills baseball cap approaching from behind the house. He was transparently thin and unshaven. He also carried a 12-gauge shotgun casually in his right hand.

"They didn't seem well-disposed towards me," Mako said, keeping an eye on the shotgun, which the man held pointed at the ground.

"Well, that's their goddamned job, I guess," said the old man. He spit into an old Maxwell House coffee can he carried and looked at Mako with exasperation in his watery, half-shut eyes. "I'd be justified if I shot you, mister. What are you doing on my property?"

"Are you Preston Grady?" asked Mako, recalling the name that he was supposed to ask for. "I'm Ma....."

"Yeah, yeah, I know who you are. Follow me and don't kick my dog again."

Mako followed the old man, who walked with a limp, half-dragging his right leg behind him. He might have had a mild stroke or perhaps a horse or cow had kicked him years ago and left its indelible mark.

"Be careful where you put your foot. Haven't got around to repairing the porch."

Mako strode over the missing step and wondered if the old man ever got around to repairing anything. The run-down house had a Dust-Bowl look to it. For that matter, the old man looked like a 1930s Okie straight from the pages of *The Grapes of Wrath*. Mako kept his thoughts to himself. It is never a good idea to compare a Texan to an Okie, at least not aloud.

He opened the front door and motioned Mako in.

"They're in there," he said. "Make yourself at home."

The old man tried to smile, but he seemed out of practice. The corners of his mouth rose and he showed his teeth, but there was no mirth in his expression. Mako walked into the living room and immediately saw two recognizable figures sitting in chairs. They both stood up when they saw him.

"Sonofabitch! The things you see when you don't have a gun!" joked Mako and embraced each man and shook his hand. "You had me scared, boys, I'll have to admit."

"It took you long enough to get here," groused the taller of the two men.

"Well, rumor had it you two were dead. Corpses usually don't stick to their emergency commo plans."

***

"Preston Grady!" Creed Taylor called out hoarsely. "Don't you have any goddamned liquor in this house?"

The old man limped into the living room. Mako could almost see his cheekbones through the pale blotchiness of his parchment-thin skin.

"I told you not to go into politics," he said shaking his index finger at Creed. "Now you're cussin' and drinkin' and Lord knows what else."

"Oh?" asked Creed. "Since when did you get religion, Preston? And where's that pint bottle of Old Crow you used to keep in the cupboard?"

"You mean this?" The old man frowned as he extracted a small bottle from the front pocket of his overalls. "Leave some for me, you old coot."

He handed the half-empty bottle to Creed, who unscrewed the cap and took a drink. He grimaced as the old man watched him drink. When Creed smacked his lips, the man nodded, turned on his heels, and left the room, dragging his bum leg behind him.

"So, that's basically what happened, Mako," said James Brazzle when the old man disappeared. "We stayed longer than we expected and had to let the plane go. Its owner is a rich oilman from Dallas, a heavy contributor to Creed's political campaign. He was flying some of his high-roller cronies to join him in Las Vegas. They never made it. Creed and I don't even know who was on board."

"When we heard about the crash, we thought McGinnis might be behind it. We knew we were supposed to be the targets and so we hightailed it back here in a rental car," said Creed.

"Before he found out we weren't on the plane," added James.

"So, the president refused to see you?" asked Mako.

Creed nodded his head.

"Couldn't even get close. Even the vice president couldn't set up the meeting once Ian McGinnis got wind we were in town."

"We didn't realize he had that much cachet with the president," said James.

"Did you see Ian?" Mako asked.

"Hell no, he avoided us like the plague, but Throckmorton told him what we brought with us," said James. "After that, nobody in town would even answer our phone calls. That's when I noticed the surveillance around the hotel."

"Jesus, and now the governor of Texas is hiding out in a ramshackle house in the Hill Country," said Mako. "In his own state, I might add. And I guess you want me to bail you out?"

"The thought had crossed my mind," said Creed. "Isn't that what 'security consultants' do?"

"Is that what I am?" asked Mako.

"That's sure as hell what your contract says."

The rain had started again and a gust of wind rattled the warped siding of the old house. Water began to drip from the ceiling in the corner of the living room. The *ping* of the droplets as they splashed on the floor was the only thing that interrupted the silence.

"How does that old man live in this house?" asked Mako.

"Old Grady doesn't need a whole lot," answered Creed. "He hasn't changed much since we were in elementary school together. When he got back from

Vietnam, he didn't want to have much to do with people anymore. He's been living alone on this place for almost forty years. He's happy...in his own way."

"Got any ideas, Mako?" asked James, getting back to their predicament.

"One or two."

The men were quiet for almost a minute. The rain had let up but the water continued dripping from the ceiling. Mako had been staring at the rusty nail heads in the floorboards, deep in thought.

"You know what needs to be done," he said quietly.

"Yeah, we know," said James.

"It'll take some planning," Mako said absentmindedly.

"Of course," said James. "What do you need from us?"

"You still got your contact at NSA?"

"Yeah."

"Well, that's a good start."

"Anything else?" asked James.

Mako reached into the pearl snapped pocket of his blue plaid western shirt and pulled out a folded sheet of lined notebook paper. He handed it to James.

"Here's a list," said Mako.

"You've been giving this some thought, I see."

Brazzle took the paper and quickly scanned the barely legible writing. He looked up at Mako with alarm.

"Are you serious?" he asked.

"You got a better idea?"

Chapter 35

There were some things the director of the Central Intelligence Agency would not discuss over the phone, encrypted or not. Contracting Antonio Salcido and the Sinaloa Cartel to kill Mako Sloane was one of them.

Not that Ian felt any compunction about out-sourcing death. The CIA had long morphed from an intelligence-gathering organization into a killing machine, albeit a rather inept one. The transformation had even become a subject for public discussion, at least for the few political pundits who cared one way or the other.

Maybe that was why the taking of human life held such little significance for Ian McGinnis. It had become part of his daily routine. If something or someone got in his way, there was no need for Ian or his staff to rack their brains to come up with a seamless, über-devious, covert response. The solution was always straightforward; the lowest common denominator. Eliminate the obstacle. Kill it, if necessary. That the obstacle in this case was a former CIA officer was immaterial. Mako Sloane represented a personal threat to Ian, and he had to go. It was that simple.

Ian might have looked at the matter differently if he personally had ever killed a man. But he hadn't. Killing was an abstract term for him, almost a theoretical concept. Just an intel report with names and numbers.

Nonetheless, he had no desire to go back to Mexico for a meeting with Salcido to make the necessary arrangements. The cartel's version of hospitality; the unbearable ordeal in the trunk of a car, the humiliation of being hosed down as he lay naked in the gravel of Salcido's driveway, the whine of the chainsaw, and the hissed threats from the Russian did not make for pleasant memories. Ian had not forgotten any of it. He would get his revenge in due time, but right now he needed Salcido for one last favor.

When Salcido answered his cell phone, Ian was pleasantly surprised. The drug lord certainly had ample reason to cut his ties with the Americans after the recent unpleasantness in Veracruz, but he obviously was still weighing his options. The man's arrogance would be his undoing, Ian thought.

"Ian, is that you?" asked Salcido.

"It's good to hear your voice." Ian responded.

"I'm sorry I can't say the same. I thought we were on the same team. Do you mind telling me what happened?"

The Mexican's directness was refreshing. Despite his diplomatic posting in Beijing, Ian had never been one for subtleties, something for which the Chinese never forgave him. Most Mexicans also viewed themselves as more sophisticated than their northern neighbors and thought the North Americans' penchant for getting right to the point was nothing more than backwoods lack of tact. Ian, for his part, always thought the Mexicans used diplomatic mumbo-jumbo to cover up their tendency to dissemble and, quite frankly, lie through their teeth.

"You surprise me," said Ian. "I think my dealings with you have been quite satisfactory. You should be pleased at what we've achieved."

"I have no problem with you personally, Ian, or what we've done together," answered Antonio. "I told you that in Mexico. But you obviously can't control your men."

Ian inwardly bristled at the mention of his "visit" to Mexico but was pleased at Antonio's response. It was a perfect lead-in.

"Let's get together, Antonio," he suggested. "That's exactly what we need to discuss. I have a proposition for you."

"Can you come to Mexico?" asked Antonio. "Mazatlán is lovely this time of year."

Salcido's brazen reference to the scene of Harvard Bank's brutal murder was not lost on Ian. He could not tell if the Mexican was joking or not.

"N-n-not this time," he stuttered. I'll call you tomorrow with a suggestion."

"*Espero tu llamada[45],*" said Salcido succinctly in Spanish and hung up.

***

Ian had never received any clandestine training. In fact, he had never even been to the Farm except to make a cameo appearance at a senior management graduation ceremony. Ian thought that treating clandestine operations as some kind of arcane science or designing courses to teach it was laughable. There was nothing more to running a secure operation, he thought, than exercising common sense. He was quite comfortable with his own ability to arrange a secure meeting with Salcido.

Ian refused to get any closer to Mexico than Port Isabel, Texas, but he knew Salcido would never agree to meet on U.S. soil. A rendezvous offshore in the Gulf of Mexico was a different story, though. Salcido liked spending time on the water, and Ian doubted he could resist the temptation of seeing how the director of the Central Intelligence Agency relaxed in the Gulf. A few emails, a favor or two called in, and Ian had all the pieces in place.

---

[45] I'll be expecting your phone call.

It helps to be wealthy beyond all rightful measure, and it certainly did not hurt to be D/CIA.

Three days later Ian lay in a lounge chair, soaking up the early spring sunshine on the fly bridge of a 98-foot Hargrave motor yacht rocking gently at anchor in twenty-five feet of water approximately two miles from the mouth of the Rio Grande River, or the Rio Bravo del Norte as the Mexicans called it.

The *Eye of the Tiger* was a striking vessel, drawing only six feet of water and boasting almost 1,500 horsepower from two diesel engines, which allowed her to cruise at 18-20 knots. The fact that her keel had been laid in the Kha Shing shipyard had nothing to do with Ian's earlier tenure as ambassador to China and his frequent visits to Taiwan. She belonged to a former close business associate, who knew nothing about the real purpose of the day's outing. Ian had spoken of "needing to get away" for a few days, and his friend had been happy to oblige. The yacht came with a four-man crew and a 15-foot Novurania tender, which might come in handy if Salcido showed up for their meeting. Ian was sure he would.

"I've got something in sight," said the captain of the yacht, standing on the fly bridge with a pair of binoculars trained on the coast. "There's a boat coming out fast from Laguna Madre."

"Laguna Madre?" Ian exclaimed. "That cheeky bastard was in Texas! What's he in?"

"Looks like a little MasterCraft. Maybe the X35. That would make it twenty-three feet long with a 5.7 liter engine. Three hundred twenty horsepower. That's if he's got the small version."

"I'd have thought he would try to impress me with something a little fancier," mused Ian. "That's just a big speed boat. A toy."

The captain was quiet as he watched the boat approach rapidly.

"Your friend's idea of making an impression is apparently a little different than yours. Take a look." The captain handed the binoculars to Ian, who stood beside him.

Ian looked through the binoculars and laughed aloud. He could see Salcido himself in the cockpit piloting the boat with three women in bikinis in the bow seats and two others relaxing in the stern.

"That figures," he said.

"What?" asked the captain.

"Oh, never mind. Just a private joke."

Salcido maneuvered the MasterCraft around the yacht in his version of a victory lap, the women waving and flaunting their skimpy bikinis. McGinnis noticed that two of them were sunbathing topless. He could not help but stare at their suntanned breasts before mentally switching back to the task at hand.

"Captain, have your crew move to the stern, please, and get ready to transfer to the MasterCraft. We'll go ahead and use their boat instead of our tender. Take the girls to South Padre and give us at least an hour alone before you come back. Stay sober," Ian admonished.

"You're the boss," said the captain, delighted with the unexpected turn the day had taken.

"Ian, how do you like my little boat?" called out Salcido as the yacht's crew lashed the speedboat to the stern of the yacht for the transfer of the crew.

"Let me see their green cards!" joked Ian as the captain extended his hand to help Salcido step onto the stern of the yacht. Salcido whispered something in the captain's ear that Ian could not hear, and the captain smiled and shook his hand. Salcido clapped him on the back and turned to Ian.

"Do you want to frisk me?" asked Salcido grinning. "No weapons, just as we agreed."

The yacht captain made his way to the cockpit of the Mastercraft, and Ian untied the boat and tossed the rope to one of the girls, who was dancing unselfconsciously in the bow to the loud reggaeton music coming from the boat's expensive sound system. The captain backed the speedboat slowly away from the yacht before accelerating and heading back towards the coast. Ian heard the women laughing and the men shouting something incomprehensible. He knew they would not be back for a while and wondered whether this had been Salcido's reason for bringing the scantily clad women along. Ian swallowed nervously.

"Nice hardware," said Antonio, looking around the yacht. "You travel in style, Ian."

"Let's go up to the fly bridge. Can I offer you a drink?"

"By all means."

As he walked up the stairs toward the upper decks, Ian glanced back towards the coast where the Mastercraft was by now just a dark speck trailed by a long foamy wake that extended behind it like the tail of a comet. On the fly bridge, Salcido squatted on his haunches and ran his hand appreciatively over the 10 mm thick teak flooring.

"Nice!" he exclaimed. "Real teak."

Ian handed him a mojito in a tall icy glass that had been chilling in the freezer. Salcido accepted the drink with a nod of his head.

"This boat reminds me of my own yacht. It's about the same length and has a fly bridge just like this except I've got a jacuzzi on mine. It gives the girls an excuse to take off their clothes. I named it *High Jinks*, for obvious reasons," said Salcido smiling.

"Is it true what Elkins told me about Harvard Banks on that yacht?"

"You mean the sharks?" asked Salcido.

"Yeah."

"How do I know you're not recording this conversation?" asked Salcido.

Ian laughed.

"When you hear my proposition, you'll understand. I'm not the kind of man to put a noose around my own neck."

"I'm listening," said Salcido.

"First things first, Antonio."

Ian leaned back and sipped his drink. The meeting had begun well despite his misgivings about seeing Salcido alone. He felt in control of the situation, and his confidence was growing.

"Listen, what happened in Veracruz was out of my control," said Ian. "I want to make that clear. It was regrettable, but I had nothing to do with it."

"It was that fucking Mako Sloane, you know," said Salcido.

"Yeah, that's what I assumed," replied Ian.

"My family has a history with that sonofabitch," said Salcido.

"Then you wouldn't mind taking care of him for me?" asked Ian. "Say, for five million dollars?"

Salcido turned and spit angrily on the teak floor of the fly deck. Ian felt the skin on the back of his neck prickle but said nothing.

"You're offering me money to kill someone?" asked Salcido. "Why do you have such a poor opinion of me, Ian? Is it because I'm Mexican?"

Even unarmed and on a yacht that Ian McGinnis ostensibly controlled, Salcido had the ability to intimidate with a mere gesture or a change in his tone of voice. The predatory gleam in his eyes made Ian's hands tremble.

"I-I-I-t wasn't my intention to offend you," Ian began and stood up. "I better get another drink."

"Sit down, Ian," barked Salcido. "You think I don't know you've got a gun hidden in the wet bar?"

"What?" Ian asked. Damn! How the hell did Salcido know that? he wondered.

"Yacht captains are greedy," Salcido said, almost as if he had read Ian's mind. "Yours was more than happy to share that bit of information with me for a $1,000 tip. That's what I mean about controlling your men. Maybe they don't fear you enough."

Chapter 36

"You think five million dollars is a lot of money for me?" scoffed Salcido.

"Well, how much would it take?"

"I'll do it for nothing," said Salcido. "As a favor to a friend." He leaned over, slapped Ian on the shoulder, and laughed so hard he choked on his drink.

"You need to relax, Ian," he continued. "I don't kill my friends, except under rare circumstances. Besides, I'm the one that should be afraid. Surely, the CIA is more powerful than my own modest organization. At least I hope so, or my childhood fantasies of *gringo* omnipotence would fall well short of the disappointing reality."

Ian's could not conceal his relief at Salcido's sudden display of good humor. He sighed deeply and tried to control his breathing.

"There's only one problem," said Salcido, sipping his ice-cold mojito.

"What's that?"

"We lost track of Sloane after he left Veracruz," Salcido said matter-of-factly.

"You were following him?"

"Of course. I've had a contract out on his life for over a year. Ever since he killed my brother. He's a slippery one, though. Are you telling me this is news for you?" asked Salcido.

Ian did not respond.

"He and his men killed four of my employees at a police roadblock about two hours northwest of Veracruz. We picked him up again near the border, but he crossed into Del Rio before we could grab him. He was alone."

"You mean he's in the United States?"

"He was two weeks week ago, but I don't know where he is now. I thought you'd have that information."

Ian sat back and considered the implications of what he just heard. Sloane was sure to suspect him as the source of the leak that led to the Veracruz bloodbath. The fact that the SVR Rezident knew the Armenian captain betrayed the operation to the Americans had to have tipped off Sloane. The leak could only have come from Washington. Together with the timing of Creed Tucker's trip, everything implicated Ian.

"When he comes back to Mexico, we'll be waiting. I'm preparing something very special for Mr. Sloane this time. It will make my artistry with Harvard Banks look amateurish. I'll be sure to send you some photos or maybe his balls in a jar of formaldehyde. You know, 'proof of death' and all that".

Ian shuddered but nodded his head appreciatively. Salcido's confidence was contagious, and his mind was already leaping ahead to his next challenge, getting rid of Salcido himself.

"What the hell's that?" asked Salcido, pointing out to sea with his free hand.

"What's what?" asked Ian.

Salcido continued to stare towards the horizon. "I thought I saw something splash out there."

"Probably a pod of dolphin. They come inshore to feed. Saw a bunch of them earlier."

"I guess." Salcido shielded his eyes from the sun with his hand and walked nonchalantly over to the railing on the starboard side of the yacht.

Ian leaned back and relished the light sea breeze on his face. Several seagulls circled directly above the yacht, and a flock of Brown Pelicans cruised by twenty yards off the port bow just above the surface of the water like a formation of bombers trying to avoid radar detection. It was peaceful with the small Gulf waves lapping rhythmically against the fiberglass hull of the yacht. Ian began to relax despite the close proximity of his one-time nemesis.

"Mako Sloane is the only remaining thorn in my side. As soon as he's gone, we're basically home free," said Ian.

"What do you mean 'basically'?" asked Salcido.

"There's an officer in our Mexico City station who's been freelancing with Sloane, but I can take care of him myself. That'll eliminate all possible leaks on my end."

"There it is again," interrupted Salcido, pointing out to sea. "Are there whales around here? I swore I saw something moving, but then it disappeared."

"Let me get the binoculars from the cockpit," Ian offered and ran up the stairs to the wheelhouse. He picked up a pair of binoculars that lay on a shelf next to the GPS display. He slipped the strap over his head and ran back down to where Antonio stood.

"Here," said Ian, handing him the binoculars. "Where did you see the whale?"

"Let me have those," said Salcido as he removed the strap from Ian's neck and slid it down over his head. He pointed the binoculars due east, away from the coast and panned back and forth, searching for the disturbance on the water's surface he thought he had seen.

"There it is." he said.

"Must be dolphin feeding near the surface."

"Well, here come two of them swimming straight towards us. Christ, they're fast!" exclaimed Salcido. He handed the binoculars to Ian, but the wakes of the two approaching marine mammals was already visible to the naked eye.

"Those things are coming in at almost 40 knots, I'd say," said Salcido.

"That's not dolphin!" Ian blurted out.

"Well, what is it then?" asked Salcido and then he looked at Ian, his eyes wide with the horror of sudden realization. Their eyes had time to meet and register disbelief. Ian opened his mouth to scream a warning, and then the yacht disappeared in a monstrous fireball. The explosion obliterated the small vessel and sent fiberglass and steel debris and body parts hundreds of feet into the air. The almost full fuel tanks ignited simultaneously, propelling a plume of flame and billowing black smoke skyward. Two minutes later all that remained of the luxury motor yacht were floating pieces of flaming wreckage and oil slicks spread over a quarter mile of smoking water.

The sound of a siren from the U.S. Coast Guard Station in Port Isabel broke the eerie silence with a piercing wail, and a Coast Guard crew scrambled to launch a 45-foot Response Boat to investigate the explosion.

Two and a half miles to the east of the wreckage, the blue water of the Gulf roiled and bubbled at the surface and then parted as the conning tower of a small submarine reluctantly emerged from the darkness below. The vessel surfaced slowly. Water still gushed off its deck when a hatch at the bottom of the sail opened and a tall stooped figure emerged and immediately scanned the horizon with a pair of binoculars. Several other figures followed quickly, speaking in low, solemn voices.

"I told you one torpedo would have been quite sufficient," said a man in Russian.

"I just wanted to make sure," answered the tall man, also in Russian. He handed the binoculars to the man who had addressed him, turned to the third man on the deck of the submarine, and spoke to him in English.

"Now do you believe the weapons officer knows his business?" he asked.

"Jesus Christ, Mako!" said James Brazzle, breathing rapidly. "There's nothing left of the yacht."

"What did you expect? That Black Shark torpedo is 21 feet long and packed with high explosives. It would do serious damage to an aircraft carrier. Plus, we hit 'em with two at the same time. Overkill, admittedly, but damned efficient." answered Mako. "Now hand me your phone. It's time."

Brazzle reached in the pocket of his jacket, retrieved his cell phone, and handed it to Mako.

"Are you calling Creed?" he asked.

"Yeah, I hope he's ready."

"He should be in the vice president's office waiting for your call. As soon as you tell him it's over, he'll call the president and request an urgent meeting," said Brazzle. "This time I think the president will see him."

"The captain's log and NSA intercepts should do the trick this time. We've got McGinnis dead to rights," Brazzle continued.

"Dead is right," said Mako. "There IS one small detail, though. We executed the bastard before he was tried and convicted."

"That's a minor procedural consideration for this administration," commented Brazzle. "Do you really think the president will object?"

"He won't in the end," said Mako. "Not when he's faced with irrefutable evidence that he bombed a country that had nothing to do with what happened. He's going to want to keep that real quiet. And not when he hears the recording of McGinnis conspiring on the phone with head of the Sinaloa Cartel to kill me to cover his tracks. That was beautiful, by the way."

"Yeah, it was, but my contact at NSA is shitting bricks waiting for the other shoe to fall."

"He's got nothing to worry about."

"It's time to submerge if we want to make our rendezvous on time," said the weapons officer in Russian.

Mako took one last look through the binoculars in the direction of the fire and nodded to Brazzle.

"Ever seen a submarine scuttled?" he asked.

"It'll be a first," Brazzle answered.

"Well, let's get out to deeper water," said Mako. "We're on a tight schedule."

He ducked his head instinctively as he entered the sail and climbed down the stairs into the interior of the submarine and followed the weapons officer to the control room. Brazzle had to hurry to keep up.

"You think Armando will be at the rendezvous coordinates?" asked Brazzle.

"Unless both diesel engines on that gorgeous 135-foot yacht malfunction, he'll be there," said Mako.

"Creed almost had a conniption fit, you know, when he saw the price tag for that thing."

"That tight old bastard! He's got the money in his budget. The hardest part was finding a crew that had the proper clearances. This can't get leaked to the press."

"Believe me, Creed knows it'll be worth it, but right now he's got bigger concerns," said Brazzle. "It's not every day you have to tell the president that your people just killed the D/CIA."

"Oh, I think you'll find the president will be more than happy to meet our demands when he realizes what his choices are," answered Mako.

Orders were shouted in Russian and the 135-foot Ukrainian-made Andrasta knock-off began to submerge. Mako adjusted his feet to maintain his balance and turned to Brazzle.

"Under the circumstances I don't think fifteen requests for political asylum and resettlement are too much to ask," he said.

"Fifteen?" I thought there were only fourteen crew members left," said Brazzle. "Are you counting Armando?"

"Hell no, Armando would never ask for political asylum in the U.S. I suspect he'll take Salcido's place and run the Sinaloa Cartel. Says he has plans to take the cartel legitimate. I just hope they don't kill him first."

"Then who's the fifteenth asylum request for?" asked Brazzle.

Mako flushed slightly and turned away.

"You'll see," he said.

"Mako Sloane!" Brazzle exclaimed. "You old sonofabitch!"

"She'll be on the yacht," Mako said softly. "I'll introduce you in...." He looked at the submarine clock on the wall. "Exactly thirty-three minutes."

THE END

ABOUT THE AUTHOR

Clabe Taylor is a fifth-generation Texan and a former U.S. diplomat, who spent most of his career abroad in Europe and Latin America. He speaks Russian and Spanish in addition to his native English. You can read more about Clabe and his novels at www.clabetaylor.com, and you can follow him on Twitter and Facebook.

ALSO AVAILABLE FROM CLABE TAYLOR

Mako Sloane is a CIA legend, but his dizzying rise to stardom in Moscow is matched by his precipitous fall from grace after he discovers a secret that vested interests in both Russian and the U.S. want to keep quiet. Ten years after Mako's mysterious disappearance, investigative reporter Max Crandall is writing Sloane's unauthorized biography. Max's research inadvertently dredges up ghosts from the past, and he finds himself the target of a manhunt as unidentified operatives try to derail his project. Max lures Mako out of self-imposed exile, and the two discover the truth behind a bizarre conspiracy that threatens to send the world spiraling into a superpower confrontation of unprecedented proportions.

Creed Tucker is an old-school Texas cowboy who finds himself at the epicenter of a firestorm when a Mexican drug cartel moves its operations across the Rio Grande River. With the help of a team of retired CIA operatives, Creed learns of a bizarre conspiracy to seize political control of South Texas involving the drug cartel, the leading Mexican presidential candidate, and a high-ranking U.S. politician. Creed and his allies navigate their way through kidnappings, murders, and assassinations that threaten to unravel the very fabric of Texas society and destroy the Tucker family...only to discover that the real threat lies much closer to home.

Clabe Taylor stars in his own novel as an author of cheap narco-spy novels, who is struggling to break out of the bonds of literary obscurity. When the *Ganja Times*, a popular national magazine, agrees to publish his new serialized novel, Clabe figures he's made the big time. There's only one problem. Everything he writes about comes true shortly after publication. The CIA, the Russians, and the most powerful drug cartel in Mexico are not amused. Clabe is forced to go on the lam. He flees cross-country, accompanied by his best friend Goose, a pot-smoking Mexican ex-con, and a flatulent Blue Heeler cow dog. Just when you think things can't get much worse, they do!

Other Spymasters Literary Guild Series Books

Michaelrdavidson.com

Michaelrdavidson.com

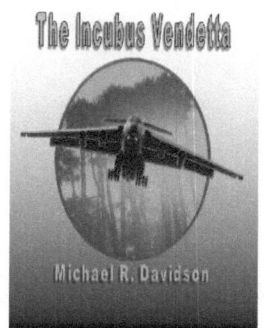

Michaelrdavidson.com

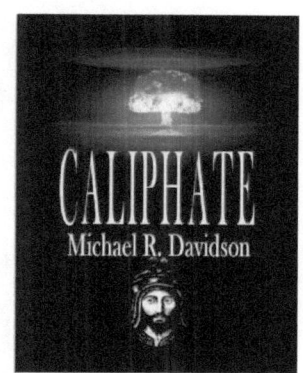

Michaelrdavidson.com